QUEEN OF LAST HOPE

THE FOURTH BOOK OF THRICE DEAD

JOSEPH SALE

TWC
THE WRITING
COLLECTIVE

First published in Great Britain in 2018 by Dark Prophets Press as part of "Nekyia". Second edition published in Great Britain in 2020 by The Writing Collective under the title "The Fifth Horseman".

This edition published in Great Britain in 2022 by The Writing Collective.

Joseph Sale has asserted his right under the Copyright, Designs and Patents Act 1988 to be identified as the author of this work.

ISBN: 9798847650830

Cover design by Dan Soule. Cover image by Warm Tail.

Chapter headings by Linda Sale.

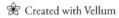 Created with Vellum

In This Series

Nekyia: In ancient Greek cult-practice and literature, a **nekyia** (Ancient Greek: ἡ νέκυια) is a "rite by which ghosts were called up and questioned about the future," i.e., necromancy.

'Caught in faded photographs, irretrievably caught between Kodak paper and photographic chemicals, as real as Coleridge's dream of Xanadu; gone up in smoke like an addict's hopes.'

— *THE NINJA*, ERIC VAN LUSTBADER

'My empire is of the imagination.'

— *SHE*, H. RIDER HAGGARD

'The miracle of order has run out and I am left in an unmiraculous city where anything may happen.'

— *DHALGREN*, SAMUEL R. DELANY

THE FOURTH READING

Beyond Death, we can sometimes find redemption. That which never dies is changeless, but that which dies can yet become something new. The Fool, The Devil, Death... A strange journey, to be sure. I rarely see so many major arcana in one place. I rarely see quite so many of the Big Three, either. But we are living in "interesting times". Realities stand upon the knife-edge. Existence, perhaps, steps perilously close to the precipice.

The Fool represents beginnings, naivety, perhaps even innocence. The Fool is the void that might be impregnated with potential. The Fool is creative potential, in other words. The Devil, on the other hand, suggests power, addiction, domination. It is fitting, is it not, that the temptation of the Devil comes so soon after an act of creation.

And once Adam and Eve tase of the forbidden fruit, they become capable of Death. But this is not always such a negative thing. To die, as we have seen, is to be reborn.

Now you're beginning to sense how this story is going to go.

But still, sometimes there are surprises in store...

Well, now you have the complete set! All of the Big Three in one reading! Either you are a major player in this game of shadows, or your desire to know burns extraordinarily brightly. I can see it, in fact, not just in your eyes, but in your chest: the white flame of the spirit. It is good to know human inquiry and curiosity is not dead, even in The Wasteland.

The Tower... This is a card of dark omen. The edifices are going to collapse. The seeming certainty of civilisation, order, and ambition will be destroyed. Our own world, its towers and palaces, was brought to ruin. Now, you are going to see another world brought low. And more, like Nimrod with the Tower of Babel, the one who built the tower will come crumbling down with it...

PROLOGUE

You know this place; the world of unkillable dreams...

The Tarmac King lived.

He slid from the formidable darkness of the water onto the formidable darkness of the land. Unlike another who had crossed the waters mere hours previous, he experienced no joy in discovering his journey was not over. He'd longed after silence. His feet had known more miles than most would in three lifetimes. Pain was his reality: every day the struggle to wake, to eat, to breathe, to do, to think. Always the road. He'd hoped his struggle was over – nothingness beckoned, a god whom he'd always believed in – but instead he found himself born again; regurgitated into reality. At least, it felt like reality. He hadn't opened his eyes.

He lay on his side. He could hear the sound of the water and beneath him felt a substance like sand. His body was warming, fractionally, as the waters withdrew back into the onyx sea. It seemed like the motion of a tide, but even in his half-conscious state he suspected it was an illusion to conceal the truth that the water, itself, was a living thing. He'd felt it while immersed: a beating sentience smothering him, its synapses firing around his bodiless mind, like electrical charges, as the water remade sinews and limbs out of some coagulated essence.

That was the feeling, eerie though it was to come to terms with. He had been *recast*, minus the tumour in his gut and the bullet-hole in his heart. Like the one who had arrived here before him, the Tarmac King had a way of seeing into the truth. Unlike the one who had gone before him, however, he did not always act on that truth.

An atheist his whole life, he'd denied any possibility of an experience after death. Even as the waters birthed him a second time he had wondered whether this was only the last acidic action of chemicals in his dying brain. But now, he had to face he was wrong. He had died – shot through the chest by a man in a mask – and now he was somewhere other than the world he'd left. This was no hospital bed. He didn't need to open his eyes to prove that.

If I lie here, the waters might take me back.

A dim part of his brain chided him for that. It was the part of his brain that sounded like his best friend Cris Orton, the person he'd taken the bullet for. Of course, Cris wouldn't have found anything surprising in the fact there was life after death. He was a believer, through and through. Sometimes Cris had spoken in such a way (not like the mad evangelists but with quiet certainty) that the Tarmac King could have almost believed it was possible.

Now, he had no choice.

Though, of course, he wasn't expecting a big white man with a beard, either.

Pike Malory opened his eyes.

———

A BEACH.

It wasn't much like any beach he'd seen before, and Pike had travelled more countries than he could remember. It was Cris used to call him the King of Tarmac. Better than what most other people used to call him: 'fucking gypo'. Perspective was everything.

The beach curved like a scimitar beyond any determinable end point. The sand was black as the water, and glittered as though made from ground down jet-stones. A city stood at the edge of the beach, as though it was encroaching outwards over the sand and into the water, reclaiming territory. Pike hated cities. He hated the dismal stink, the way that people move liked ants through them, and most of all, the way they seemed to behave like miniature gods, toying with their inhabitants as though possessed of their own demonic will. The city that loomed over him now seemed an assemblage of all the darkening cities he had seen in his life: grotesque, empty skyscrapers cutting the skyline like dagger points, patches of black breathing between them like the shadows of colossal monsters. A stink was coming from it – the unmistakeable smell of *poverty*. Not financial poverty: poverty of morals, poverty of the soul. There was no single aspect of the city that repulsed Pike, it was a jigsaw assembled from the bottom-scrapings of his consciousness, arranged in a way that rivalled Frankenstein's monster for ugliness.

Behind all the skyscrapers stood a pyramid. Most bafflingly of all, it did not look out of place next to the modern towers. They looked like they had grown together.

There was no-one waiting for him on the beach to greet him in this new world. There was certainly no way back over the waters. Pike was a strong swimmer, but there was no end to the ocean, not even a horizon: sky and ocean seemed to stretch like parallel lines, never touching. Pike, of course, had never had that maths lesson like most British kids: the one where the teacher draws a crude diagram of two lines and asks you to imagine them stretching forever. *They'll never intersect,* or words to that effect. But Pike didn't need the lesson; he understood what he was looking at because he'd spent his whole life understanding things by looking at them.

He was looking at infinity.

He turned, and began to walk into the city.

———

HE DIDN'T REALLY KNOW what he was looking for. He wasn't hungry. At some point he felt he must go towards the pyramid, but it could wait. That icon of the landscape felt terminal, and now that Pike understood he was not dead (although he wasn't sure he was alive, either) he intended to stay that way. The Tarmac King knew better than most that not everyone keeps themselves alive for some burning crusade or great purpose. Sometimes it is a tired habit of survival – a beaten patience that one day something good will come along to make it worth it, if not in the immediate future.

He saw the poverty he had smelled: a dilapidated chapel sitting like a babe between two towering monoliths. There were figures standing around the chapel. They looked human but their eyes glinted yellowish, like moons. They were wrapped in thick, white shawls and cloaks that instantly made Pike think of plague communities in Asia. Perhaps he was jumping to conclusions, they might be wrapped against the cold, but he wouldn't have shaken their hands.

As it happened, they did not approach him. They were too fixated on cooking a meal, which was no surprise given how loosely the shawls hung around their frames, like coats on a stand. There was a small pot propped up on crude metal rods. A fire burned beneath it, the dry logs giving off a greenish, poisonous-looking smoke which they all stood well back from. Within the pot, large rib bones were stewing. He smelled pork.

Then Pike saw a satchel by the pot from which a human foot protruded and he knew it wasn't a pig they were cooking.

He hurried on, feeling their eyes, though they did not look at him.

Further on, he saw a puddle in the road. As he got closer, he realised it wasn't a puddle, but a writhing pile of maggots. He backed away, repulsed. The maggots were podgy, each the size of a thumb, their bodies glistening like saliva. They made towards him, sliding and drop-ping over one another. At that moment, Pike had a vision of a beggar running up to him and clasping his knees, rejoicing at seeing another compassionate face. The beggar's face was clear as a stained glass window, its lines and faults and scars so vibrant in his mind's eye it made him reel. Pike did not know why this vision came to him or how it was so clear, but his gut instinct told him it was connected to the maggots and their bid to draw near. This thought disgusted him even more and he circled them, continuing up the road.

After a while, he started to hear the unmistakeable sound of a crowd roaring. It was coming from the direction of the pyramid, rolling over the city like a thunderhead. Pounding footsteps fired alarm bells and he wheeled. People were running up the road towards him. Some looked like the cannibals from the chapel. Others were less sick and famished, but all of them had a ragged and careworn look, like toys favoured by a child who hasn't yet learned to anthropomorphise their playthings. Pike's fingers itched and he shot his hand into his leather jacket. Once, there had been a berretta stashed there, but not now. He guessed guns didn't cross over. He considered running, but now they were closer he saw their eyes weren't fixed on him. They were fixed on the pyramid.

The people streamed past. They cried two syllables over and over, but given how breathless and strangled their voices were, he didn't quite make them out. It might have been *not since.* Or maybe even *the prince.* He didn't know. Whatever they were chanting, it had the same ring as the low, rumbling of the crowd in the distance. Some kind of gathering was happening. He was pretty sure he didn't want to be there.

He walked for miles before eventually finding a bar (of all things). There was a faint hubbub coming from within; next to the eerie chants and the things he had seen, it was comfortingly mundane. He went through the door, aware suddenly of his height, his gait, his *presence.* Pike had never been able to sink into a background. He had about as much of an ability to remain unnoticed as Clint Eastwood. This was the one time he regretted the fact.

The interior was dreary. It had the look of a place reconstructed from memory, but without the tools or heart to do it properly. A few grubby tramps cradled sour-looking drinks, sticking to the corners of the rooms where shadows hid most of their features. He knew they were watching him, but as of yet, they had made no rash decisions. Although Pike's presence got him noticed, it was also a deterrent for those seeking an easy victim.

There was an empty table in the centre of the bar that looked, merely by the way it was positioned and its relative cleanliness, like it was reserved for something. *Or someone.* He caught the barman's eye and walked up to him.

'What do you want?' the barman said.

'A drink.'

The barman nodded, as though Pike had successfully navigated a trick question.

'Beer?'

'Got a Carling?'

The barman snorted.

'New, I see. Though I didn't need to hear a request like that to tell me. Your clothes say enough.' The barman frowned all of a sudden, looking at Pike's leather jacket and jeans as though they had ancient runes scrawled over them. 'You're not related, are you?'

'To who?'

'Doesn't matter. You'd know who I meant.'

Pike felt his teeth gritting. He hated mind games like this. If he'd been standing in a real bar back in the world he knew, he might have grabbed the barman and threatened to beat straight talk out of him, but this was not the real world, and Pike didn't yet know the rules. He knew in the real world he could take on someone tougher than him and get socked a few times and get back up. Here, he wasn't so sure.

'You gunna pour me that beer then?'

The barman gave him an evil look but went to one of the pumps and pulled. Black liquid filled a cloudy pint-glass to its rim. The barman clunked it down.

'What do I owe you?'

'Nothing,' the barman said. 'Enjoy it. You'll be doing your time soon, unless he changes it.'

'Doing my time?'

The barman grinned and showed yellow teeth.

'Bless you. Are you still hoping for choirs of angels? Wait – no – don't tell me. You're a non-believer eh? Didn't think you'd be waking up at all?'

Pike hated it when other people were as perceptive as he was. He was thinking he might say 'fuck the rules' and beat the barman anyway.

'Something like that,' he said, with difficulty.

'Well, sorry mate, but this is definitely *something*. Don't matter what language you speak, they've all got a word for it. And in case you hadn't noticed, we all speak the same one here anyway. *Hell*. The place of suffering. Welcome to it!' The barman raised an imaginary glass and drank from it. His eyes looked like there was something crawling behind them, worms and ghosts. It chilled Pike, and he wasn't easily scared.

He took a sip of the beer. It was the most god-awful thing he'd ever tasted but he went for a second sip anyway. There was a nullity that came after the taste which was comforting: the nearest thing to the oblivion he'd hungered for.

'You said "he" might change it. What do you mean?'

The barman's face soured.

'Knew he was going to cause problems moment he came in here. First, asked for water. Then he fucked with Fay: turned all her cards white. Except one. Printed his dirty great big eye on it. Now he's giving speeches from the pyramid like he's some kind of god-emperor. A thousand, thousand people have been where he's been and they all fall in the end.'

It was too much information to swallow, so Pike drank. Before he knew it the pint was gone and he ordered another. Hell. Yes. That was pretty clear now. He'd given his life to defend his friend, and he'd ended up below all the same.

Two pints turned into ten. Pike had always been a drinker and he supposed this was living proof of the sentiment that what you did in life echoed beyond it. He found a seat and squatted it, downing bitter after bitter.

'Where's your "just god" now Cris?' he said, not noticing his slur. The beer was overpowering stuff. He also failed to remember that Cris had never used that particular descriptor, because like most real men of faith, he'd had his doubts too.

A hand touched him on the shoulder after what might have been the twelfth or thirteenth, he wasn't sure. He looked up and saw a woman in a white dress looking down at him. She was unbelievably beautiful – not just by comparison to the dismal surroundings. Her eyes held a kind of starlight in them that made Pike think of the word *magic.*

'Who are you?' he stammered. He was not embarrassed at being drunk: the Tarmac King did what he wanted when he wanted. He was angry, however, that he couldn't think straight at what seemed to be a critical moment.

The woman smiled. Her lips were thick and red.

She sat down opposite him, as though he had invited her. Pike wasn't about to object. She was the only thing he'd encountered so far that didn't repulse him, and she gave him more than a little hope things might not be so bad after all. Of course, if he had been in his right wits he might have considered that if this *was* hell, a beautiful woman could be the very deadliest trap. But Pike didn't really understand the mechanics of temptation and sin in the Bible. Not through lack of intelligence, but through asserted lack of trying.

'Who are you?' he said again. The more she watched him, the more he felt clearer in the head. It was as though those eyes had a purifying quality to them.

'Fay,' she said, as though that explained everything. He noticed she had a sickle slung across her back. It was curved and fine, as elegant as she was.

'And what are you doing here. In this...' He indicated the unsightly bar with a sweep of the hand. The barman gave him the finger.

'I'm the resident fortune teller.'

'Really? I used to know one of them. Funny fella' covered in moles. Went by the name of Albric. Ended up making a little boy into a monster.' Pike felt a stab of pain in his chest and swigged again. He needed a little numbness to tell this story. 'That monster ended up growing into a big monster who abducted my friend's wife...' He swallowed. 'And put a bullet through my chest, so...' He leant forward and gave her a psychopath's smile. '...I'm not too hot on fortune tellers at the moment.'

Fay did not draw back from him or blink. Her gaze was focused and even.

'But that doesn't change the fact he was right about you, does it?' A sly smirk crept over those curiously heavy lips. 'You *died for love.*'

Pike surged to his feet and roared. His pint glass went flying and smashed on the floor, a stain appearing like an omen of blood to be spilled. His chair cracked as it hit the floor. The barman watched him, as did Fay, who had not shifted an inch.

'How do you know that?' he snarled.

Those were the words Albric had said to him what was quite literally a lifetime ago in a dingy little caravan that smelled of crumpled cigarettes. Albric, against all signs and odds, had told Pike Malory the nihilist, Pike Malory the atheist, Pike Malory the lonely wanderer that he would die for love, that he was, in fact, a knight. And it had come true. In that last moment, it had been *love* that filled him up and made him take that bullet for Cris. Just when he'd thought there was only survival. Getting through.

'I told you,' she said, her voice sinking into him like music. 'I'm a fortune teller. It's my business to see.'

He was shaking. He hadn't shaken this bad for thirty years, since he'd been doing two or three lines of coke a day. That'd been when he was twenty three. The worst part of it was he couldn't even afford his own fix at £50.00 a gram. So he'd leached it all off his friend Dom. He visited Dom every day (a different reason why each time). Every visit, his friend was too nice to say 'no' to sharing his scores. Until the time he *did* say no, of course, because everyone has a breaking point. That's when Pike had started shaking so bad people noticed. People used the word junkie, which was a lot worse than gypo. What Pike called the 'dark days' rolled on. Houses got broken into. Fights happened. Things were done for dirty money. He wasn't proud of what he'd been, but he was proud he'd gotten through.

But here, now, twelve (or was it thirteen?) pints down, confronted by his past, a little echo of the junkie could be heard. Weakness. He was angry because he was weak.

Knowing that made it easier to fight it. He swallowed and counted to ten. He grabbed his chair and sat back down, slowly tucking himself back into the table.

'Sorry,' he grunted.

'It's okay. Most people react that way when they realise this isn't a sham.' Now she leant forward. The simple movement revealed a restrained litheness and power. Pike believed she would have been more than a match for him if it had come to a fight. No wonder she was so confident. 'So, do you want me to read your future?'

Pike nodded, but said:

'I thought your deck got wiped?'

Fay smiled. Her eyes sparked.

'I made a new one.' She produced a raggedy-edged hand-made deck of cards. They were larger than playing cards and flecked with dull-coloured paint blotches. 'And besides, I was glad he wiped it. He showed me something.'

'Who is "he"?'

Fay's smile deepened and the lips finally parted to reveal dazzlingly white teeth. Pike wasn't able to get the image of a shark out of his head.

'That's a very good question, but hard to answer. I could tell you his name and you'd still be none the wiser. It might be easier to show you.' She placed the deck on the table between them and lifted the top card off. She handed it to Pike. It was the card the barman had mentioned with the gleaming dark eye printed on it. At first, Pike saw only a black circle. He glanced at Fay's face to check she was not making a joke. When he read no humour there he looked back to the card. This time, it seemed there was something within the blackness, a deeper blackness that might have been a pupil, or a ring, or a doorway. He wasn't sure, but staring into it made him feel like he was standing on the edge of something and if he allowed himself to plummet down, his sanity would topple as easily as a house of cards. The worst thing about the image was that it seemed to be *moving*. The eye was roving, hungrily in search of something. Pike did not want to know what. He handed her back the card and she placed it apart from the deck. She then placed one hand on the top of the pile but didn't draw.

'Are you ready?' she said.

'Show me what you've got,' he said.

ACT I: LIKE MOTHS TO A FLAME

CHAPTER 1

'I have come to tell you about another world...'

Jubilation filled the madman's heart as he stood beneath the black ziggurat and heard the words of the red prophet.

It had been a dark and lonesome road. There had been pain, unimaginable pain. At the very moment of his triumph he had experienced the double agony of defeat and death – but death was not the end! How he'd laughed (between screams) as that revelation sank in. All those years he'd spent at the facility following failsafe procedures to ensure no one died. And then, those final hours where he had turned the tables on them all, turned the facility into his playground, watched people and animals tear each other apart (and done some of the tearing himself). All of that meant nothing because *death was not the end.*

It took someone as insane as Dr Monaghan to laugh when learning all their work was meaningless.

Tears ran from his aching eyes down the coruscating metal of the menpo. The Japanese war mask had been soldered to his face in the death moment: melted into the flesh of his chin, temples and cheeks. After the searing burning had ceased and he was no longer drunk with the smell of his scorched flesh, his first concern had been how he would

eat with the limited mouthpiece the mask afforded, but it seemed he did
not need to eat in this place; there was no hunger, only thirst.

The red prophet stretched out his hands. Even from the immense
summit of the pyramid, his dark eye was visible, an ecliptic spot,
dazzlingly baleful and void, casting negative rays out amongst them. Dr
Monaghan felt those rays piercing his heart, his being, searching his soul
for fault. *You will find none, prophet.*

'You have suffered here,' the prophet declared, his voice powerful
enough to shake mountains. It easily reached the back of the thousands-
strong audience. More were arriving even now, as though answering its
call, scurrying from between the buildings' shadows. '...but I am
different to those that have gone before. I offer you a new world where
you can take back the joys you have lost.'

Silence greeted this sentence. Dr Monaghan could not believe it. He
looked around at the crowd of yellow-eyed ghosts. How could they not
be captivated? How lost must they be?

A woman stepped forward from the crowd. She wore a white dress
and a sickle-blade, her figure cutting like a lightning bolt against the
stones of the pyramid. He felt a mixture of intense arousal (so intense
his cock was already throbbing in his pants) but also fear at the brilliance
and strength which exuded from her like radiation.

'You cannot cross the waters. They are the boundary between here
and the other life.'

'Oh, but I can,' the prophet answered, without hesitation. 'And so
can all of you. You've done it once before. You thought that everything
would end – or perhaps that there would be a heaven. But what you got
was hell... You suffer and suffer and suffer and then just when you think
you will have your sweet oblivion you suffer more! Where is the justice?
Where is the reward for what we have earned? There is none! We make
our *own* justice. That's why I want to give all of you the chance to come
with me. I *will* cross the dark waters. I will find the world again. And I
will take it back for us just as I took this one!'

And then the roar came. It ripped from every throat, as though
pulled by the dark vortex of the eye. Dr Monaghan added his war cry.

'It is a world ripe for the taking. It is levelled with conflict and death;

it is empty and barren. But we are the seeds that will make it grow again! Then, we will *all* be the masters of our own fate!'

It seemed as though the dense air hanging over the throng suddenly began to congeal and form into an image. Dr Monaghan stopped shouting and became transfixed. The air was breathing into substance. Clouds formed, like low-hanging atmosphere. Then, they parted, revealing a vision of bloodshed; an atom-scorched earth spun, a thousand World Trade Centres collapsing in on themselves over and over to the tune of an instrument made from the ligaments of slaughtered children. Acts of carnal depravity filled up the streets of unborn cities until there were no streets, only inescapable flesh and abhorrent acts performed upon it, acts done in the name of discovery, discovering to what depths human beings could be plunged. Yes, Dr Monaghan had taken his research into this particular line far, but he could go further, there were depths as yet untouched which he had now been given a second chance to reach...

The *ultimate game*. Yes, he had played a great game back in Facility 2-13, but there was a bigger game, a better game, a game where worlds could become playgrounds rather than a mere facility. His breath hissed from the mask, heavy, sluggish, hot. A new thirst had been awoken in him.

Dr Monaghan believed everyone saw the vision of blood, a shared glimpse of the greatness to come, but he was the only one. Whether that was because the prophet afforded him a special window into the future from his eye, or whether it was to do with the slow corrosion of his mind, is difficult to determine.

Suffice to say, Dr Monaghan was sure it was the former.

'Will you come with me?' The prophet roared.

We will. We will. We will.

Dr Monaghan's voice was loudest of them all.

The woman was now raising something – a white, perfect square – and on it was the dark eye. A banner, a sign.

'He is our leader, our Prince!'

'The Prince!' Dr Monaghan screamed.

And they all followed.

The Prince. The Prince. The Prince.

Except, there was one who didn't follow. Dr Monaghan noticed him and they locked eyes. For an eerie second, Dr Monaghan thought he was looking into some kind of mirror, but then he realised that the ugly, distorted visage glaring back at him was not a mask, but an *actual face*: bulbous tumour-growths mangled the left eye and right cheek, reminding Dr Monaghan of some of the more hideous specimens he had operated on in Facility 2-13. The man's lips looked like they were in the late stages of necrosis. His flesh was leprous. Dr Monaghan had also been fooled by the grubby white suit he was wearing which, at a glance, resembled his own white lab coat.

As they stared at one another, Dr Monaghan got an uneasy feeling in his belly. It took him a few moments to think what the source of this feeling was. It wasn't the ugliness of the face: he had seen plenty of far more horrifying monsters in his time at the illegal government lab. It wasn't the fact he wasn't joining with the rest in cheering on the red prophet. Dissenters could be dealt with.

No, what gave Dr Monaghan the feeling that worms were crawling down his oesophagus was the realisation that this man was not in the least bit frightened of him. After all the things the doctor had done, after the countless moments he had looked into the eyes of men and women he was about to end and seen their terror, it was disconcerting that someone could look at him without fear.

Cursing himself slightly, Dr Monaghan tore his gaze away first. Let the stranger in white think he had the better of him for now. He would find him later and put an end to that ugly face.

The crowd's cries were growing louder and more delirious. It only took a moment to realise why, the prophet was descending the side of the pyramid towards them, coming to walk amongst his people. An electrical current rushed through the doctor – he felt as though a drug was kicking in after hours of deceptive dormancy. It reminded him of those drops of caffeine and gin into the eye to keep him awake, working through the night.

A thought had formed along with the energy that was now coursing through his veins: *He must reach the Prince. He must reach him and declare his loyalty.*

Dr Monaghan ran. Screaming men and women barred his path but he threw them aside. Some stood and raised their voices to him, but when they saw the masked face and the zealot's eyes, they backed away and let him past. He fought his way through, always trying to keep the bloody figure in view. The Prince was magnificent, sunlight shining in his wounds, his eye like a gemstone.

The pyramid loomed over him, large enough to split the world in two. He almost baulked out of fear, daunted and overawed (but *he must reach the Prince*). A man stood in his way and even though he was afraid of the doctor's wild eyes, tried to punch him down. Dr Monaghan took the punch without feeling and then jabbed his index and middle finger into the man's eyes, dragging him to the floor (*he must reach the Prince*). He scooped out the goo from the sockets and spread it over his mask like war paint, laughing to himself about how it must look like semen stains. The man cried and rolled around in the dust, shrieking. The others backed away from Dr Monaghan, and his path was clearer from then on.

He reached the foot of the pyramid just as the red prophet leapt down the last few steps. The woman in white moved as though to stop him but Dr Monaghan threw himself to his knees. He wouldn't chance it against her. Not yet, anyway.

'I mean no harm. I mean no harm. Let me speak to him!'

The woman turned and looked at the Prince, who nodded. He walked to Dr Monaghan, and though awe filled every eye (except perhaps the eyes of the man in the white suit), no one dared interrupt the exchange. The prophet motioned for the doctor to stand, and he did. Up close, Dr Monaghan could see the blood was the prophet's own, from innumerable lacerations which had shredded his rag-tag leather jacket, his dusty jeans, and his face. *What a face!* Dr Monaghan could have devoted a lifetime to studying it. It would have been far more interesting than all the specimens of Facility 2-13 combined. The lines were impossibly deep and complex, their own labyrinth.

'Who are you?' the Prince asked, a small smile curling his lips.

'My name is Dr Monaghan,' he said, in a hushed whisper. 'I will wage a war on *god* for you.'

The Prince laughed.

'We'll see.'

It was then Dr Monaghan found himself staring fully into the dark eye, the eye that lived in the empty socket. He knew in that instant he could hide nothing. The entire story was going to come out: the principle act of it was how he'd converted the containment facility into his own arena of death and driven thousands to madness, suicide or death. In seconds, the events played before Dr Monaghan's eyes; a quivering smile appeared behind his mask as he was reminded of some of the more delectable moments. He knew these scenes were also playing before the Prince's eyes. They were sharing experience. It was intimate, perhaps the most intimate Dr Monaghan had felt with anyone, and his throbbing erection returned. The eye seemed to be panting, as though a separate entity to the prophet which possessed its own will and desires. It hungered for the violence in the doctor's mind, for his twisted thoughts, for the savage detail of the acts he had committed. He was feeding the eye, he realised. And as long as he could, the Prince would love him.

The visions ended.

The prophet's smile was like a black scar in the earth.

Slowly, he stretched out a hand and laid it on Dr Monaghan's shoulder. Spasms of pleasure fluttered through his body at the touch.

'You have done great work,' the Prince whispered. 'But there is *more* you can do if you will follow me.'

Dr Monaghan could not speak, the joy was too overwhelming.

'...will you answer me?'

At first, Dr Monaghan had thought it was the Prince that'd said these words, but then he realised, it had come from behind him, and the voice conveyed nothing of the depths of power that the prophet's did. He returned. The crowd had also turned. There were two desolate figures approaching the gathering. They did not look like the others – for one their eyes were not yellow. Perhaps they were also fresh souls like himself? More players for the game...

The Prince began to make his way towards the two figures. The crowd split like the sea in the Old Testament, allowing him through. Dr Monaghan fell into step behind the Prince, a vanguard. The woman in white followed too. *Stupid bitch. You doubted at first. You denied him. I believed from the start.* He then checked himself. What if she could read his mind? Better not think too loudly...

You never knew what women were capable of.

CHAPTER 2

They had shattered one city of illusion only to find themselves in another.

Hagga did not know how much more she could bear. Her limbs were almost too weak to lift; her head felt like it was still set alight by the invisible fire of the demon. Larri had had to carry her out of the crumbling foundations of Yin's labyrinth - and he was a cripple. She couldn't believe his misaligned legs were still supporting him. The more she learned about Larri, the more he surprised her. When she'd first seen him limping up the road she thought there was no one who could be of less use to them in the fight against the illusion-master. He had ancient, white hair, a stumbling gait, hunched shoulders that meant he was eternally stooped, and a kind of twist to his body like a chewed up tin can. But now, as she watched his face, she saw there was stone beneath the outer flesh.

Besides, who was she to judge for scars?

The flesh on the left side of her body and arm were discoloured; motor-function in the fingers was intermittent at best, and would be for a good long while, perhaps even permanently. She had seen the look in Larri's eyes as he carried her down the long tunnel which had led them to this desolate city: the regret of something beautiful marred.

So much had happened to them both these last few days she could scarcely believe any of it was real. What if she woke up and found all of this was another trick of Yin's? His final joke? Somehow she didn't think so. They had destroyed Yin in the heart of his citadel, or at least, they had destroyed his hold on the Circle. If he was still alive, he would be changed and reduced, his true form exposed to all.

But this was the past. She had to concern herself with the now, though it was hard to remain focused through so much pain. Simon had said to take the word of God to those outside the Circle. Hagga didn't know much about God, but the people she saw now did not look ready to receive him. Hell, she wasn't sure if she was, either.

Like the first upright hominoids scanning the horizon for danger, they watched as the windows of the titanic buildings filled with yellow eyes like stars being birthed. Crowds were gathering in the streets. In the distance, a black pyramid tore a triangular rend in the universe.

Larri stood, suddenly, as though a voice in his head had told him to do so.

'I am the voice of one calling in the desert. Will you answer me?'

At first, the figures did not answer. Blank stares greeted him. She wondered if they understood his language. Then, the crowd parted.

A man made his way toward them, flanked by two others that looked like they guarded him. All three were imposing. The women in white looked like a goddess. Hagga could not think of anyone more opposite to herself. Where the woman in white was fair skinned, bright eyed, and clothed like a royal character out of a picture book, Hagga was dark haired, brown-skinned from years beneath the illusionary sun of the desert Circle, and deep inside of her a darkness still pulsed, the dreadful Need. She shuddered. Why was she thinking of that now? Hadn't Simon cured her? Simon, the hermit. Simon, who had given his life for them to reach here.

The other guard was a man in a war mask and a white coat; Hagga had never seen a coat like it before. The mask was metal and grotesque, barely human, an expression of maddening rage formed by bulbous, distorted features. More terrifying than the mask though were the eyes of the man, which grew brighter and more alarming as he drew closer, like the torch-fires of the cannibals who had come for her friends month after month as part of the Circle's offerings.

But the man who stood between them was the most frightening of all.

Where there should have been a right eye, there was a hole, like a sink-hole, and Hagga was sure if she looked into it long enough she and the rest of the universe would be drawn into it like dirty water and disappear forever. She wanted more than anything to take her eyes away from the hole, but she couldn't. The hole was drawing in but it was also looking out, like the absent eye would have done, and *feeling* its way across her being.

Deep inside, the lupine form, the slavering hunger that was the Need, shivered. Its hair bristled, as though the eye had *touched* it. That, more than anything else, made her afraid.

She struggled to her feet and went to stand beside Larri, who was also transfixed by the dark eyed prophet approaching them.

'There are no answers here,' he said, with a grin. He had a face that should have been handsome to Hagga (though weathered) but somehow it wasn't. Somehow it made her want to scratch until there was nothing to look at. 'But there is purpose.'

'What purpose?' she said, challenging him.

The prophet seemed to find this amusing, because the grin expanded.

'To find our way back.'

'To the Circle?'

The prophet shook his head.

'No, let me show you.'

He stretched out his arms and looked up to the sky. As if answering him, it darkened. The atmosphere drew in, as though the perceivable world had shrunk around them like a tight blanket. Hagga felt breathless. Her feet were unsteady. Colours shifted and though the prophet was covered in blood, he seemed to be flashing a myriad of impossible hues.

Tendrils erupted from the darkness of his eyeless eye. Black, snake-like, they coiled and morphed, an octopean, chthonic creature that wriggled towards the heavens as though seeking to topple it. A monster capable of demolishing gods. The crowd became a pop of gasps, shudders and even screams. Everyone took a step back from him save the man in the war-mask, who was laughing deliriously.

'It grows and grows!' the prophet said, triumphantly. 'The power grows!'

The monster uncoiling from his socket stretched, writhed and then began to melt until its limbs were no longer limbs but buildings like the skyscrapers around them, each window lit with moving pictures of a world Hagga could not even begin to recognise.

'But...'

Impossible images flickered and flashed: children and mothers and fathers, all clad in clothes of impossibly lavish design, walking silver streets whilst musicians and glowing screens surrounded them with dazzling sound and light. Forests rolled for miles beyond discernible end. Hagga did not know where to look: she was being shown so much she thought her brain might fall into a seizure.

But she could not look away, either, because something was happening. A light was building behind the innumerable windows, a fizzling, ecstatic light that for some reason made her bones ache. It was expanding, rippling. Some of the windows showed people looking to the sky. What was it? An errant star? A comet?

The light multiplied a hundred times, becoming a sphere of impossible whiteness that swept over the scenes, shattering the windows, and creating a noise like a thousand hurricanes. Hagga clapped her hands to her ears and felt the Need quiver. Larri was bleeding from the nose, a single red line forming on his upper lip like the beginnings of war-paint. The whiteness throbbed and seethed. Within it, a hissing of melted flesh and stone and metal reverberated like the greatest serpent. The sphere became a snowglobe of ash.

The light ended. A city was visible, clinging to a coastline, its proud towers much like the ones which stood around them (although Hagga could barely remember them, the vision was so real). There was only one window now. One image. The silent, dark city next to the desolate waters. Slowly, the city began to expand. It was as if they were moving towards it, like birds. They sailed down through its snow and ash laden streets until they saw a figure, standing amidst the desolation. That figure was the prophet.

And he was laughing.

Defragmenting, the window split apart. Once again they were looking at a shadow of the towers around them. These shadow towers flickered, their windows changing shape and becoming watery, more like the suckers of a tentacle. Their oblong shapes curved and glistened, gained rubbery motion. The monster was there again, retreating into the dark socket.

Only when it was gone did the light return.

'You... you did it... you caused it... you're the Cataclysm!' Larri whispered. He was as white as his hair.

'Yes,' the prophet said. 'But the world I levelled is not your world.'

'What do you mean?'

'You come from a place that is not unlike this one. An alternate world, tucked away behind the supposed reality of the *primary* one. Which means...' A strange laugh broke from the prophet's mouth. '... you were both born in a kind of afterlife.' He raised his voice. '*Christians hear this and know you know nothing!*'

'That's impossible,' Hagga growled. She was beginning to feel this prophet was no less a deceiver than Yin. What did he hope to achieve by convincing them they were somehow not real? Was he really implying *they* were illusionary? Hagga hadn't fought cannibals and demons to be told she was less than human by a lunatic.

'At this stage, nothing is impossible,' the prophet said, with surprising calm. 'The souls assembled here come from all different times and some from other worlds like yourself. Fay...' He pointed to the woman in white. 'Was born of *this* world. Dr Monaghan and I...' He indicated the man in the war mask. '...were born of the same world but he died many years before me.'

'Died?' Larri interjected. 'Afterlife? What are you trying to say – we're in Hell?'

'I somehow think Hell would be a little more crowded, don't you?'

Hagga had to hand it to him: the prophet knew how to speak and win.

'If we all come from different times as well as places, then that must mean we've all been brought here for a reason,' Hagga said. 'Chosen, if you will.'

The prophet turned his full gaze on her for the first time during the conversation.

'Smart,' he said. '*And* beautiful...'

Fay twitched.

'Dangerous,' Hagga growled.

This seemed to amuse the prophet.

'Come now, there's no *Need,* to get defensive.' The way he emphasised the word, and the way he looked at her, made it more than clear he knew. How, Hagga wasn't sure, although the memory of feeling as though he had somehow touched the Need inside her surfaced, like a warning dream. It was clear the eye had power to show and to see. She had to be careful what she thought from now on, keep parts of her mind walled from him; otherwise, he could so easily use her secrets against her.

The prophet walked towards her, closing the distance. Her body felt as though the joints were cementing. At the same time as the paralysis, she thought she could hear an angry dog breathing heavily in her ear. It was the Need, surfacing, aware of the danger.

She hadn't been cured at all; Simon had temporarily subdued it, but the curse would never fully be gone.

Larri made as though to halt the prophet's advance, but just as he did, the prophet stopped.

'There used to be a guardian in this place. A dog. He was much less sophisticated than you. He needs replacing. There's much I could offer you in return for this service.' He extended a hand. Like his face, it was full of trenches, canyon-deep scores in the skin. 'Where I come from, those with gifts become kings and queens, not exiles.'

Hagga shivered. He had been reading her and she hadn't even known.

She looked at the hand. She had been tempted like this once before, in the heart of the city of illusion, by Yin. Yin had offered her a vision of those who had driven her out of Law Town bowing to kiss her feet, of an endless feast – the Need chewing through the bodies of children – of men awaiting her every command, satisfying her every want. Because the

Need was a hunger of many forms: body, mind, and soul. It had been a long time since that physical urge was sated. She had offered herself to Simon whilst they journeyed together, but he loved men.

The prophet had called her beautiful – his hand was outstretched. She had no magical eye, but she could feel the throbbing energy of him, a power that promised so much.

Yin had been the master of illusion, but the temptation she had felt in his citadel paled with what she felt now. She could feel Larri watching her, but even that was hardly a deterrent. *Larri saved you. He carried you out of the collapsing city.* But Larri was also weak. Larri was foolish. It wasn't through accident that he had become a cripple. It had been through his cowardice – he'd let his own son be raped and taken by the cannibals.

She forced herself to *look* at Larri, but that made her feel no different. He was pathetic. Meagre. Yet...

The white of his hair triggered memory of the ash, the white light, the ending she had been shown by the prophet in the vision. This man caused the Cataclysm. This man caused the end of the world.

'I'll take my chances on my own, thanks.'

The prophet withdrew his hand. There was a moment when she sensed that her life was being assessed for its value, as though a human soul had weight and metallic properties.

'If you change your mind, you know where I'll be.' He smiled. 'Hagga.'

He turned and began to walk back towards the crowd. Dr Monaghan was still looking at her. Hagga was sure he would have killed her in a heartbeat if the prophet had commanded it. But he hadn't. They were free to go, for now.

Dr Monaghan turned and followed his master. Fay remained. If there had been any indication the prophet's words to Hagga had enjealoused her, all traces were gone now. Her eyes were squinted slightly and her head cocked to one side.

'Don't think too long,' she said. 'And watch out for the dwarf.' She slid through a crack between two buildings and was gone. Clearly she had other errands to run that did not involve the prophet; Hagga was not sure whether that meant she was more or less dangerous than she appeared.

Larri turned to her, wiping the blood from his upper lip.

'You were tempted, weren't you?'

'Yes,' Hagga answered, quietly.

'He isn't human,' Larri said. 'He's like Yin – some kind of demon.'

Hagga shook her head.

'He's nothing like, Yin. He's another beast entirely.'

CHAPTER 3

The world disintegrated and he was left with the memory.

The boy with the disfigured face stood in a clearing in the wood, tears streaming down his face. He was fifteen. Somewhere, Albric called to him. Albric the liar. Albric who had pretended to be his father. He would not go to him. He would not speak with him. All these years the old beggar had fed him a myth of who he was. He would not hear it anymore.

'Come on, girl,' he said, between tears. The border-collie followed him as he walked, attentive as a careful nurse, glancing up every now and then with the approval-seeking eyes the boy had come to love. If indeed, love were real.

'We're both strays now,' he said, to Found, who panted, tongue lolling like an old sock. Perhaps he imagined it, but he thought he saw the dog's brow was furrowed, as though sensing his distress.

He walked for a long time, until Albric's cries had melted into echo, and then his legs gave out from under him and he collapsed and cried again, resting against an old tree.

Found started barking.

'What is it girl?'

She wouldn't stop. He reached out to stroke her neck, but the dog just kept up its chant. Slaver flew from her mouth. Her eyes were fear-wide.

'Girl what's...'

A man appeared. He was tall – impossibly tall to the young boy – like a giant. He wore a torn up leather jacket and had only one eye. Though his flesh said that he was youthful, perhaps only in his twenties, the eye that stared out of the sockets looked older than sunlight. The boy had grown up in the woods. He had a knife in his back pocket which he knew how to use. He was not afraid of anybody. Except, this man did not seem like anybody. He did not seem human.

'What's the matter, kid?' He was American. The boy had never met an American before. Despite how frightening he was, he reminded the boy of one of the cowboys from the old movies Albric sometimes let him watch.

'Nothing.'

'Your father let you down?'

The boy's blood ran cold.

'How'd you...?'

'My father let *me* down too,' the man said, grinning. He had shark's teeth that glinted like moonshards. The forest suddenly seemed a lot darker, night very close at hand. 'He wasn't who I thought he was. Is that what happened to you?'

The boy nodded slowly. Somehow he sensed there was no point hiding anything from this man.

'I don't know what to do.'

The man nodded and then took careful steps towards him. Found had stopped barking, but she mewled and shivered. The man in the leather jacket knelt beside her and reached out a hand. As soon as he touched the dog's fur she went limp and lay down, submissive as a sheep. The boy had never been able to exert such control over the animal, and he had taken the dog in a year ago, saved it from death.

'Good dog,' the man said.

He turned his eye on the boy. This close, the boy could see that the man's empty socket wasn't exactly empty. There seemed to be something in the hollow. An orb, or maybe a circle, like an Egyptian coin placed over the eye of a deadman.

'You want to know what I think?' the man said.

'Yeah.'

'You gotta hurt something, kid. You gotta get back. It's the only way you're gunna make that pain go away.' The man sniffed, reminding the boy eerily of Found. 'You got gifts, kid. Maybe one day you could find me. I got plans for this world. I'm getting a team together. One day, you come and find me in New York.' He grinned. 'But meanwhile, you've got to get rid of this pain. The only way is by making an offering. A sacrifice.'

He stroked Found's coat.

'No,' the boy whispered.

The man stood. He put his hands on his belt like a prospector. He seemed more solid and rooted than any tree.

'Yes. And I'm going to watch you do it, boy.'

The boy launched to his feet, drawing the blade from his back pocket and lunging.

But the man had started moving *before* he'd even gotten to his feet. He slapped the boy's lunging hand, knocking the knife clean from his grip. His other hand snatched out and fingers closed around the boy's throat.

The man lifted the boy from his feet and held him nose to nose.

The boy looked long and deep into the empty socket.

The man set the boy down, who gasped for air.

'Pick up that knife,' he grunted.

The boy obeyed.

Found whimpered.

'We have work to do, kid,' the man said.

And his smile was like atomic light.

———

T<small>HE</small> T<small>AKING</small> M<small>AN</small> shivered and came to slumped against the wall. He wiped the drool from his lips. The memory was chokingly vivid, every detail etched as clearly as hieroglyphs.

It was the Prince that had made him the monster he was. It was the Prince who had made him kill the dog he so loved.

He had taken away the last thing he loved. Made him nothing. Made him the Taking Man.

Now, the Taking Man would make *him* nothing.

He got to his feet and peered out from his hiding place.

His quarry was still in sight: he watched the fortune-teller from the shadows. If he could get at her, he would pull at the central thread holding together the web of the Prince's lies. She had been the one playing the crowds – at first appearing to contradict him, then being won over. The others, like that masked man, might be too dim to see it, but the Taking Man saw. The Taking Man knew. Making examples out of people was everything.

Nothing had changed since his death. This world he now inhabited was frightening and dark (no different from the murky streets of London), there were several dangerous players in the game (no different from the other *gifted* ones), and he had a mission to complete. He had failed to make Cris Orton understand the truth, all because of that wretched thug Pike Malory. He had been trying to show Cris how *he* had been the one to destroy his life. How *he* was the real villain of the story, but it had all gone wrong. When he presented Cris with the choice between his best friend and his wife, his friend had made the decision for him.

This time, he wouldn't offer a choice. He would kill everyone surrounding the Prince and then the Prince himself. But first, he had to do what he did best. He had to *take*. With Fay out of the picture, missing, the Prince would panic. He might then go looking for her – over-extending himself – or he might hole up in the pyramid. Either would suit the Taking Man just fine.

Fay turned into another alleyway. The Taking Man followed slowly. He had mastered the art of treading softly. It came from being raised in the woods, hunting for food from the age he was first able to hold a blade. Even then, he'd known the power of taking. Kill a doe and you had a few nights' meals. Take one of its fawns and leave it bleeding and tied to a tree, and you got a few weeks'.

She reminded him of a doe. The way her legs moved, a suppleness conveying weightless power, as though her bones were carbon fibre. If she was a doe, she was the white one, elusive, mythic. She would not be as easy as the stupid, fat gypsy woman Cris called a wife, or the children, or any of the numberless people he had taken back in the 'living' world. No.

He lost sight of her around a corner, and though he was cautious of being discovered, he was also aware he did not know the city and could not lose her. He quickened his pace, and reached the edge of a building. He peeked around and saw her crossing a desolate highway (but there were no cars, so what purpose did it serve?). On the other side of the highway was a bar within which a feeble light shone, the only light that wasn't the eerie convulsion of a permanently storming sky.

As she crossed the highway, she paused. The Taking Man had no hairs on his body; his flesh was fishlike and oily. The smell that came from him was like a fish's carcass, a smell that did not give away his presence as one might expect but rather masked his approach. Though he did not have any hairs, he felt the prickle as though they had stood to attention all down his spine, neck and arms, a warning that some would call a sixth sense. *She is about to turn around.* He slipped back into the alleyway and waited. He counted to fifteen. When he looked again he saw a sliver of white dress vanish behind the door to the bar.

His black, cracked lips curled into a crescent shape.

'I wonder if you read this in your cards, witch.'

————

HE DID NOT WANT to confront her in front of the patrons if he could help it, so he waited outside. The other side of the highway would be too far away, so he'd crossed and nestled himself behind swollen garbage cans sitting out the back of the bar. Flies hummed around them, seeking a perforation point to get at the liquidated contents. He didn't mind them. The Taking Man had grown up in the muck.

As soon as she emerged, he would overpower and take her. That would be his first blow to the Prince. He was already imagining the look of rage on his face when he learned his chief agent was gone.

Hours went by and she did not emerge. He'd have to make sure she was still in there. Besides, he could always leave if he was found out. He had time. If he didn't grab her today, it could be tomorrow or the next.

He'd spent decades planning his revenge on Cris. He could afford weeks if needed for this.

He emerged from behind the garbage, not bothering to waft at the flies, and entered the bar. He scanned the room. No one paid his hideously disfigured face any attention, which was one thing different about this world.

He saw Fay, sitting in the middle of the room, cards laid out on a table in front of her. There was a man sat opposite, wearing a leather jacket. There was something vaguely familiar about the torn up jacket (for a brief moment it had reminded him of the Prince's, but he was certain this wasn't him).

The sensation of hair rising returned; prescience awoke, it was as though his body had split into two, one part rushing ahead into a dimly glimpsed future, and the other chained into the past. But it was too late to heed the warning; there was nowhere to go.

The man turned around and he found himself looking into the eyes of Pike Malory.

Time is not a boring, metric tool. As Einstein said, it is relative. It stretches and compresses and twists and coils back and repeats itself. In that moment of revelation, it stretched, not only for the Taking Man and Pike, but for the rest of the bar's patrons, who sensed, in the primitive way animals sense impending disasters, that something had changed in the air.

Then, time compressed.

Pike was on his feet in a heartbeat. The Taking Man lurched across the room, a roar tearing from his throat.

Just before he reached Pike there was a flash of light like needles being driven into his pupils and the roar became a howl. He held up his hands to shield against the blaze, adrenaline making his limbs jittery and elastic.

The light cleared a moment later. Fay was stood between them, her sickle blade forming a dividing line. For a moment, the Taking Man considered throwing her aside, but something about the gleam of the sick's edges held him back. It was no ordinary, crude blade. He could smell that much about it. *It* was what had issued that burst of impossible and disorientating light.

'Now, now,' she said. 'Didn't your mothers ever tell you to play nice?

'My mother abandoned me at birth,' the Taking Man said, grinning. Though Fay was the greater threat to him, he couldn't stop watching Pike, imagining his rugged face purpling under the touch of his powers. 'So I guess I missed that lesson.'

'Boohoo,' Pike said, 'You going to cry about it?'

The Taking Man grit his teeth and bore the chemical rush inside his veins silently. However much he hated Pike, he knew that sickle blade and the steady-handed woman who wielded it, could end him. Or near enough to it. He wasn't sure death held any meaning in this place.

'One of you needs to leave,' Fay said. 'And given your appointment is over, Pike. I suggest it should be you.'

Pike's lips curled back to reveal his teeth. He glanced at Fay then nodded with what looked like great effort.

'I was on my way out anyway,' he said. He walked around the blade and to the door, not looking over his shoulder, bearing his back like a fighter intending insult.

He opened the door and paused in the threshold.

'I'll pay you back for that bullet, *Orton*.'

He went through the slammed the door behind him. The Taking Man felt vomit creeping into his throat. *How dare he use that name!*

'Why don't we sit?' Fay said, redirecting the sickle so it was solely focused on him. He grimaced. The tables had certainly been turned, but then again, what had he expected? He had lost patience. Foolishly blundered in. It was the kind of thing he expected from his enemies.

He took a seat at her table. The barman gave an audible sigh and continued polishing the dirty glass he'd stopped cleaning the moment the two men had faced off against one another.

Fay sat, sliding the sickle back into place on her back. It was held there in a small, translucent pouch that looked like it'd been made from the fronds of a jellyfish. Unlike a traditional longer sword (which was actually nearly impossible to draw from the back at any speed) the sickle was short and light enough to be brought to bear almost instantly, as she had just demonstrated.

The Taking Man noted all of this. He had acted without any information, but information was exactly what he needed. He closed his eyes for half a second and visualised the world substantiating, turning fleshly coloured, becoming a body. He visualised him opening his mouth and sinking fangs deep into its tissue, piercing a vein and drawing the blood from it. As he drew the blood, knowledge poured into his mind zoophagusly.

Of course, when Albric had first taught him this technique, he had said to imagine the world as a flowering garden, from which petals could be plucked, but the Taking Man preferred his version. It was realer.

When he opened his eyes he was calm. Pike was an unpleasant revelation, doubly so now that he had gotten away, but not for long. He could be dealt with. Fay was no longer within his power to take. She was stronger than he had given her credit for, an oversight of judgement he cursed himself for, but she would not be invulnerable forever. He also was certain she was not about to kill him, otherwise she would have done so.

'It's funny how these things work,' she said, playfully. 'I bet neither of you expected to meet each other here, and yet you sent each other to this place. In a way.'

'You'll have to do better than that, fortune teller,' the Taking Man said. 'You heard his bullet remark. And you're wrong. He didn't send me here.'

Fay only smiled.

'I said: "in a way." Laura might have pulled the trigger, but Pike weakened you, didn't he? Was it a syringe?'

The Taking Man swallowed. So the witch did have a kind of gift. She reminded him of Cassandra, except Cassandra had been stupid and easy to manipulate, despite her talents. Fay posed an entirely different conundrum.

'And you didn't even use your cards,' he said. 'I'm impressed.'

'I've been learning from *him*.'

The way she said it could only mean one person. The Taking Man felt his face twisting without him willing it. There were times when he was angry the tumours felt like sacs of poison, burning against his face. His breath shortened, cutting off as though someone had gripped his lungs in their fists. The asthma had followed him here. He clenched his fist and slammed it on the table, pain flooding his chest. He fought for control over himself for a few moments, and eventually the breathing smoothed. He was dizzy but lucid. His tumours still burned.

'He is a liar. He'll only betray and leave you.'

'He sees the truth. The eye...'

'Is not a part of him,' the Taking Man cut across her. 'He is not in control of it. He cannot always predict when its powers will flare and when not, but he goes with it. Hence his surprise when the vision unfolded before the cripple and that woman.' The Taking Man had watched it all, from the shadow of an alley. 'He is powerful, yes. But the power does not come from *him*. Hence, he is a liar. The eye is a lie. And he will lie to all those who follow him.' The Taking Man had an idea and he seized on it. 'He has already undermined you. His offer to the woman. Didn't you see how quickly he was prepared to take another woman?'

Fay laughed. For all the beauty in her voice, it conveyed no real amusement.

'The Prince is not interested in women. If he seemed to suggest that to her, it was only to manipulate her.'

'If he will manipulate her, why not you?'

'Because he knows I can see too. Perhaps not as vividly as him, but sometimes much further. I'm the only one who knows his real name.'

'Which is?'

'If you give a demon a name, it has power over the one who carries that name.'

The Taking Man grinned.

'You know more about me than I realised.'

Fay shrugged and gave a sly smile. She lifted her feet and placed them on the table. She had elfin toes and a perfect arch. Her legs were like the work of a master-sculptor. The Taking Man had the bizarre thought that perhaps deformed, wretched physical specimens like himself were merely practice for art like her. Despite that, he felt no desire for her.

'You're like him, you know,' Fay was saying. 'You don't have any kind of desire for this.' She took her legs off the table and leant forward. 'Perhaps that's why you don't like him. He reminds you of you.'

The Taking Man felt his face twitch.

'But you're also not alike,' she continued. 'He wanted the world to lie at his feet when he set off those bombs. You just wanted one man.' She smiled. It was a confusing expression: at once filled with pity and mockery. The Taking Man, though he'd believed himself impervious to these kinds of games, felt the smile physically twist something in his body. *She's playing with you. End her! Take everything! Leave only a husk.* Her beauty could be destroyed. He could wrench it from her with a touch alone. Of course, it would not repair his own face: that was the one thing he couldn't steal with his gift. He could absorb strength, knowledge, even powers, but he could not keep beauty. He could take it from another, but he couldn't own it. The universe had a wonderful sense of humour, black as a hole in space.

All you could do was match it.

'I did what I did for a reason,' he said. 'He does what he does, because the eye tells him to. When you've had enough of following the eye, let me know.'

He stood.

She rose with him, a calm smile on her face.

'Are you sure you don't want me to read your future before you go?'

The Taking Man grinned.

'What future?'

He swept from the room.

Chapter 4

The one who now called himself The Magician sat cross-legged in the throne-room of the pyramid, a mantle of blackness enrobing him.

Twelve robed figures stood in a semi circle. These were the keepers of the pyramid, the ones who allotted the suffering of those who arrived on these shores. Only, the Prince had changed all that. The Prince had changed many things.

When the Magician had been driven from the Circle, he had been a piece of trash scattered on the wind, swept up with the other detritus and garbage of the world. He had no agency left. No power. No will. He was swept to this place and quickly enslaved by the twelve. There was a time he could have thrown them aside with a single soul-crushing illusion, unmaking the fabric of their insubstantial being in the same way a child could unwind the thread of feebly knitted clothing. There was a time he could have taken the whole city hostage, made shadows dance through its streets, turn friend on friend in the delirium of cannibalism, risen high on the winds of suffering until *he* became the new god, the new prophet, just as he had once been in the Circle.

But none of that had happened. The winds had blown him into the gutter. He had been overpowered and forced to act as guardian. That was until the Prince came. The Magician would never forget the first time he saw him, striding out of the dark waters. Everyone else was washed up like lifeless driftwood, but he *walked* from it. And the eye. The eye that had seen him even whilst he wore his cloak of invisibility...

The Magician shuddered.

'Is there anything else you require of us?' the twelve said, singular and many at once.

'Nothing further.'

And with that, they were gone. They weren't happy with the new way of things, but it seemed as long as the Prince remained in the seat of power, there was little they could do. He had conquered the pyramid somehow. The Magician knew enough of the magics of illusion to understand the pyramid was much like his own citadel had been: a labyrinth designed to invade and haunt those who trespassed with visions of the past. It drew in an image, reflecting it back, but also producing its own copies. In essence, the past lived again, doppelgan-gered. But it could also be tampered with: fears and horrors expanded and enlarged to leviathan proportions. That was how a will could be crushed.

The pyramid was more complex than the Magician's citadel. Each of the thousands of doors that lined the cylindrical interior column was charmed with a different kind of illusion. And the well of darkness beneath, the one into which prisoners had previously been lowered for millennia, remained as yet un-probed. He would investigate it, in time. First, he needed to know how this place was constructed. The twelve were not proving helpful. Clearly they were instructed to conceal the intricacies of the design. But the Magician would break through eventu-ally. He always did.

The Prince had set him this task in the hope of discovering a way back to the living world, but of course, the Magician had his own reasons for wishing to understand the city, the pyramid and the twelve.

But I must not think of that. The Magician was better than most at concealing his thoughts. He was one of a handful in the city capable of hiding them from the eye. But that didn't mean a momentary lapse of judgement would prevent them becoming clear. He was a slave (once he had been a god) and he would remain a slave. Until he discovered a way out.

'Honey we're home!'

The Magician gritted his teeth. He waddled over to the circular opening in the centre of the throne-room. His legs gave him pain. Back in the Circle, he had been freed from his stunted physical form, but now he was trapped within it. *Until you acquire the power again. Until you become what you once were.*

He scalded himself for the thoughts. *He* was in the pyramid, too close to be safe.

A gigantic chain pulley hung over the hole, the chain-links two feet long, plummeting down through the column of the pyramid. Previously, prisoners, or The Allotted, as the twelve referred to them, were lowered into the blackness via the pulley. The Prince had ordered it made into an elevator. The Magician pulled a lever and the pulley began to grind and growl, like a cumbersome beast of burden awakened to some monotonous task.

After a few moments, the crude platform appeared. The Prince, and with him another figure: a man in a white lab coat wearing a Japanese mask.

'May I introduce, Dr Monaghan,' the Prince said. 'Dr Monaghan, this is my magician.'

MY magician. He takes ownership of everything.

'A pleasure,' he forced himself to say, making a slight bow.

Dr Monaghan ignored him and paced into the room. There was a manic hunger about the man. He was like an animal constantly in the panic of the thunderstorm.

The Prince took his seat on the throne. A stone slab. He'd asked for no more and no less.

Dr Monaghan stood as though awaiting robotic input, forcing the Magician to do the same despite how much his legs protested.

'Dr Monaghan has just told me something very interesting...' There was an edge in the Prince's voice. It made the Magician think of a psychopath hiding razors in their guest's food. *Go on*, it said, *dare you to bite.*

'What is that my Prince?'

'He was watching the two newcomers very closely –'

'Newcomers, my Prince?'

The Prince's face darkened. The Magician regretted the impulsiveness of his interruption. He hated the Prince with a passion, but that did not mean he wasn't afraid of him.

'Yes,' he said. Then his face started to glow, and the eye *pulsed* like a maggot enjoying a particularly rich carcass. The Magician felt dizzy; he knew that was a sign the Prince's power was at work. 'A cripple and a wolf.'

The Magician felt a shock through his spine. The Prince's face continued to glow and one side of his mouth curled upward.

'I thought you might be familiar.'

'But I... I brought down the city on them... I...'

The Prince stood, shaking his head. The Magician felt his consciousness become a whirlpool. He had failed. Failed to destroy them. Not only had they dealt him and his illusion a crippling blow, but he had not annihilated them as he initially thought. As the whirlpool thickened, pulled and deepened, the stone slab of the throne began to vibrate and then lifted into the air, weightless. Its surface shimmered, changing from the sandy stone to marble then to steel girders and lastly to a textureless white box.

'Yin,' the Prince put a hand on his cheek; it was almost tender. The Magician looked up into his master's eyes. 'Don't you know how powerful *belief* is? Even false belief can carry human beings to the stars!' He looked up, as though he could see through the walls of the pyramid to the infinite skies. *He probably can. He sees the illusion in everything.*

The Magician nodded. The Prince smiled.

The throne sank to the floor and changed back to its original sandy colour. He had a hold on it all again. The Prince sat back down, never doubting for a second the magic would be in place.

'As I was saying, Dr Monaghan observed something very interesting. The cripple had dirt all around his shoes. A kind of oily muck. It couldn't have come from the beach or the roads. There must be tunnels beneath this place. If there are tunnels, they may prove our way out.'

The Magician cleared his throat.

'There is at least one tunnel I know of, my Prince, but I did not think it was relevant before. It leads back to the Circle. An enclosed realm. A desert of my making. It would do you no good.'

The Prince pulled a simpering face.

'You weren't afraid I thought you were hiding something, were you?'

'No... I... I merely wished to state the fact.'

'Because you can't hide anything from me, Yin. I know what you are and where you came from.' The Prince pulled a sorrowful face. 'Which means I also am the only one who understands your true value.'

The Magician looked up. He searched the face for the lie but could find none. The lines of the face were too deep, too solid, and the human eye gleamed like the surface of clear water, displaying compassion the Magician would not have thought possible.

'Thank you, my Prince.'

His face burned. He had been humiliated by Dr Monaghan's discovery. Of course, he should have thought of the tunnels first. He had even built one. But the Prince showed forgiveness, understanding: it was unbearable. And the thing which made his heart feel like it'd been filled with tar, the worst thing, was the knowledge that however much he hated the Prince, he did crave his approval. Pathetic.

'Dr Monaghan,' the Prince had turned to his new follower, the mind-breaking focus of the voided socket shifting. A magnetic current seemed to release the Magician all of a sudden, and he could control his emotions again. 'If I give you a team of people and tools, will you go down into the tunnels. We must leave no stone unturned in our search for a way out.'

Dr Monaghan knelt, like some ancient, bloodthirsty knight. His words similarly echoed this medieval imagery.

'I shall, my lord.'

'Lord?' The prophet laughed. 'No lord. Nor king. *I am the Prince.* Never forget this.'

Dr Monaghan seemed confused. His eyes darted left to right, as though reading writing which was written on the floor.

'I shall not,' he said again. He stood.

The Prince rose from his throne and clapped the iron-masked face in his palms, as though addressing his only son.

'Go forth and conquer!'

The Magician watched him march from the room, the taste of poison in his mouth.

CHAPTER 5

The shadows of the obelisk-buildings concealed an underworld of furtive iniquity.

There were tradesmen dealing human limbs which had been fashioned into everything from weapons to walking aids. Male prostitutes lined the sidewalks (far more common than female) with signs sporting slogans such as 'ORGASM GUARANTEED' and 'FORTY MINUTES OR YOUR FORTY BACK'. When they saw Hagga (who despite her withered arm was still a striking beauty) they surrounded her like eager crows. She forced them back, a black glimmer surfacing at the bottom of her eyes. Larri shuddered. He had never seen Hagga transform into the creature she called the *Need*, but if he had pieced the story together correctly, she had destroyed the cannibals of the Circle overnight, torn apart their city, and left only blood and bone in her wake. According to Simon she'd also killed the cannibal leader, the Blood Mare, and she hadn't even had to transform to do that...

As they got deeper into the city (or at least, what they thought was deeper) the prostitutes and the dealers became less frequent. Instead, there were yellow eyes watching from blinded windows, and crooked shapes in the dark nooks, shapes which moved like insects but had human feet. Larri thought he was starting to understand the prostitutes.

At first they had seemed bizarre and out of place, a carnival piece in the midst of a tragic play, but he was beginning to think that the chief suffering of all the people who lived (perhaps 'inhabited' was a better word) in the city was that they had no way of experiencing pleasure anymore. But, despite the slight alterations to their being, they were still human, and so were going to try anyway. He wondered how long some of the people had been here, how long they had been deficit of any kind of joy or spark of excitement. Larri did not feel any different. Was it that this place muffled sensation in the body the longer one remained?

They reached a crossroads. To the south (or rather, what they had taken to calling the south – there were no true compass points without a sun and so they marked the black sea as southward) a long narrow road ran until it reached a small crouched building; the building stood out from the rest because of its squatness. From its shape, it might have been a kind of chapel. Larri wasn't really sure as he'd not seen many in the Circle. There were columns of greenish smoke around it which sparked his curiosity, if also a note of warning.

To the north, the pyramid. Always the pyramid.

To the east, straight ahead, there was a cluster of sunken brick-a-brack hovels with sloped shanty-town tin-roofs and rust-coloured doors. Sprays of yellowing grass grew from the cracks where house met concrete. Hagga and Larri had never seen a modern city or green fields: they knew only the desert. Had they been familiar with these things, they might have noted the oddness of those tufts of dying grass growing there and nowhere else in the city: they might even have thought it was as though whoever had built this place had only a fading memory of reality. They knew grass and weeds grew in these places, but they could not remember its true image, hence the spidery over-long stems and the wheat-field colour.

Hagga paused at the crossroads.

'We can rest before making a decision,' Larri said, anxiously. His knees felt like they had nine-inch nails through them. They were so stiff they hardly bent when he took a step.

'My wounds are healing,' she said, misinterpreting his offer as gallantry. 'I can hardly feel them. It's this place.'

I wish it would heal my damn legs then.

After all, Larri hadn't been born a cripple. Ten years in a coma had done this to him.

'You're looking for something,' he said. 'What?'

'I don't know.' Hagga turned to him. She was biting her lips, and her eyes quivered. It was strange how someone so powerful could also look lost and confused. She was over six feet tall, towering over Larri much like the skyscrapers, and muscled as a Grecian sculpture. She had feminine beauty to go with all that. No wonder the Prince, or whatever he called himself, had wanted her.

Larri winced at the memory. Another time he had been weak. Jealously had clouded his sense of loyalty, turning him *against* Hagga, resenting her for being tempted by the prophet. The whirlpool in Larri's head which relentlessly pulled him back into self pity was painted with all the familiar thoughts which paint a depressive's mind: *of course she would be tempted by him and not me, look at him! You're just a cripple, a hunchback with weak legs and a feeble heart. He is a demigod, a warlord.*

A monster.

However deep down the whirlpool dragged him, there always seemed to be an answering voice to drag him back out again. Larri hoped it was that god Demus and Simon had spoken of, and not just the beginnings of hopeful madness.

He tried not to think about the fact that the only people he knew who believed in God were both dead.

'Look, we should find somewhere to rest for a while. We need to talk. About the Prince, this place, who we are.' Larri swallowed. 'I don't know whether we can believe him. But what we saw, it didn't seem like an illusion. We'd know one by now, wouldn't we? All those years of Yin. No. There was *some* truth to it at least. But how much?'

Hagga nodded.

'Ever since we met *him* I've felt like we were supposed to find something. Like we have a purpose being here. The Prince even said I was right.'

'He said you were smart. It's not the same thing.'

Hagga frowned.

'I suppose you're right. Still - '

The door to one of the shanties burst open. A bare-chested ebony-skinned woman strode towards them, pendulous breasts swinging like weapons. Her nipples were pierced with nails and she was holding what looked like a signpost that'd been ripped out of the ground. There was a lump of concrete on the end that made it into a club.

'Fuck,' Larri said, momentarily unable to feel alarm for the sheer weirdness of what he was watching. The woman was carrying her massive weapon as though it was nothing more than a small bat. Her eyes were so bloodshot he wondered she could see out of them.

'We don't mean you harm,' Hagga said.

The woman snorted and continued to approach. Larri realised her eyes were on *him*, and their expression suggested she viewed him much like prize horse to tame and capture.

'Fuck,' he said again.

She began to circle the huge mace round her head, straightening her legs to compensate her balance. She looked something like a fat stalk wielding a medieval war-cudgel.

Hagga did not budge or flake and that frightened Larri even more. Was she about to transform?

'Stop,' she said, calmly to the crazed mace-wielder.

Larri's mouth was open. *Do something you coward!*

'Hagga.' He ran forward, grabbed her hand and tried to pull her back. She shrugged him off.

'Get back.' She ran forward. Larri's heart began to quiver. He watched the concrete mace-end like an arachnaphobe watches a spider. One revolution, two, then Hagga sprinted, coming in just as the pole and concrete orb went past. She punched with both fists. The woman squealed, let go of her cumbersome weapon, and toppled back. The maul span twice and crashed into another shanty house, which came down in an avalanche of shoddy metal parts. The woman staggered ten feet, never toppling, bloody-trailing from her broken mouth like a ribbon, until she snapped the back of her head on the metal corner of her shack. Pink exploded over the shack wall and a v-shaped groove appeared in the rear of her skull.

She slid down the side of her house and lay in a bloody heap.

'I didn't mean to do that...' Hagga whispered. 'I just meant to knock her down.'

'You were defending yourself.'

Larri felt nothing for the whackjob; his relief they were both unharmed was too all-consuming. He wondered whether that was how this place got to you, first reducing you to the impulse to survive, then, below even that.

'Is she... decomposing?'

'That's not...'

But even as his mouth formed the words, he looked closer. The woman was disintegrating, or rather, morphing. He wasn't sure which. The blood from the back of her head was changing colour and attaching itself to the crude welded plates which made up the shack's walls. It'd sprouted nodes like fungus, and was beginning to exhibit mossy mould-clumps which crept up the house, oxidising and browning as they went. Her ebony flesh was brightening, turning the same hue as the rusted house. It gained a grainy, uneven quality, and as a gust blew, some of it blew off in sandy granules which were swept into the cracks and gaps in the building's structure. Her black hair turned yellow and sprouted purple flowers, flowers which promptly shrivelled and shed petals. Moments later there *was* no woman, just a lumpy piece of weed-choked metal and brick. A face could still be discerned, its expression one of someone deeply sleeping, but he had to look hard to find it, and its features were indefinite and impersonal.

'What did we just see?' Hagga said, quietly.

'I don't know. But I don't like it. It makes me think this whole place was built like that. From people.'

Hagga shivered.

'Let's go.'

She was right. Larri could see more yellow eyes watching them from the gaps in the shanty houses and from the windows behind them.

And how many more from the walls of the city itself?

———

HAGGA'S FEELING drew them south. Larri was more than happy to follow that way: anything to avoid looking at the pyramid. It surfaced memories of their encounter with the Prince, the eerie feeling the eye had given him: the feeling that his ugly naked self had been exposed to a kind of darkness that shone, a glow-worm light that could only be kindled in the infinite depths. Even when Yin had confronted him with his sins, played with him, taunted him with illusion after illusion in the heart of his labyrinth, Larri hadn't felt the same level of vulnerability. The Prince had the power to tear memories and thoughts from inside his head, and more besides, that much was clear. How else had he known so much about Hagga's 'gift'?

But he didn't test you, not in the way he could have.

There was that stronger voice again; Larri welcomed it like rain in the Circle. It was right, the Prince had clearly thought him of no worth or importance, otherwise he would have driven more deeply into him, tried to tempt him like he did with Hagga. Though this rekindled a small spark of Larri's feelings of self pity, a greater part of him recognised that the Prince had underestimated him. Larri had been the one, after all, to strike the killing blow (or what he hoped was the killing blow) to Yin, shattering his city once and for all. And Larri was also the one chosen by Simon to carry forward the word of God. He had seen the strength God gave Simon, and if that was anything to go by, Larri hoped he would learn that strength in time. Maybe it would be enough to vanquish the Prince?

But then again, what if the Prince was right and there was a way back to this other world? A chance to start over? A chance to learn what it might be like to have a real human existence? Then they would need the Prince because he clearly knew more about this world than they did.

The chapel was starting to acquire definition; it did not promise anything other than what they had already received from the city. There were a cluster of figures around it, smoke coiling from what looked like cooking fires beneath crude pots.

'Hold up,' Hagga said.

'What's wrong?'

Her eyes were intense, bird-like.

'I just got a sense of déjà vu. Those fires, the people. It's like the Stricken, the cannibals in the White City. We shouldn't go there.'

Larri nodded.

'It's strange though,' he said, 'Have you felt hungry at any point?'

Hagga shook her head.

'And I'm always hungry,' she said. 'A side effect of *it*.'

'Why would there be cannibals in this place if no one needs to eat?'

Hagga grimaced.

'Why has everywhere and everything got to be fucked up?'

Larri felt the weight of her statement like shackles. He thought of the woman and the mace and the crazy way she'd looked at him, like she'd found a toy.

'Nice punch, by the way.'

'Oh, thanks. Wish it hadn't killed her.'

'I don't think it did.'

Hagga looked at him.

'You thinking about that afterlife thing?'

'More and more.'

'Come on, there's something down here.' She pointed at an alley.

The 'something' turned out to be a graveyard.

It looked more like a collection of vine-haired gargoyles, fossilised creatures, than a place where the dead were buried and honoured. In fact, it did not seem a dead place at all. Something always seemed to be moving, but whenever Larri focused on it, the motion was arrested. Broken wings formed a canopy over them from which contorted faces looked down with maddened, drill-hole eyes. Ugly forms tore at their own warped flesh. Had Hagga or Larri ever seen a sprawling mansion gardenscape, they might have thought of one, but as it was, they'd never had the luxury.

The iron railings which fenced in this carnival of stonework looked like something out of a Lovecraftian novel. When Larri examined them, he saw that intricate, hellish faces were graven into the tip of every vertical rail. His guts were starting to feel like they weren't arranged right in his stomach and dryness kept invading his mouth. Something wasn't right with this place. Everything was made of some*one* rather than some*thing*. He looked around him. Every statue had an expression of pain. The few gravestones he'd seen in the Circle all had solemn-faced angels depicted in their stone (if any angel at all) and their features were incoherent and vague. These statues all looked like the work of a deluded artist with a mania for mania.

'Hagga, have you...'

But she had walked ahead. He saw her long shadow disappear around a corner created by an open mouthed statue. The mouth was larger than Larri's head and the inside of his throat was exquisitely carved. It resembled a starfish's maw, receding forever, teeth within teeth within teeth. It made him shudder.

'Hagga?'

He rounded the corner, despite his unease with the weird statue, and found her standing beneath the largest tomb in the graveyard. It was colossal, twenty feet high, reigning over the other stone forms with misplaced grandeur. At first, Larri wondered how they hadn't seen it coming down the road, but the skyscrapers boxed it in. *Almost as if hiding it.* He was starting to attribute will and sentience to this place, and that made his guts feel even worse.

'Who was this?'

He joined Hagga and looked up at the colossus. The statue depicted a man sitting on a throne. At first glance his features and expression appeared to be that of a king. He had a sharp nose, powerful cheekbones high (perhaps too high) on the face. Piercing eyes, the pupils six-inch wide holes, stared out with a sick man's intensity: their concave depth reminded Larri eerily of the Prince's empty socket and the seeing thing that lived there, except this statue had *two* dark eyes. A crown adorned his head, made of some kind of natural plant stem. The mouth was lopsided but smiling, as though it had just been told a joke.

And the more Larri looked at that smile, the more he noticed odd things about the statue, things that made his brain itch like returning motifs in dreams.

The crown was *also* slightly lopsided. He hadn't noticed at first because it was aligned with the tilted smile, but now he held his head straight, he could see it was askew. Was this bad craftsmanship or deliberate? The eyes were too-wide. Solemn eyes are always half-closed, lidded, as though pensive. These eyes gave the impression of a kind of ecstatic rush, more suitable to a root-dreaming poet than a sober leader. The statue's hair poked out through the crown and flopped either side of it, mimicking a jester's bell-ridden hat. This was no king but the court fool they were looking at. He turned to Hagga and saw her eyes roving over the statue and lines creasing her forehead, clearly thinking the same thing.

'Is this a kind of... joke?' It sounded so feeble. And what did it say? In the midst of apocalyptic desolation they'd found a statue twenty feet tall that had been meticulously crafted and resourced purely for the purpose of a brief, unfunny trick. 'Can't imagine anyone having a sense of humour in this place.'

Hagga snorted.

'You got that right. Question is: if this is a gravestone, who is important enough to get this after they die? If it's a statue, then who made it and are they still alive?'

'I'm starting to think everyone is still alive in this place, Hagga.'

If that's so, then death is the greatest trick of them all.

He felt as though a cold blade had perforated the frontal lobe of his brain. Hagga's mouth hung open, making her look like a parody of the strange statue which had so unnerved Larri. The coldness spread to his feet – then he realised it was *real* coldness, and he looked down to see a dark gloop was exuding, as though porously, from the base of the statue's throne. Larri skated back from it. The liquid continued to bleed out of the statue in thick, leech-like globules, sliding down the stone and forming into an expanding puddle. It had been so cold. Unimaginably cold. Like becoming death.

Don't be so surprised. The voice sounded excited, eager to talk. *You've known it a long time cripple-man. In this place no one dies. They just change into something new.*

Hagga swallowed.

'And is that what you are?'

Of a fashion.

The black liquid paused and then solidified like oven-baked mixture, forming a perfect circle around the statue. The smile didn't seem so jolly all of a sudden. There were teeth behind it and those teeth were pointed.

There is a point at which one form cannot be sustained, and so it crumbles. The tolerance threshold is different for everyone. Some of us, of course, choose this fate. We choose to become one.

'And why would you do that?' Larri could think of nothing worse than becoming immobile, a brain detached from its body. He had been in a coma for ten years, and that had been the nearest thing to hell he could think of: the haunting dreams, the paralysis, and the memories that chased like rabid hounds. Some of the harrowed in the Circle had cried out to be freed from their physical, earthly suffering, but Larri knew better. Your body was freedom, and if you lost use of it, that was the end. To willingly choose an eternity of that prison seemed insanity.

Because when one gives oneself willingly, one acquires another type of control, agency. The city's body welcomes...

'And is it all you thought it was cracked up to be?' Hagga said, eyebrow raised.

Soft laughter echoed – but Larri suspected only inside their heads.

It is different. Parts of me have been lost, it is true. But parts remain. Memories...

Larri shuddered. Had he heard a sigh following that word or was it the wind?

Well, I have work to do, but I thought, as I had guests, I would introduce myself.

The blackness began to recede towards the statue. It was like watching time reversing. Larri felt nauseous.

'Wait!' Hagga marched forward and put a hand on the statue, giving Larri the sensation his teeth were being attended to with a nail-file. 'We have questions. Do you know who the Prince is? Do you know if there is a way out of here?'

The liquid continued to withdraw, but there was a last shudder of speech.

Oh I knew the Prince before the Prince was.
I have danced his dance and fought his war.
And so will you.
And so will you.

CHAPTER 6

The cannibals watched him with white eyes as he dangled the babe over the cooking fire.

'Pl-please,' the mother begged. The men circled, eyeing him like a tiger eyes a wounded elephant. The Taking Man did not move an inch. The babe cried. Occasionally a spurt of wind blew the greenish smoke into its face and it choked, causing the mother to howl, her knees buckling then recovering like a feeble attempt at dance. Her outstretched hands were like tree branches in a storm.

'Listen to me carefully,' he said. 'There is one who has fed you lies. His name is the Prince.'

'Please just give me back my baby!' the woman cried.

The Taking Man grimaced.

He lowered the baby towards the fire. The woman shrieked, looked as though she was about to fling herself forward, and then held back, crumpling into a heap. Two men moved forward and caught her. A third looked at the Taking Man as though considering killing him, but the babe was now so close to the flame that a drop meant certain immolation. The smog made the baby cough like a 40-a-day smoker. The Taking Man didn't know what the green tint meant, but he couldn't imagine it was healthier than normal smoke. Quite the opposite, most likely.

'I told you to *listen.*' He hissed.

'We'll listen. Please. Please. The smoke. The wood is poisonous. When it burns the poison is released in the smoke. Please.'

The Taking Man begrudgingly lifted the baby, careful to watch the men who seemed poised to attack. The third one still watched him. The Taking Man smiled.

'You're judging me, but look at you. You're a *cannibal.* Only vermin eat the dead. You're scum.'

'Better to eat them than let them become the city,' he spat.

'What are you talking about?'

The woman crawled forward, breaking away from her two supporters and coming to the Taking Man's feet.

'Haven't you seen it? Faces in the stonework? In the mud? Bodies in the shape of the city itself? When you die you go *into* the city. Feed it. Grow its hold over us. Unless you eat the body. That's why we take the human flesh. There is no hunger here. Thirst, yes. But no hunger. We eat to save the souls of the dead from becoming tied to this place.'

The Taking Man searched her scarred, gaunt-eyed face, every line of the ebony skin, and realised she was telling the truth. Whether that justified the obscene act was another question, but then again, he had been called a monster many times himself.

'If that's true, then you must help me.' He spoke slowly. Thoughts had formed, but he needed to order them, needed to present them right. 'Because there's a man who's going to destroy us. He's going to feed the city more souls than you can possibly imagine. He's in the pyramid now. He thinks he can find a way out of this place. He's wrong. You know he's wrong. You've been here long enough to know.' *Since the days of ancient Egypt,* he thought.

'Who says you're better than him?' the third man, growled. His fists were still clenched. He edged forward as he bounced on his toes. *Big mistake.*

'I certainly never did. But I am *against* him. Because I want to make the best of what we have.' He smiled.

'Give her the baby back, then,' the warrior said. 'Prove yourself.'

The mother only looked up, imploring. *This is almost a biblical scene.* The chapel looked like a temple from old Jerusalem, framing the picture. A mother. A child. *And a saviour,* he thought, with relish, then laughed at the thought; disturbing glances were shared between the cannibals.

'I think I will. Prove myself, I mean.'

He dropped the baby into the fire.

The mother issued a scream so loud it threw him out of himself, disjointing soul from body. The third man ran forward in a foam-lipped rage. The Taking Man knew now that he was the father, and glowed with the triumphant knowledge. The man leapt over the fire and swung a blow which missed. The Taking Man caught him around the throat and squeezed, as he did so, he thought of the corpse and the leech and began to drain.

First youth bled away from him. Then muscle and strength. Fire died in his eyes and he murmured like a drooling loon. His knees broke and bent the wrong way, like a canine's. Finally he collapsed, a shadow of himself. The Taking Man kicked the fire over his corpse. The mother would not stop screaming.

The other two men stared with mouths open.

The Taking Man dusted off his white jacket. The man had gotten greasy finger-prints over it.

'Well, now that's done with, I'll be needing you to prove yourselves to me.' He stepped forward, past the mother, who was digging with her bare hands into the still flaming corpse of her babe, her disintegrated lover by her side. 'You can start by going to the pyramid and telling me what goes on there. I want to know about the Prince. But also his servants. The dwarf. The woman. And the man in the mask. I want to know about him, especially.' The Taking Man saw they were not moving. Their eyes showed the kind of fear that paralysed, an early rigour mortis. He sighed. 'Do it now, or you suffer the same fate as him.' He pointed at the deconstructed remains. They nodded, rose and ran off into the city, slipping like knives into the cracks of the alleyways.

He turned to look at the hysterical mother. There was no longer a sack of bones by her side. The remains were morphing, greying over, the hair becoming moss, the flesh turning into the stone of the city. *So it is true.* The wind picked up the babe's ashes and cast them into the air. The mother followed them with her eyes and hands, tears streaming down her face.

'It's a terrible thing, isn't it, for a babe to be taken from its mother,' he whispered. 'It happened to me, you know. I was dropped in the fire. Taken from mommy.' He grinned, black lips peeling back to reveal blacker teeth. 'But look at me now.' He held out his hands as though on a gameshow. 'I'm doing just *fine.*'

ACT II: AN ARK OF POISON WOOD

CHAPTER 7

He sat in the throne room. Before him, a black disc spun, or rather, it *spiralled.* The walls of it were being sucked down to some central point beyond definition. Within its boundaries he saw the city stretched out like a skin-cancer on the land. Behind it and the glistening mole of the pyramid was a mess of black hair – the forest – which stretched beyond where even his magical eye and the black disc could see. At the other end of the city there was the water, also limitless.

Within the city, there were crawling things. They looked like insects from the height at which the disc's perspective was situated. Sometimes the Prince guided the disc and brought it closer to the streets, examining the souls like bacteria under a microscope. Other times he did as he did now, soaring like an eagle, alert for signs of uprising, gatherings, resistance.

When he had claimed New York and demolished the edifice of American society, raising his tattered banner over its ashes, he had been able to see things in his sleep. Dreams. Visions. Prophecies. Now, those dreams had become part of his waking days and substantial to the point where the rest of this dismal realm was becoming more and more dreamlike. It was hard to hold on – to conversations, to the tangible things. No one felt like a real person anymore.

Had they ever?

'Michael.'

Her voice – infected atoms which slipped through the cracks in his armour. He hated her using that name, his birth-given name, but he also found some forgotten part of him responding to it. At times this forgotten part walked in front of him (another vision) like an entirely separate being: A young boy who still had both eyes. A young boy so full of fear he did not know the meaning of the word *sleep*. A young boy who's father locked him up in a shack at the end of their garden and day after day forced his cock into his mouth and came down his throat.

The Prince shuddered.

'Don't call me that,' he said.

The disc swallowed itself.

He stood and turned to face her. A window in the throne room (newly constructed by the Magician so as to look out on the city but deny anyone sight of what lay within) let through beams of palefire which illuminated her, making her flesh glow like superheated magnesium. Even the Prince's eye found it hard to look at.

They had no moon, but the palefire made up for it: a sickly aurora borealis which danced like a ghost on a grave. It was the only thing they had to mark time. In 'day', stormclouds. By 'night', palefire.

'Everything is going to plan, and yet, you're afraid. Was it like this in New York?'

'No.' He could not treat her as he treated the others. She had proven herself too often, and besides, she had something of the future sight like him. He could see it growing in her. The seed had been already planted before they met, but he had watered it, and now it was blossoming into a carnivorous plant. He never feared it would challenge his own gift, of course. But he did fear that like so many of the apostles and followers who had gone before her, she would turn on him. 'In New York, I did not see the danger until it was too late. I... made an error of judgement.' He smiled. 'It happens to the best of us.'

'But you're still haunted by it?'

He growled.

'Are you reading me, priestess?'

Fay laughed.

'No. You don't need a gift to see that. And my name is *Fay.*' Her eyes looked like they were studded with diamonds; her sickle blade glowed; she was not afraid of him. Mirth made her cheeks rosy without detracting from the marble beauty of her face. *Beauty.* There was a word that did not often enter the mind of the Prince. He found himself thinking it now though. She was beautiful, and in that way, she was perhaps more powerful than he could ever be. He shook himself. *Strange thoughts.*

'Fay,' he said, lightly. 'Where are my manners?' He grinned and paced towards her. His shape interrupted the palefire and cast a shadow over her. 'And yes. I am haunted. I can still see his ugly face as he drove his fingers into my neck.'

Impulsively he reached out a hand and touched her slender neck. He touched it only with the tips of his fingers, brushing the throat with his thumb. A swan might have envied that neck.

'Brian Mor,' she whispered. Her eyes flitted to his hand, the skeletal fingers, grooved, dirty-nailed, flesh so wrinkled it looked like it was tattooed with snail-shell spirals.

Her speaking the name was like spitting acid in his face. He wanted to scream and strike her, but he fought the urge. Yes. Brian Mor had killed him. Brian Mor. The Man in the Black Hat. The man who faded into the background and no one saw coming, not even the Prince.

'It doesn't matter now though,' he said, voice shaking. 'I was given another chance. He didn't destroy me. He *couldn't.* Neither he or anyone else knows what it would take to end me. They cannot begin to imagine it. They have not dreamed it. Not even God has spoken it, unless perhaps in his sleep, troubled by a bad dream.'

'I won't betray you,' she said. 'If that's what you fear?'

She stepped closer. Her presence, the radiance which permeated from her which only his eye could see, was running over him, like the shockwaves of a continuously detonating explosive device. He could have reeled from it. Her smell filled him up until he wanted to be sick but he never wanted to stop smelling it. The desire was burning in him to own her, to penetrate and bind her to him with some carnal, ritual act. He felt the calling.

She reached out and put her hand on his chest. The eye screamed – as though a note had been hit at such an octave as to make its darkness crack like glass. His body shuddered. He drew his hand away. He felt stripped. *Who are you? Who are you Fay? You are not a woman. You are not human. You cannot be.* No one, not Brian Mor or even Joel Nether, the mad Fool King, had ever overwhelmed him like this.

'I am yours,' she said, running her fingers down him. 'Whatever else happens, I will never leave your side.' Her fingers touched his belt buckle.

They slipped beneath it.

'Leave,' he stuttered.

Her eyes reached for his. She swallowed.

'Are you –'

'Go.' It took an effort to say. 'Go. I can't. Go.'

Fay nodded, solemnly, as though she had been entrusted to deliver a message bearing bad news. She swivelled and walked out of the throne room. The Prince stood there, electrified and paralysed, and finally sat back down on the throne. Palefire lit one side of his face with glorious white light. The other remained in shadow, and in it, a deeper darkness.

———

DR MONAGHAN WAS LAUGHING. He was laughing because he had just realised how funny it really was. He'd spent the final years of his life working in an underground containment facility, hating every moment of it. And now, having died and arrived on the shores of a strange alien world, where did he find himself?

Working in an underground facility.

Of course, this time it was different. He had been one of many researchers in Facility 2-13. Here, he was the master. The labourers obeyed his every command. Largely, that was due to the six-foot claymore he'd smelted for himself out of the greenish ore he found beneath the city. Well, it was more a meat-cleaver in design than a claymore, but it had the length of an old knight's sword. Veins, like emerald coloured scars, ran across the otherwise black sheen of its surface. The ore he'd used was no ore which existed in the world he had come from, that much was sure, and Dr Monaghan liked to believe it had special properties – namely *hunger*. He used that to torment the slaves who endlessly tunnelled these mines. *Don't let her get hungry now,* he'd say, if a worker fell to the floor from exhaustion. *I've already starved her for so long...*

Another factor of working underground was that no one really checked up on Dr Monaghan, which was good, because Dr Monaghan had long ago abandoned following the Prince's plan. Of course he still idolised him, the red prophet, the bleeding messiah, but Dr Monaghan was perfectly insane (or perhaps brilliant) enough to hold two completely contradictory ideas in his head in the same time: he could worship the Prince and disobey him. They weren't related in the slightest as far as he was concerned. The Prince had asked him, shortly after Dr Monaghan had offered to investigate the tunnels, to search for a substance that resembled pitch or coal tar.

How boring.

He'd been hoping to be asked to find the new oil, or an explosive, or more of the luminous green ore to fashion weaponry and arms.

Pitch. What could you do with that?

The Prince had told him but he'd already forgotten. It was unimportant. What the Prince should have asked him to do was find whatever this world's equivalent of explosives was. So that's what Dr Monaghan would do. He was actually doing the Prince a favour, in a way. Better serving him. After all, the Prince would inevitably come round to that, whatever his plans were. It was always came to that eventually. Nothing ever got achieved except by men with bombs.

Men, specifically, which is why Fay had no place on the Prince's council. Dr Monaghan hated the idea she was hanging around him whilst he worked beneath the earth, but it couldn't be helped.

He realised it was about time he checked up on the digging progress.

His 'office', as he called it, was a circular space dug out from the solid rock, a feat which had cost three lives. It was filled with tables upon which a cluster of unorganised items were heaped: the hand of the one of the perished diggers (it hadn't yet decomposed – which was interesting), a slab of the green ore, bone fragments, a section of what looked to be rubber tubing (but it was the only sample he'd found in the whole of this place) and piles and piles of what would have looked like simply dirt to most. On the other side of the room was a large metal cage made out of re-formed rail tracks.

Yes, that had been a little strange.

They hadn't needed to drill down into the earth. Dr Monaghan found an entrance to what looked like a subway station. First he'd followed the tracks to see where they led but the tunnel was collapsed in both directions. A railroad to nowhere. That was when he commissioned the digging.

They pulled up the tracks and began making a tunnel in earth which they found was, surprisingly, soft. He'd thought they'd need pneumatic drills and explosives to crack through (neither of which they had). Shovels had served well enough, however, and now they were burrowing down to some core, if this place even had a core. It probably did, because it seemed to mimic and echo the living world (what the Prince called the 'primary plane') if in an incomplete, forgotten kind of way.

Dr Monaghan swept from the room. He wanted to fill that cage with something soon, but hadn't found the right specimen. There was a pre-emptive part of him. It wasn't like the Prince's foreknowing. It was simply that he started doing things before he realised why. There always was a why. So, he'd taken the tracks up to the surface, felled a few of those poisonous trees beyond the pyramid, started a fire and heated the metal rods until he could bend them. He did it with his bare hands, which were now blistered and black – he'd experienced pain, but his body didn't seem to sustain damage in the same way as it did in the living world.

His 'office' was midway down through the tunnel network, what he had taken to calling The Cove. It sprawled like a nervous system, hundreds of volunteers from the surface labouring to discover clusters of ore, oil, anything unusual. Dr Monaghan had promised the first one to report something useful that he would personally carry them up the steps of the pyramid into *ascendance*. Religion was a great tool. He had to hand it to them.

Of course, he also had to hand it to the Magician. He might be a short, fuck-ugly little bastard, but he had some moves. His illusions – broadcast like Times Square neon signs throughout the city – had caused people to come flocking. They promised salvation, a new world. No spin artist could have done better. Once the volunteers were *in* the mines, leaving was difficult, especially when someone wearing a mask and wielding a six-foot long blade kept the keys.

Dr Monaghan made his way down the earthen tunnels. Beams of the strange wood held up the low-ceilinged shafts. Occasionally these beams snapped and part of the tunnel collapsed and had to be re-dug; other times an overtaxed worker slipped and set one alight with their candle. This was most disastrous, because the poisonous fumes of the wood could gas out miles of The Cove.

Numerous ways branched off from the central downward sloped shaft, but Dr Monaghan did not have time to investigate them all. He had a feeling that it was the direct route which would yield what he wanted. The sound of weeping echoed up from the mouth of one branching line. He rolled his eyes. You couldn't get the staff these days.

Finally he reached an end point where five or six of the workers were hacking away at a slab of wall. When they saw him their efforts doubled despite the fact most of them looked ready to fall down dead. Their eyes were set so deep into their heads they seemed close to disappearing. They no longer had lips, just cracked peeling flesh. Their bodies were hideously scrawny, like hairless dogs.

'Report,' he said.

One of the workers turned his head but did not let up his efforts. His pick was so blunted Dr Monaghan doubted he could have broken through a sheet of paper with it.

'This wall is proving difficult, sire.' The appellation 'sire' was of Dr Monaghan's devising. 'We cannot break it down.'

'Stop!'

Instantly the workers dropped their picks and shovels and scampered back until they were behind him. The doctor strode forward and put a hand on the wall. He had no fear they would attack him. Even if they did, he doubted any of them could swing a rock hard enough to break his skull. They were far too emaciated by now.

Dr Monaghan stroked the wall for a few minutes. There was much of his past that was vague and foggy to him now. It'd been lost beneath the vividness of his final day on earth, the exhilaration of the hunt, the pain, the ascendency of discovering his carnal power. He was scientist no longer. He'd always thought that was the way in which man most resembled a deity: tampering with DNA, with the laws of physics, with *theory*. That final day, however, he'd discovered there was more that was godlike in physical acts than there could ever be in the mind.

But he still remembered.

'Stone,' he said, to himself. 'This isn't earth it's stone. We've hit the next rock bed.' It had the qualities of sandstone but was paler. Granules of dust came away at his touch.

And there was something beneath it. Something *glittering*.

He tapped the wall twice with a balled up fist. The sound echoed, hollow. The stone was not solid but a shell for something.

He raised his claymore over his head. Uttering a scream he swung it down and shattered a segment of the wall. Like an egg it cracked and started to bleed a juice which looked like tree sap. He reached down and swabbed it with his fingers and brought it to his tongue which chaffed on the edges of his mask. He swilled it around his mouth. Bitter. It induced a moderate synaptic spark followed by a dullness in the mouth. *Alcoholic.* That was the quality he would ascribe.

'Candle,' he barked.

A worker scuttled forward and offered his candle. The worker wore a crude metal bowl on his head – evidently to protect from falling debris. Dr Monaghan took the candle and the hat from his head. The worker treated it as a blessing and scampered back to his colleagues.

Dr Monaghan collected the juice oozing from the crack in the wall using the bowl. He then dipped the candle into it.

There was a crack, a *shoooshft* noise, and a gasp of flame which lit the chamber like a firework. Smoke followed, issuing from the bowl like a lazy Djinn. The metal had bent and warped.

Dr Monaghan smiled.

He tossed the smouldering helmet back to the worker who received it with a yelp.

The doctor walked up to him.

'Notify the surface. We need containers: as many as can be made or found.' The worker sprinted off up the shaft, delighted, perhaps, to have a reason to leave the mines. 'The rest of you: collect this substance and bring all of it to The Cove's entrance.' They nodded, shivering, grateful he would do nothing further. Dr Monaghan was rather like a wild dog in that they never could guess whether he would bite or not. He started to walk away from them; the workers scrabbled to pick up their tools. He turned.

'Do this for me and you *will all ascend!*'

Their eyes opened fully. Their ribs flexed with the motion of their breathing. Yes, they hated him, but they were also *devoted.*

Smiling beneath the mask, Dr Monaghan returned to his office. He was beginning to wonder whether he did have the foresight, after all.

CHAPTER 8

The Prince walked through the woods.

There were few who had the courage to walk between the poison boughs. The canopy hung too low, and the green light which emanated from the trees produced an effect of creeping unease, like being exposed to something radioactive.

He was trying to think of a name for the trees. The workers had taken to calling it *poisonwood*, but the name was too prosaic for him. There wasn't much to appreciate in this dark purgatory – so why call something ugly by an uglier name?

'Silva – Siliva – Sylva.'

It was strange what you could remember: Latin had never been a favourite class, and he hadn't been paying attention even in his favourites. He'd been too busy dreaming – half an act of horrified remembrance and half an impossible escapism into the future. He had always been torn between the past and future. Most people couldn't decide between left and right, one course or the other, but the Prince was being pulled forward and back, haunted and possessed at once. Sometimes he was sure he had the eye even before he fell into the manhole with the infected water. The burning just gave it a shape.

He stroked a trunk gently. His flesh crawled with a rash of red spots, which then subsided. He smiled. The wood was becoming dark. Only thin white slivers, like the arrow ports set into the tower of some ancient castle, afforded him a sense of direction. He would go a little further. Just a little.

He ducked under a jagged branch and it brushed his scalp. A faint stinging sensation spread, like a nettle prick.

'Supremely venomous,' he said, and continued to mutter under his breath.

Inspiration took him.

'Silvenom!' he cried, laughing. 'Silvenom trees.'

He turned, as though looking to the trees to supply him with their approval. As he did so, he caught sight of something not thirty yards away and froze. He bent his knees, lowering the level of his eyes and readying himself to run; no sooner had he done this then he realised there was no need to be afraid. *It* was more likely to flee from him if he moved suddenly. But the Prince, despite the boundlessness of his rage, knew when to be still.

'You're a pretty one,' he whispered.

The white stallion stared back at him. Its eyes were inky globes, each one a match for the Prince's own distorted socket. Its coat was sleek as silk, but the body structure was nightmarishly thin, the skeleton of a horse dressed in rags. Hunger gaped within the hollow-looking ribcage, the lips-pulled-back mouth, and the angular stilt-legs. It was a creature at once familiar and strange – a horse made the wrong way. But still beautiful. *That word again.*

'Come here,' the Prince said. He had never been one for animals, but he had an urge to ride this beast. He sensed, rather than understood rationally, that if he sat atop it he could become undisputed king of the world.

As it happened, the horse turned and trotted off into the shadow of the trees.

The Prince wandered back to the pyramid: a sadness in his smile.

———

PIKE STARED up at the pyramid. In front of it a spectral scene played out – a great voyage across an impossible ocean. Smiling faces. Discovery. Freedom. *The American ideal is alive in the land of the dead,* he thought, but Pike was a Brit and he didn't buy it.

He'd consoled himself with the thought that at least *this city* didn't have the bombardment of corrupt advertising, but now it had succumbed even to that. But it wasn't the advertising that made him go to the pyramid, though, it was her, or rather, what her cards had revealed.

For the first part of their interview, Fay hadn't needed them. She told him more about his life than he could remember himself. Drugs and alcohol had a way of allowing you to let go of stuff like that, and even when the cocaine had stopped the drinking never had except in those last few days in London with Cris, hunting the Taking Man. But then, he'd had a mission. Maybe that'd been the first time he felt like he had a mission in his whole life.

'Now for your future,' she'd said and finally drew the top card of the deck.

Because she'd so accurately described his past, and because a strange mole-ridden man in a caravan had once told him he would die for love (and he had), Pike took what came next to heart. The first card had been The Emperor.

'You will find a new *father figure,*' she said, smiling as though she'd known it would be that card all along. Her smile also told him that she knew he'd never had a father.

'Fifty seems a little late to start.'

'It's never too late,' she said. 'Some people are only born at fifty. It takes them that long to realise it's no good waiting. Or, in other cases, they need a catalyst, some kind of disaster to remind them time is short.' She shrugged. 'Besides, I'm not sure age will be a problem for you in this place.'

He sighed. For weeks he'd scoured the city in search of the Taking Man, but no luck. Pike was sure he'd gone to ground somewhere. Pike hadn't forgotten about him, but he had come to the conclusion it was time to move on. He couldn't chase a memory through the city forever, even if he was the Tarmac King. If he ever *did* see him again, he'd kill him. And Pike was fairly sure it wouldn't be long before he did. This place seemed to have a habit of throwing people and events together, like a great alchemical mixer. There was a formula it was seeking after – Jesus, he'd given it sentience. But that wouldn't be the weirdest thing he'd seen.

He made towards the pyramid's base. Beneath the eternal storm was an open plateau on which myriads of the devoted knelt and prayed and begged to be *ascended*. Pike didn't know who had started the myth. He was fairly sure it wasn't the Prince, even if Pike distrusted him. The Prince didn't seem to want to be worshipped. He wanted to be *obeyed*. There was a difference. An important difference. Hitler had started out wanting to be obeyed, and that's when he'd been unstoppable. It was only at the end when he wanted worship that he fucked up.

As Pike strode past the abject 'faithful' they cried out that he should bow his head or be struck down by lightning. Despite his disbelief in these claims, the sky was ominous. It seemed a battle using godlike artillery raged in the clouds, discolouring them, cutting shapes and shadows in their swirl. Was the whole sky just a great big mirror of what was happening below? Pike didn't know. He didn't do well with strangeness. His life had been secular and material right up until he followed Cris to London. That's when it went crazy, and people started talking about *gifts* and *powers* and *prophecies*. Shit, maybe he was locked up in an asylum somewhere? Maybe this was all imagining.

He reached the pyramid. The faithful wailed behind him.

'Do not ascend lest you be struck down! Lest you be struck down!'

'It's in my cards you morons,' he shouted over his shoulder, and began to climb.

The rock was slippery, as though slick with rainwater. The steps were chipped and uneven, a mishmash of variously sized stones jigsawed together with impossible intricacy.

But climbing was one of the things Pike was good at. He couldn't hold down a job. Couldn't say the right thing. Hell, couldn't be a friend except sticking with someone like a dogged cold. But he could climb, he could swim, he could delve. He was an adventurer. He'd been born to walk. Born to traverse any and every plane.

The first few hundred feet he didn't slip or stumble. Some of the crowded worshippers below were standing and jeering him. Others watched in strangled silence. His work got more difficult when he reached two hundred and fifty feet. The stones were worn away. He was trying to move towards an opening like a square window, but it seemed to be moving away from him. That or the distance was greater than it'd looked from below...

His fingers started to ache with tiredness. He didn't feel hunger in this place, but he sure felt thirst and exhaustion. His leather jacket was glued to his back and the clefts of his knees and elbows were grimily damp.

He took a rest about four hundred feet up and looked down on the worshippers, rolling, shouting, smashing their heads into the floor in obeisance. Behind them the city stretched – a labyrinth of secrets.

He realised that if he stopped too much longer he would not be able to start again. The window looked to be only another hundred feet away, but he was prepared for how deceptive that might be.

Driving his nails into the stone, he pulled himself up. He was more crawling now, the slope had eased somewhat. His toes (able to feel the stone through the thin soles of his shoes) never felt like they had a good grip.

'I thought this would be easy if it's my destiny.'

He regretted talking to himself, it cost too much air, but then again, it motivated him to crawl a few more feet. He looked up. The window was just above. If he jumped, he could grab its edge and hoist himself in. That was, if he could lift his own bodyweight. He was fairly sure that would be impossible at this point.

With dismal, snail-like progress, he clambered up the last few steps beneath the window and flung one arm over its edge into the interior. He flung a leg over. Something felt like it was tearing in his stomach. He shoved with the leg still on the steep of the pyramid, pushing up as hard as he could. It felt like he was moving the weight of a building and not just his own scrawny form.

Then, like a babe, he slid smoothly through and into a small square room.

He lay underneath the window for a moment, crouching in darkness. The occasional lightning fork outside lit the room with blue and white splashes. He blinked several times. Rubbed his eyes. He wasn't sure whether it was exhaustion, but the room looked dimly familiar.

He forced himself to his feet. His legs wobbled, as though the joints were missing a few key muscles. He threw out a hand and steadied himself on the wall. He felt inside his jacket and pulled out a lighter. It was strange what he'd carried over from the living world. He got to keep his lighter, but not his cigarettes. The urge to smoke them was gone too.

He offered a brief, serviceable prayer that the lighter was now dry enough from the waters that it would work. He rolled his thumb over the bitter wheel and a spark emerged, leading to a teardrop of flame. The room's features softened with the light, but were still familiar.

It was the room he had been born in, the room which belonged to 'little spike' and not the Tarmac King.

There was a door on the other side of the room and Pike ran for it as fast as he could. On the door there was an engraving: 'The child is the father of the man.'

He didn't know what it meant, but he flung the door open anyway.

The vision which now greeted him was like something out of an industrial nightmare. A cylinder, lined with an infinite series of doors, stretched higher and lower than he could see. Metal-wrung ladders led up through a series of circular levels. Beneath these levels was a black pit; he went up to the railings and looked down. The pit stung his eyes and reminded him of the Prince. *No wonder he likes this place.* When he next closed his eyes, the pit had left a circular imprint on his retina which danced and transformed in multicoloured strobe.

A rusted, colossal chain plunged from the levels above, down through the centre of the cylinder and into the absolute blackness.

A section of the railings had been removed, clearly to allow access to some kind of platform. He could easily cast himself from this level down into the deep below. As soon as that thought reached him, there was a sound like metal grinding against metal, a thunder that might have been the storm outside or the awakening of a deep engine. The chain rose, dragging something out of the pit. Pike's heart began to feel bloated in his chest and pain him when it beat. He stepped back from the railing and waited. Whatever came up from that darkness, he would face it. After all, he hadn't made the climb for nothing.

———

A PLATFORM EMERGED. Fay stood on it, a look of surprise creased her face, throwing Pike into even greater disorientation. *So you don't see everything, then?*

'I'll be honest, I didn't expect to see you here,' she said. 'I had you down as the stubborn type.'

Pike grinned. She had a sense of humour, at least, which was more than could be said for most of the whackjobs in this place. Maybe that was another reason for coming here too: his conversation with her was the only meaningful one he'd had since he got here.

'I am,' he said. He took a running jump and landed on the platform as it continued past his level. 'But I guess I realised there was no getting round it.'

'There's always a way round,' she said, looking him up and down in a way that made Pike uncomfortable. 'The future is a living thing. It changes its mind, and sometimes you can persuade it to do so.'

'Is that something he taught you?'

She smiled – but her eyes showed something else. Was it grief? Sadness?

'Yes. Before I met him, I was bound to the cards and what they said. Now I see they are just a tool, a window.'

The crude elevator ascended for a long time. There were so many doors it made Pike dizzy. He wondered where they might lead, whether to other rooms from his life. What was the magic of this place?

'You love him, don't you?'

She smirked.

'You have a way of cutting to the point, don't you?'

'I keep asking until I have my answer.'

Fay turned away from him. He could not stop his eyes following the curve of her back right down to her perfect calves.

'There are many definitions of love,' she said. 'I'm not sure yours is the right one.'

They emerged into a kind of throne room. At the far end there was a black doorway suspended six feet up the wall. Beneath it was a sandstone block upon which a ragged figure sat: a ragtag man in torn clothes.

He looked pensive, but the eye remained alert. A window, or rather, a kind of phantasmal screen, allowed a view of the entire city. The electrical lighting of the thunderheads poured through. The room was re-coloured by intermittent flashes.

The Tarmac King was not afraid of anyone. He'd stood up to men with baseball bats twice his strength and two feet taller than him. He fought foam-mouthed druggies, gangs and of course, the Taking Man himself. But he shook as he approached the seated figure now. The dark sphere, the eye, seemed to be breathing out of rhythm with the Prince's physical body.

And all of a sudden, it was looking at him.

The Prince stood. His normal eye was still fixed on the window, the city, his thoughts. The dark socket was all on Pike. He crossed the distance and stood before him.

'Pike Mallory,' the prophet said. Pike had to get used to everyone knowing everyone's names around here. 'The Last Knight.'

'Why'd you call me that?'

The Prince grinned.

'Because you died for love, didn't you? Like some chivalrous soul in old Thom Malory's book.' He laughed, a sound which made Pike's legs feel like they were unstable again. 'You share the name; you share the honourable deed. You come from the right country too. I find there are no American knights. Only cowboys.' The grin widened. 'So why not? I'm the Prince. You're a knight. It was only a matter of time before you came here.'

Pike nodded, sucking it all in. The Prince was impossible to read. He talked with an almost childish energy, the energy of a young hopeful man. But his face looked like a thousand years had ravaged it. And the eye, it seemed to be *listening* as Pike stumbled over his next few words.

'I heard about your plan. I saw the signs. I wasn't sure. But Fay...' He glanced at the woman who was leaning against the wall, watching the whole thing as though it were no more than a casual family interaction. '...she read my future. I've had a reading before. It told me the truth. I resisted it for so long but in the end it came true anyway. I'm done fighting. I want to embrace it. I want to embrace the truth and fulfil it.' Pike couldn't believe these words were spilling out of his mouth. Was he breaking down? Under what pressure? Was the eye affecting him? Or was it just that clown's grin splashed across the Prince's face, sitting so at odds with the ancient eyes? 'If what you propose works, it could give us all a second chance.'

The Prince nodded slowly.

'You died for love, Pike. You died to save a friend. Many would say that there's nothing greater to do in life. Why would *you* want a second chance?'

Pike got the feeling from the twist at the corner of the Prince's mouth that he already knew but he wanted to hear it.

'I might have done one good thing at the end, but...' Pike breathed. His chest was tight, as was his throat. His eyes felt raw. '...I wasted so much before then. I see it now. I couldn't see it while I was in it... But now I'm here. I see it. I want to go back.' He took a shuddering breath and stared fully into the Prince's face, not shying away from the frightening abysm, accepting it, *welcoming* it.

'I want to help you build your ark.'

CHAPTER 9

The release was coming. They were almost there, just one last
push...

And then it happened, shakingly, ecstatically.

For a moment, their dismal surroundings were irrelevant. The
dirtied mattress, the hungry broken windows, the shadows, the insects,
none of it held any threat or reality to it. She was climbing. The Need
roared in triumph as pleasure exploded in the core of her being, a point
just above her sex. That point seemed to glow with red light, a light
which blossomed like sun-rays and enveloped her whole body. *Pleasure.*

Then it was over.

Larri slumped and lay back on the bed, panting; she rolled off of
him and curled into his arm. They must have looked funny, she
thought. She was a good foot taller than him, and her legs dangled off
the end of the mattress.

'Good?' he asked.

'Good.'

At first, they had been awkward together. Larri had been unwilling
to put his maimed hands on her: she assumed because of her scarring,
but later, she realised, because he was ashamed. His hands had holes
right the way through the palms from when he had offered himself as a

sacrifice to Yin in the place of a little boy. Hagga knew that Larri thought they were repulsive, but it only reminded her of his best moments, when he found his courage.

Just as she accepted his faults, he accepted hers. The fire-burn scarring down her right arm spoiled the perfection she'd so often used to get what she wanted. The twisted, discoloured skin sprawled all the way down to her wrist and crept partially over her right breast. But if that revolted or deterred Larri, he did a good job of hiding it. He attended to both her breasts with great and equal enthusiasm. It was funny how the men she'd slept with who prided themselves on bedding scores of women didn't show anywhere near as much of an ache for it. She supposed being ten years in a coma taught you to be grateful for what you could get, but it didn't seem entirely like that. Larri wanted *her* body. And there was still a faint pride in that.

They were not in love. That much was certain for Hagga. At least not yet. If they kept going as they were, who knew? At the moment, it was physical companionship. Comfort, more than a need for sexual venting. When they were together, the bleakness of the world seemed to press in around her less. It was good for Larri too. His confidence was growing outside and inside the bedroom, the awkwardness of his body falling away as he found his rhythm. He didn't just *please* her, he *satisfied* her. And Hagga had slept with a lot of men (she'd wager she'd had more sexual partners than all the men she'd known who boasted about their scores of women), so he was doing well.

She ran her hand over his chest. The hairs on it were a mixture of dark brown and grey, and bristly like stubble. His body looked like it was trapped between two ages: a man in his thirties and a man in his sixties. She supposed it was the coma, the incomplete the recovery, the stress and the torture, all taking their toll.

'You've got that look on your face again,' Larri said, grinning. It was a semi-smug grin, but she could forgive him for it. He'd never thought he'd get this lucky.

'What look?' she replied, with forced innocence.

'That look that says you're trying to solve the universe's mysteries.'

She snorted, flicked her hair out the way, and laid her head on his chest, listening to his heart. Outside the window of the room which they had made their home, they could hear the loud declamations of the Prince's holographic call; a new life 'beyond the dark waters.' The signs irked Hagga more than anything because they reminded her of Yin's tricks. Every time she saw them, she couldn't help but think of the woman in white's words: 'watch out for the dwarf.' In Yin's final illusion he had seemed a dwarf. Could it be they hadn't killed him and he was now working for the Prince?

No, the entire city collapsed. You heard his scream when Larri drove the dagger into him. The mountains surrounding the Circle collapsed. It's over.

'I'm not sure we'll solve even the mystery of this city.'

Larri reached down and stroked her hair, gently smoothing behind her ears.

'I've been meaning to talk to you about that.'

'Oh?'

'I think we should go back to the statue. The King.'

She lifted her head and looked into his eyes. He returned her gaze with the steadiness of someone crafting a master-weapon.

'You think he actually knows something?'

'I don't know. Can't get what he said out of my head though. *And so will you.* I couldn't decide whether that means the Prince is an enemy or...' He shrugged. His eyes became bright like searchlights. 'What do you think?'

Hagga had hoped he wouldn't ask that question, because she was as unsure as he was. On the one hand, the callings reminded her of Yin, his tricks and illusions, but on the other the promise of discovering a world they had never had a chance to see seemed like the escape they'd been searching for so long. Defeating Yin and getting out of the Circle was almost meaningless now – this place was no less a prison. But if they volunteered for the ship, there was a chance they could get to this other place. A chance for them to experience a world without illusions. For all the warning bells ringing in her head about the Prince, his determination seemed unquestionable.

'I think it can't hurt.'

She stood and began dressing. There wasn't much in the way of clothing here (even less than there was in the Circle, as it happened) but she'd managed to find a serviceable pair of men's jeans, a black women's coat with a high collar (which concealed the burn-marks stretching up the side of her neck) and a navy blouse. None of it was particularly clean. There was a shortage of water, save for the black ocean, but she didn't think that would serve. Occasionally a spring of water erupted through a crack in the concrete and the dishevelled city dwellers danced around it for days, collecting it in bowls, bottles, anything they could get their hands on. Some nakedly bathed. The women didn't seem afraid of showing their bodies here. After their encounter with the concrete-wielding matron, Hagga didn't wonder at it too much.

Larri was ready shortly after her; it took him a while to get his trousers on because of the crookedness of his legs. They set out. The journey was uneventful, though as always she felt they were being watched. She didn't doubt they were, even when they were making love. There were so many windows and holes and cracks in these destitute skyscrapers (she had heard someone else call them that) privacy was impossible.

As they passed between two high square towers, a suspended image made up of glistening blue particles unfolded and began to portray a ship heroically cutting through a turbulent water. The Prince stood at its prow, boldly leaning out into the wind, a manic gleam on his face. *Well, at least they don't try to hide how crazy he is.*

They saw the chapel with its unhealthy smoke and ducked down the alley into the cemetery.

———

'WE CAME to ask you about the Prince.'

Hagga felt stupid watching Larri talk to what seemed to be an inanimate object, but it didn't last long. The statue began to bleed again and the voice groaned, as though waking from a bone-aching sleep.

The cripple-man and the wolf-woman come again! No one visits a second time. How kind.

'You know about...' Hagga couldn't finish the question. Of *course* the statue knew. Everyone seemed to know everything about everyone around here. The place forbid secrets to be kept, and yet the entire city was one big secret itself.

Darling, don't take this the wrong way, but you smell like a bitch.

Laughter followed, a kind of squealing laughter, like a child that'd found a new source of humour and was enthusedly exploring it.

'The Prince,' Larri pressed. 'Who is he? You said you had fought his wars. What did you mean? Can we trust him? Will he succeed?'

I never said I could see the future, cripply. I said I knew him.

The same nerve-tingling sigh issued from invisible lips. The amused face of the statue gave the impression it was listening in on the conversation and enjoying it, like a mildly entertaining sketch. *How can I begin? He is all that is iniquitous personified, and he is also just a man born like any other. He is godlike but has never claimed to be a god. He is the Prince, only, and will correct you if you call him lord or master. He knows his place but his arrogance knows no bounds. He is an oxymoron. He is the death of civilisation and the flame of humanity, burning up its own fuel and reigniting itself for eternity.*

Does this help at all or is that too vague?

Larri and Hagga exchanged a glance. Hagga burst out laughing.

I'm glad that tickled you. Now, it's rather hard not to be portentous when talking about said Prince and I hate being portentous. Let's talk about something else.

Larri looked dumbfounded. He opened his mouth and then closed it again. He looked at Hagga again.

'Who are *you?*'

Ahhhhh, another boring question. Time's up I'm afraid. Things to do. This city is a part of me, you know. Got its best interests at heart. Teehee.

The liquid sucked itself back into the stone. They stood in the quiet graveyard for a while longer, but the voice did not speak again.

'Can you hear that?' Hagga said, after a while.

'I can't hear anything.'

Hagga smiled.

'Which is a first in this place, right? The storm's fading.'

They looked up. The clouds were paler and looked less heavy. A layer of mist, like a thin bride's veil, separated the city and the sky, making it seem remote. There hadn't been a lightning flash in twenty minutes.

Then it began to snow.

Hagga flinched from the white flakes, thinking it would burn like hot ash, but then she saw Larri laughing and cupping the white in his hands, letting it fall into his hair.

'It's cold,' she said. 'What is it? Ice?'

'It's snow,' Larri said. 'God, my grandfather used to have a picture book with this stuff in. It was all about the seasons. Of course, there weren't seasons in the Circle. No *weather* even. Grandpa used to say the book was talking about the world before. In winter it snowed, he said. I didn't think we'd ever see it here.' His eyes were glistening, adding three more words to his sentence: *or at all.* Hagga ran forward and embraced him and they both started laughing.

Faintly, like the softest instrument amidst an orchestra, she thought she heard the King laughing too.

CHAPTER 10

They stood on the other side of the pyramid, an eerie feeling pervaded, like the ground was about to give way beneath them. Acres and acres of forest stretched out to the horizon. The trees were unlike any trees Pike had seen before, their bark bulbous and twisted, like a field of huge walnuts. Most of them were bent over double as though under crippling weights. They almost resembled willows, but their leaves were star-shaped and coloured a virulent green.

In the strip of earth between the pyramid's base and the tree-line sat a skeletal edifice. Even though its foundations had barely been laid, Pike could visualise the huge vessel it would become. The longboat would fit roughly thirty people, he reckoned, with some room for significant storage below decks. Even though they wouldn't need food. Water would be necessary. Barrels of it.

Workers hacked at the trees with crude implements. Others stripped the felled trunks, turning them into rounded pillars. Another team cut these into rectangular planks. Countless misshapen specimens lay discarded by the log piles, no doubt marred due to the in-precision of the tools they were using.

The Prince was smiling. Fay smiled with him. He held out his hands as though unveiling a statue in Pike's honour.

'What do you think, Limey?'

'I think if you call my limey again I'll sock you.'

The Prince laughed.

'You have spirit, Pike. I think that's why I've decided I like you.' He started walking towards the ship's skeleton. Fay trailed a few steps behind like an exotic bodyguard (perhaps that's exactly what she was, he thought). Pike waited a few moments, then followed. He wasn't used to talking with someone who was so good at controlling the flow. Pike was normally the one making the call of when and where to end a conversation.

'I need you to feed back to me on what you see. You're a well travelled man. You may not know anything about boats per se, but that's irrelevant. I'm not sure the waters we are going to cross will follow the same rules as old H2O.' The Prince stopped and stroked the central wooden beam of the prow. Pike wondered whether his dark eye was visualising the ship complete, in its full splendour. Then he supposed he didn't need a magic eye for that, just an imagination. But imagination was a human word, and it was hard to think of the Prince as human.

Pike started to pace around the ark.

'Well, I take it a motor's out of the question,' Pike said, shooting the Prince a glance. There was a huge slab of wood, separated from the rest, which he thought might soon be shaped into the slope of a primary rudder. Is this going to be oar-driven or windsail?'

'The winds here seem strong,' the Prince said, 'But there's not enough material to make a sail. Unless we find a new source.'

Pike nodded. He took a few steps back and squinted at the design, holding up his thumb and index.

'I'd say your ship's a fraction too deep. The hull's hanging low. It gives you more storage space, but it also means you got to make the oars six feet longer. At least. The longer the oar the more prone they are to snap and you don't want to have to deal with that kind of imbalance out there. Sure, you can carry a few spares, but if you're tackling heavy waves, you're gunna be breaking more than just a few.' He moved closer again and crouched, stroking the sternum-like under-beam. He imagined tickling the underbelly of a massive sea-creature. 'If it's this low you're also going to have problems if there's ice. The old longboats were long and shallow for this reason.' Pike stood and walked back to them. 'You're also gunna need some kind of pitch to coat the outside, make it water-tight.'

The Prince waved his hand.

'We're working on that one.'

He looked at Fay, who smiled knowingly.

'I told you he was our man,' she said.

'That you did, my dear.'

Did Pike hear a note of *affection* in that world-cracking voice? If there had been a soft note, it was gone as soon as it came. The Prince was looking at him again, or rather, *into* him.

'How is it you came to know all this, Sir Malory?'

Pike shrugged.

'Studied ancient history. Greeks had a lot to say about boat building. When I say studied, by the way, I mean read a bunch of books. Didn't have time for school.'

The Prince roared with laughter.

'A gypsy who studied ancient history...' The Prince clapped his hands together. 'I like it!' He slung an arm around Pike as though they were old friends. 'We'll make your changes, but first, I want to make you an offer, to thank you for volunteering, and giving your advice.' The Prince led them away from the makeshift shipyard, and Pike suspected, out of earshot of the other works.

'I'm listening,' he said.

'Well then, tell me Pike: have you ever captained a ship before?'

Pike looked at him to see if there was a shadow of a smile on his face, a twitch at the corner of the eyes, anything to indicate he was joking. But there wasn't a shadow of irony or mockery in the Prince's face, simply a fixatedness which drew everything to it. Pike considered himself one of the most stubborn, resilient men alive, and even he had felt the draw of him. Like a moth to a flame, as the old saying went.

'I can't say I have.'

'Would you like to? I need someone with me on this voyage, someone who knows what it is to travel, who isn't afraid of the ends of the earth.'

They stopped without Pike becoming aware of it. The Prince's hand was still on his shoulder, a kind of heat fizzling from his fingertips. The eye seemed to be growing, widening.

'You know me,' Pike said.

'Yes,' the Prince whispered. 'I know you.'

'What about The Tower.'

The Prince frowned.

Pike swallowed. It was hard to get the words straight with the darkness bathing you like sordid, dazzling neon. Like explaining a convoluted theory whilst a stripclub raged around you. The eye made you feel *dirty*, exposed, it questioned you and your motives. It made everything seem palpably wrong.

'The Tower... it was the second tarot card Fay drew for me. It means disaster. Surely it's referring to the voyage?'

The Prince nodded. Pike sensed he was withholding something. There was a tremor across his upper lip and the face resumed its concrete aspect.

'It *could* mean that, but remember: the future can change its mind.'

There was a quietening. The skies clouds changed colour. Snow began to fall and dress the skeleton ship in white. Pike was incredulous. The Prince held up his hands.

'You see?' His grin was like a lightning bolt. 'It's changing already.'

———

HE STOOD at the chapel altar in darkness. The Slaves (so he had taken to calling them) were seated before him in the broken pews, heads bowed. Many wept. Their weeping made him angry. What did they have to weep about? What did they know about humanity? Emotions were for people, not monsters. Whatever their beliefs, the consumption of flesh was vile. The Taking Man had done many things, things people would call barbaric, but he was not an animal.

Of course, there was one exception he would make. There was one person he would see devoured. He did not want their spirit living on in the stones of the city. There'd be no botched job when the time came. Total annihilation.

He had converted the altar into one of his own fashion. The bowl which once would have held baptising water had been removed. Instead, the altar-stand now birthed a fire. There was a tear in the ceiling which allowed the toxic smog to escape and palefire to pour through in an intermittent beam. A rod of metal rested in the fire. It hadn't been in their long. It wasn't hot yet.

'People of this dismal city,' he said, matter-of-factly. He was no false prophet, orating and impassioning. He was a man with a simple goal. He intended to achieve that goal. The only motivation his Slaves needed was that things would turn nasty if they didn't cooperate, but by now, they had learned that. 'As you know, our false prophet claims he is intent on building a boat and trying to cross the waters back to the real world. This is a lie! The only thing he intends on doing is sacrificing any who go on the venture, feeding the city.' He scanned the room. These people looked like the children of fear and darkness. Their lips were cracked, their hands shook (a side effect of their habit), and their eyes were weak. Grimy, defaced iconography stared facelessly down at them from around the walls. The Taking Man imagined these were the dark gods of which Albric had once made mention, hearing this fell sermon, judging those who would follow his path. Yes, he liked that image. And he would need their help if they were to destroy a being like the Prince. 'It has already taken its toll on you, this city. It has forced you into dark ways. Forced you to become less than human.' He offered what he hoped was a smile, the bulge of his deformed face made the action difficult. 'But you are not broken, despite all that has happened to you. And now, dear people, the opportunity has arisen for us to strike back. You have spent weeks gathering information, and now, we see our *chance!*'

Heads lifted from their postures of dejection. A few exchanged looks.

'Yes. This ark is being built behind the pyramid – an attempt to conceal it. The Prince knows that no one dares go beyond the pyramid into the dark forest. But he was not vigilant enough in hiding his efforts.' The Taking Man grinned and glanced at the iron rod in the fire. The tip was turning a molten orange. 'There will be guards, but we will overcome them. And then...' He grabbed a bough of the poisonwood and thrust it into the fire. It ignited, forming a hissing, grey-green torch of jade fire. '...we will *burn it down!*' He drew the iron rod out of the fire with his bare hands. The gods were with him. The dark ones.

'And with this rod, I will burn out the darkness of the Prince's eye and destroy him!'

They got to their feet. Some were jumping up and down. Others waved their arms as though in a hallucinogenic trance. The Taking Man could feel his voice lifting. He had refuted oratory, but now it came naturally to him, as though long ago in another life he had rehearsed the same script and was now remembering, piece by piece, how he had first performed it. He did not see the Ark burning in his mind's eye, but the forest, the forest in which the Prince had made him what he was.

'BURN IT DOWN!'

And they answered him. There was fear and terror in every face, and was it any wonder? Before them stood a devil-faced being, holding burning poison in one hand, and a spear of flame in another.

The Taking Man ran down the aisles and the Slaves let out shrieks and yammers of jubilation. They scrambled over the rotten pews after him as he broke from the doors into the palefire lit night. There was a layer of snow lying over everything like bone-white dust.

ELSEWHERE, in the pyramid throne room, the Prince stared out through Yin's viewing window and touched his throat. He was remembering his death, in the cold, cold snow-swept New York. In another world.

CHAPTER 11

'What's that?' Larri said.

But he knew. It was fire.

The two of them froze like the grave-statues surrounding them. Reason stated they should run back to their 'home' and wait for commotion to pass over, but if something was happening, if someone (or worse, something) was attacking the city, they needed to find out.

'Let's go,' Hagga said.

So they went.

She set off at a running pace Larri was just able to match. He knew her long legs were capable of much more, but she was compensating for him. The snow dragged them to an even slower march after a few minutes. Larri's toes burned. He felt like he had weights lashed to his ankles.

He'd gotten a lot more able since their physical relationship started, however. There'd been a time this pace would have been unthinkable. The sex was like a clothes-iron on him, hot pressure smoothing the kinks in his legs and back. He wondered if the city itself had something to do with it too. The burns that'd left Hagga's right side disfigured had been minutes old when they entered the city, but in an hour they had cooled. The scars remained, of course, but he wondered if given enough time even they might fade.

'It's coming from the pyramid,' she said. He could see the smoke between two skyscrapers, winking with green atoms, like the dust of emeralds. The tips of the fire he could see were green too. Was it the wood or was all fire like that here? It wasn't worth thinking about. There were too many deeper mysteries.

The snow was still falling, appearing to slow time. Each flake drifted like thoughts dropping from a zenith onto the landscape of an active brain. Larri found it hard to feel any urgency in this. The peace was so real.

'I already dislike this stuff,' Hagga growled, looking back over her shoulder. She was smiling. The snow had given her white spots in her hair. For a second, Larri knew what she would look like in forty years and it was no less attractive.

'Try being my height!'

She laughed and forged on, leaning into the not inconsiderable wind.

They were almost at the pyramid. He could now see the flames were coming from somewhere behind it. They'd need to skirt around its base.

'What's behind?' she said, voicing his own question.

'A forest, apparently.'

Of course, neither of them really knew what that was. Larri had seen pictures of trees in his book. That, and he'd been nailed to the last tree that grew in the Circle as a sacrifice to Yin. There'd been no blossoms on that tree however, only fruit made bitter from the blood its roots drank.

The idea of a *forest,* a place where many trees grew, seemed impossible, extravagant even. He was excited, he realised.

Hagga's arm caught him like a battering ram and knocked all the wind out him.

'What the –'

But even as he doubled over he caught a glimpse of what stood before them in the road and blocked their way to the pyramid. Hagga trembled violently.

There was a figure, no more than four feet high, a black square cut out of white cloth. The snow piled up around his dark robes which flowed out from him like an overlong shadow. It gave the impression of a gigantic figure kneeling, but it was not a giant, rather, a dwarf. His hair was black, as were his eyes, but what was most arresting about him was the way that he alone of all the surroundings appeared *solid,* like a slab of concrete amidst polystyrene walls.

'I've found you,' he said, and though his voice was conversational it crossed the thirty feet between them undimmed by wind. 'The cripple and the wolf. I didn't believe him, at first. I couldn't. But he was right.' The dwarf took a step forward. In the distance behind him the flames cracked and shot up, cutting the night like a neon blade.

'Who are you?' Hagga said, but Larri knew she knew, and so did he.

'It looks like we both made a mistake,' he said, clenching his teeth. The holes in his hands and feet ached all of a sudden, as though the wounds could remember their origins.

The dwarf nodded, solemnly.

'You create his illusions for him,' Hagga said. 'You're the one who makes them flock to him.' She snorted. 'The god of the Circle reduced to a door to door salesman.'

Larri saw the dwarf's fists clench and unclench.

'I'm going to enjoy watching you suffer, whore.'

He took two ungainly steps and jumped, as he did so, the dark folds of his cloak rippled out. They spread impossibly wide, growing and gaining three-dimensionality. His face enlarged and then imploded, his eyes and mouth merging into one gelatinous hole which began to suck at the air like a squid's mouth – filled with teeth. The body elongated, became that of a shadowy, feline entity. A scream sounded throughout as though the process was not without sensation. The shape multiplied its size in one last shrieking contortion, becoming twice the height and girth of an elephant but with none of the ponderousness.

The creature took a few moments, once it had attained full form, to stretch its neck and open the angler-fish maw, revealing a silver, liquid eye inside the mouth. The eye focused on Larri. His breathing stopped. He had faced this thing once before, deep within the City of Illusion. He had only been saved by Simon and the others then. He wasn't sure whether he could face it now. *You're stronger,* the voice said. *You're better. And you've got Hagga.*

It began to slink towards them, moving like a series of sketched images, cutting the corners of real movement. Its shoulder rubbed against one of the buildings and dislodged a section of concrete as easily as though it was made of plaster, rubble spilling to the snowcaked high-street in cloud.

'Two can play at this game,' Hagga said.

And this was the first time Larri saw her change.

———

IT WAS SOMETHING LIKE SNOW. Falling and falling. Burying the structure of a familiar town beneath layers and layers of cold, senseless ice. That was what turning into the Need felt like. Hagga could sense her personality, not vanishing, but receding, diminishing, becoming clouded and obscured by each new layer, layers of undiluted hunger without end.

There was physical pain along with this psychological change. The hell of her knees breaking and inverting, her forearms bursting from her flesh as they extended, her fingers snapping at every joint and acquiring claws which ripped through the skin like erupting maggots. Her head reformed to acquire a long crocodile's mouth: a process which felt like her face had been smashed in with a sledgehammer and then subjected to poor reconstructive surgery. Black fur sprouted like a disease.

But there were good parts to it too. Even Hagga had to admit it. The part when it was finished, and she threw back her head and screamed, her and the Need as one, and the scream tore the fabric of men's hearts. Awakening. Or was it sleeping? She was never sure which was more real – her days walking on two legs pretending the world was normal – or her days as a thing with no name that wanted only blood and body forever.

It had been a long time since her last transformation. Her relation-ship with Larri had, in part, been a way to assure the beast was held at bay.

But now she was here again, it felt like she had been wearing the wrong skin all these weeks. She didn't care that Simon was supposed to have cured her with his 'touch of God'; she didn't care that in turning she had put Larri at risk; she didn't even care that she had tried herself once before against Yin and lost.

All she cared about was the *Need*.

In fact, 'she' didn't care at all. The Need was an 'it', androgynous yet carnal, and *it* was calling the shots now.

KILL. KILL. KILL.

It saw the hulking creature before it, the thing with the weird eye in its mouth. The Need wanted to take that eye and grind it between teeth until it was liquid paste. It ran forward, bounding like a half-wolf-half-jackal. The Eye Creature did the same, moving with a tigress's sleek power. The two leapt.

Its jaws opened wide like a sea-monster's, the silver eye glittering between them like a jewel. Though the Need was primitive it was not stupid. It saw the trap of that jewel, and as much as it wanted to taste it, it knew it had to stay away from the fish-teeth or be snared. So it swivelled, slashing with its claws instead of going for the bite. It raked a gash along the side of the Eye Creature which let out a mewling howl. It spun and found footing, like a cat. The two monsters circled and leapt again. The dance was on. It was a dance the Need knew well. It did not fear the Eye Creature. It did not care for its size. It only knew it bled. Oily tar leaked from the gashes in its side, but whatever it looked like it smelled like blood to the Need.

KILL. FEED. KILL. FEED.

The Eye Creature pounced and snapped, like a reptile, its neck unnaturally extending. The Need skirted and dodged, swiping, and printing another score of four gouges in its face. The Eye Creature leapt back, arching its spine, hissing without true lips.

BLEED. BLEED.

The Need was ready for the kill. The Eye Creature was weakening. It could feel it.

Don't lose focus now. It's more dangerous than it looks.

The Need recognised the dim voice. The woman. The vessel. The one whom it shared a form with. The Need snorted and ran for the Eye Creature. The beast swung a gigantic paw, claws flashing like so many scythes.

Danger!

The Need drew back, desperately, but one of the scything claws ripped at its ear, tearing it fully off. The Need barely felt the wound. Pain was alien.

Wait. Wait your time.

The woman interrupting. The woman confusing.

The Need snarled and leapt for the throat.

But the Eye Creature was fast. Its second paw snapped out and caught the Need mid air, sending it flying back and crashing against one of the buildings. The impact would have broken the back of almost anything but the Need was not entirely a physical being, more an energy, indefinable as emotion. It did, however, feel pain in that moment. The sensation was so unknown to it a squeal tore from its blood-clotted throat and it writhed even as it fell. It scrambled to rise, out of balance. Hagga's consciousness and direction had become fully submerged beneath the blind panic of a wounded animal.

The Eye Creature pounced again.

Before the Need could evade the full weight of the monster crashed into it, the scythe-claws driving through its chest, piercing the torso eight times and pinning the Need to the ground.

Somewhere, someone screamed. The Need did not know who it was, but the deep part that was still Hagga heard Larri's voice.

The Eye Creature bent over the Need. Its jaws opened, revealing the silver eye, which dripped with a fluid that was neither blood nor poison but something else. The Need struggled, but that only worsened the pain. It clamped its jaws around the talons but they could not be broken. It kicked with desperate abandon.

Saliva dripped from the eye, covering the Need. The pain had been so great, but the saliva was like morphine. *Don't go. No. You have to fight! Fight!* But all the Need wanted was for the pain to end. Its lust had been sated. Hagga rose through the snow-layers of animalism, disgust and despair making her feel like she'd vomit her guts from her mouth. The beast was not really fearless. It was a coward – she had simply never had an opponent strong enough to show her.

No. No. This is Yin. Yin. You must fight. Larri...

But the Need had already slipped out of Hagga like a thief.

She did not feel any pain. She opened her eyes and saw the brutal talons imbedded in the feeble-looking flesh of her stomach and chest; she tried to speak, but blood poured out. She looked around her and behind Yin's shadow she saw Larri run and drive a broken, jagged-ended steel rod into the back of its leg. The beast howled and spun, lashing out. The blow sent him tumbling back, but he managed to rise to his feet, rod still in hand.

'Come on!' he cried and darted around the corner.

The beast took one glance at Hagga and hissed. Then it surged after him. For a moment it was like a segment of reality had uprooted itself and moved.

Hagga tried to cry out, but couldn't. She lay there for a moment, blood turning the snow around her into red spirals like a Norse rune.

She slipped into darkness.

But strangely, that wasn't the end. In the darkness, she saw a man standing there, a man with one eye that was normal and one eye that seemed a blacker circle against the black. He was looking down at her, his face difficult to understand.

Then the man scooped her up and carried her through the snow, frost touching her cheeks like deadened fingertips.

But the man was warmer than flame.

———

LARRI COULD BARELY DRAW in the air – the cold stung his lungs and throat. His legs felt like they had metal nails driven through the kneecaps.

But if he didn't stop running, Yin would get him. Or rather, the thing Yin had become. Larri never would have thought Yin had the power to do it outside of his own city, but this place seemed to empower, to give back life.

No time for thinking. Run.

He darted around a bend and listened as part of a skyscraper crumbled, the panther-like darkness shouldering down a narrow alleyway.

If he hit a dead end, he was gone. He didn't know if his crude weapon had wounded it, but even if it had, it would not be enough. He wasn't even sure it'd been enough to save Hagga. God, the blood pouring from her, the talons through her chest. She'd been ripped apart. One moment it'd seemed the Need was invincible, the next, Yin had gained the upper hand. The table was well and truly flipped. All bets off.

He wondered about doubling back and reaching her, but then he'd only be leading Yin back to her, and if she hadn't already begun to meld with the city, he'd finish her off.

Larri turned right, but didn't account for the frosted surface and slipped, tumbling on his side and smacking his ribs against the snow-packed ground. The rod went flying from his hand. He scrambled to his feet and couldn't see it. He heard the hissing noise the great creature of darkness made, and a sloshing which he thought might be its liquid eye rolling around in its mouth. He left the rod behind and kept running. The cold made his fingers difficult to bend and straighten. Everything had become labyrinthine – depth obscured by a vista of white atoms.

His feet were entrenched. The beast's padding footfalls drew closer, shaking the ground, or maybe it was just Larri's trembling legs? He didn't know. He was beginning to shiver and shut down. His lips were glazed with a frost layer that was now cracking. Blood trickled down his chin. *Colder than hell,* he thought, but had no idea where the thought came from. *Colder than the black stars.* Was it a voice on the wind? A voice like a captured lightning bolt. The voice of a Prince.

He staggered on, tucking his hands into his armpits in a desperate attempt to reverse the freezing. An alley, too narrow for Larri let alone the creature, caught his eye. He squeezed himself into it and waited, head resting against the ice-block concrete of a building wall. He listened. The snow quietened everything. Yin's footfalls had stopped. Had he changed back?

Fighting with his breathing, he took the briefest glance.

No, Yin was still in monstrous form. The beast was at the other end of the street, oozing towards him, mouth low to the ground, the light of the inner-eye concealed by the closed jaws.

Larri's knees buckled and he leant more weight against the wall.

Move you dumb fuck. Move. No angel's voice came to him. There was only his own amygdala, the desperate reptile part of his brain buried beneath rolls and rolls of pink matter: it wanted to hide but also wanted to run its ass off.

He started to side-step down the alley, moving like a man on a ledge. He was sure the creature could not fit down the alley. Even if it tore the buildings apart to get at him, it would buy enough time to get away. But he *wasn't* so certain one of its dextrous forepaws couldn't snake into the gap and seize him.

A shadow cut across the alley mouth. He brought a dead hand to his mouth and pressed. He couldn't feel the pressure or texture of his own skin. Jesus, he was never going to make it out of this blizzard alive. It'd become something else.

A silver eye gleamed,

FOUND YOU.

Larri started to skip. The alley would not permit running, but he moved as fast as it would allow. The cold lent him help here: he couldn't feel the ache in the bones of his legs anymore, so they did not protest.

The thing thrust its clawed hand into the opening but the talons merely shrieked against the stone wall. He thought he heard it hiss again and withdraw. It vanished. Was it circling round? Should he wait to see whether it appeared on the other side of the alley? Or would it come over?

Larri looked up. A skyscraper stood at his back, but the building next to it which formed the other wall of the alley was only two storeys.

He crouched, trusting the nauseous feeling in his gut, and began to crawl-shuffle along the floor towards the alley's end.

There was a rushing noise, a crash and he was cast in darkness.

He scampered forward and slipped from the alley just as the talons tore a chunk of debris from the skyscraper. Pebbles shredded his calves like grapeshot and he stumbled.

Do not fall. If you fall you're dead.

He danced, fighting with his rapidly shutting down body, his legs throwing off shapes, his hands like the coiled rigour mortis limbs of a dead person. There was now no sound to his world. Everything had receded. He was on an entirely white open plane.

'Colder than the heart of Mor.' He said, the words not his own.

He collapsed in the drifts.

His arm dangled into something – it hadn't met solid ground. Was there some kind of pit? He forced his eyes to remain open, to look, to understand what they saw. There was a rip in the street. It looked like it'd been created by some kind of explosion. The ground was torn up. It was hardly visible from the street because of the snow piled up at its edges. If he could get inside, Yin might not be able to see him...

He pulled. The thunder of the footfalls had returned. *It's too late,* he told himself. *You're too late. Hagga's dead and so are you.*

But the talons did not come, and neither did the dripping silver mouth. Maybe it couldn't see him? He could feel the snow on his back, in his hair, drowning him.

One last heave, his fingers red from a hundred cuts he didn't remember. He pushed with his good leg too, moving like the slowest and most ancient worm. He tipped, careful to stifle the yelp, and tumbled down into a cavern.

He cracked his head as he hit the ground, and the world snapped out like a TV turned off.

CHAPTER 12

He stood back and watched the skeleton set ablaze.

Around him, the Slaves devoured the corpses of the pathetic guards the Prince had set on his 'ark'. Their lips and teeth shone like the features of dark idolatrous statues. Green blazed at the heart of the fire, making the snow around them look like a poisonous ocean.

The Taking Man was alive again. He hadn't felt this good since his bomb went off in Hyde Park and ripped apart the whole audience. That'd been a moment of orgasm, of triumph, punching back against the awful cogs of life's secret and biased machinations.

Now, as he watched the wooden beams blacken, crackle and release gouts of smog, like the fumes of an industrial plant, the whole structure beginning to fall inwards like a wrinkled amoeba, he felt that triumph again. In one hand, he held a flaming brand. In the other, he held the rod. Its tip had cooled, so he thrust it into the baleful flame and it began to superheat again.

'Tonight, we tear down the false prophet!'

When the tip started to glow he pulled it out and held it above his head for the Slaves to see. Its tip shone like the multicoloured gemstone of a sorcerer's staff: orange, white and green.

'Follow!'

He turned and began marching towards the pyramid. Wordlessly, they obeyed, carrying with them the dismembered body parts of the Prince's servants. Most of them were naked. Their only weapons were crude nail-pierced bats, shovels with sharpened edges, kitchen blades and pipes. But they were fighters. The Taking Man hadn't been sure until he'd seen them in action, sweeping down on the pitiful defences like a locust plague and overwhelming it. He didn't know if it was the consumption of flesh that made them so strong or whether it was a fear of the Prince and the threat he represented, but either way, the end had been achieved.

The pyramid's surface was like something living. The snow didn't cling to it. Every other building and surface was caked in white, but not the monolithic seat of power. He reached out and touched its stone – there was something slimy coating it, like the secretion of a worm. It made him nauseous, but he pushed down those feelings and began to climb. The host at his back did the same, though with some reticence. None of them had ever mounted these steps accept when they were brought to its topmost chamber and lowered into the darkness – there to suffer punishment for a time equal to the crimes they had once committed. Maybe it was that which made them so bold? They had endured the abyss – true emptiness, the rot and famine of the mind, of humanity itself. What was war after that?

'The shadows defend this place,' one of their number said. Her name was Deela. Where she came from, the Taking Man did not know. A distant epoch of the old world's history, perhaps. She had daubed her eyes with designs which reminded him of the eye of Horus – perhaps Egypt, then? – but they also reminded him of the Prince's eye. It made him mistrustful.

'What shadows?'

'The shadows of the past. First they torture you with them. Then, with the darkness.' She sniffed, nostrils flaring. She climbed the pyramid with effortless dexterity, still holding a sharpened metal pipe that glinted like a scorpion's tail in the snow-bright night. 'A thousand years I spent in that hole.' She looked at the Taking Man. 'I don't care about this "Prince" of yours, but I care about revenge.'

'Then revenge you shall have.'

She snorted and climbed on.

The Taking Man bit his tongue. What of it? She had her own motivations. So did he. As long as these people accomplished his aim, it didn't matter.

He began to throw himself up the narrow steps, scrabbling at the black stone.

He would be the first inside.

————

PIKE WOKE and the throne room was bathed in green light, a light that lit his nerves on fire and spoke the word *warning*. He got to his feet and rushed to the strange viewing window. One glance outside told him what was wrong. The ark was ablaze – its frame curling with sulphurous looking green fire.

He scanned the throne room. The Prince and Fay had not returned. For perhaps the first time in his life he felt a pang that he would be without their guidance. The last few weeks in the Prince's service had been glorious. For once, he did not have to think where he'd next sleep, where next find water or find something to do to alleviate the boredom of wandering. All his life he'd lived hand to mouth, quite literally, but now he saw how people became settled in cosy work. There was a bliss in knowing that the next drink, the next job, the next sleep could be relied upon, and the Prince treated him like a long-lost brother.

He ran for the elevator, all the while his mind whirring with possibilities like some old computer that hadn't been started up in a long time. If the ark was on fire and the guards had been overpowered, either someone very powerful was present or there was a group. *Or both.* He thanked his inner pessimist for that last remark, but as always, it was best to assume the worst. An army of sorts then, led by someone powerful. But who was powerful enough and not already allied with the Prince? Could the weird doctor have betrayed him? It seemed unlikely: he was positively obsessed with his work. The Magician, too worshipped his master. It didn't make sense.

Although... there were moments when it seemed the dwarf was

hiding something behind the Cheshire Cat smile. A secret. A dirty niggling little maggot of loathing and doubt, wrapped up beneath layers of fawning nicety. Pike didn't know if it was just his inner pessimist projecting, but sometimes he felt the Magician was not as content as he seemed.

Manfred, a hunched-backed old man in the service of the Prince, waited by the elevator, snoozing. Pike kicked him awake. He sniffled and blinked, slabs of sleep-dust falling out of his cataract-ridden eyes.

'If I call out, bring me back up.'

Manfred nodded and fell back asleep.

Pike grabbed the lever, pulled it, and jumped on the platform. It groaned, then began its slow ascent through the central column of the pyramid. The hive of doors unveiled itself, and he couldn't help but shudder. He remembered seeing his own room behind one of them – *and* what the Prince had told him about this place.

'It's a phylactery of your past,' he'd said, grinning. 'Whole place is one great big psychological torture chamber.'

'How charming.'

The Prince had laughed.

'Indeed.'

'Who built it?'

'Your guess is as good as mine. I set the Magician working on it, but so far his investigations have proved inconclusive. The caretakers of this place don't talk much.'

Pike had only met the 'caretakers' once: their appearance chilled his blood. They reminded him of computer programs: identical, synthetic, and unable to deviate from their set courses. Though he didn't sense anything inherently malign about them he didn't exactly trust them either. It was clear they were not happy with the way the Prince had ended the 'allotted suffering' as they termed it. He didn't know to what extent they could override their programming to obey the master of the pyramid, but he thought there must be a few clauses which allowed it, and the Prince was probably treading dangerously close to transgressing one.

The elevator ground to a halt. There *was* someone there. As soon as Pike saw him he couldn't believe he'd been so blind. Of course there was someone who could lead an army against the Prince, who had the power to manipulate.

'Pike,' the Taking Man said, with a savage grin. 'I didn't expect to find you here. Lapdog was one thing I thought you'd never be, for all your faults.' He was flanked by a host of bloody-mouthed warriors. It took Pike a moment to realise what that blood meant. No one needed to eat here. *Cannibals.* He remembered the chapel, the bag of body parts, the fires. It all slid into place.

'So, you gunna feed me to your new friends, is that it?'

The Taking Man shook his head. He was holding a spear that glowed at the end like a poker. Casually, as though he was merely unshouldering a rucksack, he handed it to a tall black woman next to him. Then he began to take off his white suit jacket. He looked at it for a moment as though contemplating an old friend, then cast it over the edge; it drifted like a muddied flower-petal down into darkness.

'That wouldn't be a fair fight now, would it?' He stepped onto the elevator. His followers formed a ring at the railing edge, watching hungrily. 'And I know you're all about a fair fight. Pike the fighter. Pike the Knight.' The bulging, tumour-ridden side of the Taking Man's face drooped like a ripe, fleshly egg-sack. It dragged the smile down with it into a snarl. 'You know, we've more in common than you think. We're both gypsies. We both never knew our fathers.' He straightened his head, parodying a gentleman's posture. 'And we're both *British,* don't you know?

'Stop fucking talking.'

Pike strode forward. The Taking Man's hands became fists.

'As you wish.'

Pike swung. He'd never had any training, but he could punch like the back kick of a donkey. Cris had practiced years of bare-knuckle boxing and he said Pike punched harder and faster than anyone he knew.

He connected cleanly with the distorted face. At the last second he tensed, making his arm hit with the impact of a ball and chain. The Taking Man rocked and blood flew from his lip, which had split in several places. The bulbous flesh around his eye turned red.

But he did not go down, like Pike expected him to.

The Taking Man used the momentum and swung right back, catching Pike off guard and staggering him. The blow made his teeth snap together and pain flooded his gums and face. He lost his footing and stumbled back, connecting with the chain. He pushed himself forward but the Taking Man had already stepped in for the next hit.

This one didn't catch Pike's face, but landed somewhere under his swinging arm in the kidney, causing him to feel like a host of needles had been stuck deep through his skin, nestling in something vital.

The fight was a slugging match. Neither was interested in blocking or technique. Neither moved to avoid a swing. It was a match of wild animals contesting: clawing, goring, each blow more crippling than the last.

Pike swung an uppercut which made teeth fly like fragments of marble from the Taking Man's lips. He took one in return which ignited a splitting pain in his chest: a rib broken.

He swung back, desperate. This time the Taking Man stepped into the blow so it only glanced the side of his head. The Taking Man put one hand on Pike's shoulder, digging his thumb into where the cracked rib was. Pike screamed. The Taking Man unleashed a barrage of hole-punch jabs which made Pike cave inwards. He coughed up blood, flailing his fists, trying to land a hit that would change the direction of the fight. His nose exploded – this pain was pitiful next to the pain in his chest – and red clouded his eyes.

He snapped his head forward, like a wild stag trying to gore its assailant. He felt the hard frontal curve of his forehead connect with something squishy followed by something hard. The Taking Man screamed and the rain of blows ended. Pike blinked away blood, staggering, steadying himself on the chain. The Taking Man's face was a mess of broken flesh. Pike grinned and launched himself at him.

But the Taking Man wasn't done. He snapped out an elbow – and Pike walked right onto it, drunk with pain. Pike felt the rib *bend* inside of him, pointing inwards. He doubled over and spat out more blood, but his face met a knee which hit so hard his nose seemed to break a second time, the tiny shards that'd remained cracking into splinters. He fell, tumbling back, snapping the rear of his head against the chain. He was hardly aware of where he was. He imagined he was swimming through a red sea and had to keep blinking the water out of his eyes. And he had this *oozing* feeling, as though parts of him were escaping. He tried to prod them back in, but his fingers were slow through the red seawater.

'A fair fight,' a voice was saying. Someone stood over him. Pike looked up and saw a horrifying face, a face which brought him back to the present moment. 'And you've lost, my friend.' The figure crouched down and reached out, touching Pike's cheek. He tried to swipe at the hand and remove it. *This man shouldn't touch me,* he thought. There was a very specific reason for this, but he couldn't remember it. The ugly man was smiling.

'I'm going to take everything,' he said.

And suddenly, a cold feeling began to tingle his skin.

———

PIKE MALORY WAS in his grasp.

All he had to do was drain him – rob him of all his strength – and his revenge would be complete. It was funny that earlier Deela had been the one to say she was here for revenge. It seemed he had come here for the same reason, after all.

She had also said this place was guarded by shadows of the past. What better shadow to confront than Pike? The one who had ruined all his plans. But now, it was finished. There would be nothing left of Pike once he was through.

'I'm going to take everything,' he said.

Pike tried to beat his hand away, but it was no good. He was well and truly fucked up. His face was hardly a face anymore. *He's almost uglier than I am,* the Taking Man thought, with a chuckle.

And then there was agony, an explosion beginning in his wrist and coursing down his arm.

He stumbled away from Pike. A streak of silver had passed between them – so fast he hadn't registered it, had imagined it was just a trick of the dismal light. But he registered the pain of his missing hand. Each nerve ending seemed to be separately exposed to white-hot fire. He doubled over, wracked and bowed. He watched, mouth hanging open, as his own pale hand descended into the deep beneath them and was lost from sight. He looked at his maimed limb, expecting to see jets of blood pouring from exposed arterial veins, but the wound had been cauterised as though cut with a weapon of pure sunlight.

A talismanic sickle of silver-yellow manifested itself in the abyss. At first he thought a planet had woken in the depths but then he realised it was a sickle blade, the blade which had cut him, returning. He emitted a scream, clutching his charred wrist with his good hand. The blade circled like a boomerang and swept past him. He ducked, half-falling to one knee. It sped over his head and came to a stop in the hands of a tall, elegant woman standing amidst the onlookers.

'You!' he snarled, clambering back up to his feet.

'Me,' she said, leaping down onto the elevator platform. The Slaves watched as though they had abandoned life to become statues.

'Stay out of what doesn't concern you *witch!*' He spat.

Fay shook her head.

'I could say the same to you. You shouldn't have burned the ark. You should never have come here at all. If you'd let me read your cards, you'd know this.' Every word she spoke was a soft, melodic continuation of the last, her logic like perfect flowing water.

'Fuck your futures! Fuck your cards!' The Taking Man forced himself to straighten, though that mere act caused his arm to feel like it'd been broken in several places. He thought he could still feel his fingers, flexing to stroke Pike's face, continuing the motion even as they fell. 'I beat him and I'll beat you.'

'No you won't.'

Before he could come at her, she launched herself at him. Moving with the swiftness of an oriental assassin she crossed the distance in a single bound and snapped out a kick which landed squarely in his chest. The blow was shocking – like his diaphragm had been imploded. He tumbled back.

After a few reeling steps he knew his danger and fought with balance, just stopping himself from toppling over the edge into the vast depths below. He caught a glimpse of them, like the edges of a nightmare, where the most unreal but powerful phantoms reside. A shiver passed through him and he forced his feet to find balance.

Only to meet a second kick which launched him mid-air, back and over the edge.

He plummeted, screaming and screaming, into the place where a million souls had suffered a timeless time of suffering. Blackness closed over him like a lid. Substance ebbed. There was only the sensation of falling – not even of acceleration.

And then, somewhere, he touched a bottom.

There was an end to that blackness. And *that* was the awful part.

————

SHE WATCHED from the slope of the pyramid for him. Pike recovered upstairs. As soon as she threw down the Taking Man, the Slaves had disbanded. The blizzard had seen to the expulsion of the fire on the ark. Much of the structure had been damaged and would need to be repaired, but the venture was not lost. Parts of the skeleton remained and much of the stockpiles of poisonwood hadn't been burned, the fire not having had time or the conditions to spread. A bruise, yes. To the head? No. *He would like that,* she thought. The Prince's psyche seemed so interwoven with the Biblical texts it was as though they had created him. Or perhaps, she sometimes wondered, it was the other way around. His existence had created the texts – but how old would that make him? She had seen the visions of his childhood in New York in the early 21st century. He was mortal and explicable.

Yet...

Reincarnation was a possibility. Each version of him echoing down through history but unable to remember the deeds of the last. *And the eye* – there was another possibility. The eye itself had an age quite independent of him.

She stood, sharply. The winds pulled at her dress, making it flap around her like a war-banner. Her flesh had turned as white as the snowflakes: dropping from the sky like so many diamonds. The cold had sunk bone deep. She didn't care. He was coming back.

A black crucifix formed. It gained shape and definition as it came towards her. She'd been right: he *had* gone out into the blizzard despite everything it meant. How he could impress her, even now, when she knew so much, boggled her mind. But she felt the familiar flush down to her core, like enchanting chrysanthemum tea. Of course, she knew chrysanthemum could also be a deadly poison, brewed in the right hands, but she was tired of circumspecting her feelings about the Prince. Better to let them be.

The eye shone like a newly acquired burn. He panted; she could hear it even from the pyramid's slope. In his arms he carried the wolf-woman: unconscious. The blizzard seemed to be attacking him – ripping at coat and face with a savagery that resembled will. Perhaps it was? There were ghosts in every part of the city.

He climbed the stairs. Slowly. The wolf was no easy burden. Fay waited. Part of her urged to go down and help, but she knew he wouldn't accept it. Better to wait.

He mounted the last few steps and stood face to face with her.

'You braved the blizzard,' she said.

'I told you once that I'm not afraid of the past,' he said, words able to instil a coldness deeper than the blizzard. 'I meant it.'

'But still...' She turned and slipped in through the window. The Prince ducked and clambered through. He shivered as the temperature suddenly increased. With two of them, the pyramid's powers were confused, and as a result, the chamber was a broken splice of two rooms. Endless dusty books on arcane subjects stood next to cold, empty walls peeling plaster. There were colourful drawings and a stack of old Western VHSs.

They walked through to the elevator and called Manfred. A few moments later, the elevator began clumsy ascent.

'She must be important. You sense it, don't you?'

'I have a hunch. Yes.' He did not look at her. His face was entirely absorbed with examining his new prize. She was a lovely specimen. Fay could not help but admire the more earthy beauty of her form. There was no jealously in it. She knew the Prince held no interest in the woman, merely the wolf. Fay knew physical intimacy was beyond him but she did experience an acute rage at herself for wanting his attention so badly. Little did she know, she resembled Yin in this respect. 'She will make a useful tool.' He finally took his eyes off of her face and stared ahead, as though seeing through the walls.

'How'd she end up like this?' Fay said.

'Yin.' The Prince looked at her. 'Who is licking his wounds.'

'She did wound him, then?'

'Considerably.' The Prince flashed a smile. 'Which is why we want her on *our* side.'

There was a pause.

'I threw the Taking Man into the depths.'

The Prince threw back his head and roared with laughter, just as the elevator lifted its head into the throne room. Fay felt a spark of rage. Was he laughing at her feat? She was his *loyalist* servant. The sickle blade began to hum – sensing her rage and wishing to be activated. She enacted controlled breaths and regained control of her mind.

'Perhaps he'll meet my father down there,' he said, and waved at decrepit Manfred.

———

PIKE BLINKED. Laughter. Laughter he recognised. Light played upon his face through the window, but that was all it was, the light cast no definition upon anything, because nothing had definition. This seemed to include his face which felt like a squelching bag of bones. Still, he was alive. If it hadn't been for Fay, he might have been turned into something less than a husk.

Footsteps drew near him. Suddenly, things *were* becoming clearer, as though someone held a flame close to his eye, and the flame burned away the cataracts.

'Prince...? Prince...?'

'*I am here.*'

And there he was. Though everything else remained foggy and indistinct, his face was clearer than the startling vision of God Jung had once described in his Archetypes of the Unconscious. It was a face that could have broken dreams in its intensity, in its sheer *reality*. The words '*I am*' brought a shiver to Pike that he couldn't explain and didn't know how to categorise, as though they awakened some deep and latent fear he had tiled over.

'Are you going to kill me?' he asked the glowing face.

It split into a smile.

'No. No. No. Why would I do that? You served me well Pike. You fought to defend this place against my enemy. No. You will be rewarded, when the time comes.' He shifted, until he was hovering over Pike. The face lost clarity as the dark socket seemed to gain it. *How can darkness gain focus?* Pike thought, but it was vain to understand it, because the darkness was like perfect calligraphy smeared by a master artisan across the most perfect parchment – it shone with meaning. 'I've come to tell you something, Pike.'

'What?'

'I think I know what your Tower card meant.'

And they both shared in morbid laughter.

CHAPTER 13

L arri opened his eyes. Where was he? What had happened to him?

Images returned – like de-compartmentalised dream matter. Whiteness. Pain. Hagga – pierced and bloody. The thing that had been Yin: cat-like and reptile in one breath. Crawling. The pain. Crawling to...

He had thrown himself somewhere underground. He must have fallen. It was a wonder something wasn't broken. Or was it? He checked himself. Somehow he had lost all his clothes. Naked, he lay on stone.

He was fairly certain he couldn't have fallen *out* of them. Someone had taken them, which meant that someone was keeping him. They might, of course, be friendly. There was an eerie déjà vu of the time he had woken from his ten year coma in the healing hands of Demus. But this was different now. He trusted this place even less than he trusted the Circle. The only face he would ever find welcome now was Hagga's.

And she's dead.

'No,' he whispered. 'She can't be.'

'Talking to yourself?' a voice questioned. 'By some, it's considered a dangerous habit.'

'Apparently not to myself,' Larri forced his voice to something resembling a conversational tone but he was sure he had just seen the shadows move, and as they had moved he had the feeling of seeing a large mouth at the bottom of a deep well.

He shuffled forward, aware of his nakedness even in this darkness. He didn't get far before he found metal bars. He swallowed as he put his fingers around them. *Oh god.*

'Come now. Tell me your name.'

He still could not see the owner of the voice. Beyond his cage all he could see were patchwork segments of darkness, their edges created by a faint aura that might have been the light of the skies filtering through whichever crack Larri had fallen into to reach this place.

'It's Larri. Now why don't you tell me something about you?'

There was a pause.

'Larry? Larry? *Laaarrrryyy?*'

A thud like footsteps; a hellish mask appeared at the bars, drawn from white lines like something scrawled on a blackboard. It was the servant of the Prince he'd first seen when they entered the city, but this close, and now that Larri was unarmed and caged, he had evolved into a new level of terror. 'I knew a man called Larry once!' He talked as though he had done four lines of cocaine and was readying the fifth. 'He played the game. He played the *ultimate* game. And he nearly won.'

Was he smiling beneath the mask? It was hard to tell: the flesh was warped so badly from the soldering. Larri harboured a thought that he might have done this to himself.

'But no one wins in the end, Fred. *NO ONE.* Not even me.'

'My name's not...'

'QUIET FRED!'

It wasn't angry – the doctor simply said the words at maximum volume. The room trapped the sound in its stones, making it fizzle on the ears long after.

Larri swallowed and retreated as surreptitiously as he could with the strange eyes on him. He made as if reclining, settling in for the long conversation. His heart felt like it was trying to batter down the ribs in his chest.

'What's the game, then?'

The doctor seemed to brighten up at that question. It reminded Larri think of the way people who were attention starved lit up when someone asked them about themselves.

'The game. It's *the* game. The best game that was ever played.'

He ruffled in his pockets.

'But to play it, we're going to need this!' He produced a vial of amber-looking liquid. 'And this!' He produced a matchbox. 'Are you ready?'

Larri's heart kept ratcheting up a notch just when he thought it could go no harder.

'How do we play?'

'We?' The doctor seemed confused.

'I don't...'

The doctor put a finger to metal lips.

'*We* aren't playing anything. *I* am playing the game.'

'But I thought you said your friend, La –'

'Oh he was much smarter than you, Fred. Much smarter. Yes. And he wasn't in a cage when he started.' Dr Monaghan laughed, a sound which made Larri want to break down into tears and suck his thumb. 'You *are* however. So this is going to be a short game. Or a long game. I haven't decided yet...In any case...' He struck a match and produced an emblem of flame. He unscrewed the vial with his teeth and spat out the lid. Then he threw the amber substance towards Larri. Instinctively, Larri dodged, and the liquid only splattered against his leg. Dr Monaghan shrugged.

He flicked the match toward him.

Larri screamed.

It was like fireworks being repeatedly shot into his thigh, knee and calf. He had heard rumours in the circle of an ancient device which could fire pellets. He had never seen one, but this, he imagined, was what it would have felt like to be shot with such a weapon. He writhed and twisted: his leg had become a jigsaw of magma-orange scarring. It glowed as though something beneath the skin had been set on fire. Boils emerged, erupted, sprayed blood, and then cauterised themselves. He could hear a mounting hissing noise of the liquid in his limb being turned to steam. The pain was unreal, unquantifiable – it transcended any and all pains.

When it was over, he slumped back and vomited at the smell of his own burning flesh.

'Oh,' Dr Monaghan whispered. 'How radiant...'

ACT III: THE WHIRLPOOL AND THE DRAGON

CHAPTER 14

The Ark cut through a wave like an elegant blade. White foam grappled with the hull and deck, seething over it like an army of pearly lichen trying to overwhelm and drag them down. The ship shook off the invaders and returned to buoyancy. But each time, it was with a deeper dip, a greater shudder. Something wasn't right.

'Keep rowing!' the Prince roared. The galley-slaves (*It's no use denying what they are*) were hard at the oars, but the storm did not seem close to abating. His mind confidently asserted it would soon break and dissipate. They would once more have the clear, black waters: still as a lake. His heart warned this storm would *never* break. It would never break because it was their presence which caused it. Already the world, what the Prince called the 'falsehood of a universe', attempted trying to drive them back.

'*Magician!!*'

Yin appeared next to him, disgruntled, wrapped heavily in shrouds. It seemed his dwarfish form served him better in their current predicament. His lower centre of gravity meant he was not as easily unsettled.

'Master?'

'I need to know if this storm is natural.'

Yin glanced up at it, his piggish eyes scanning the tumultuous red-tinted clouds, the crimson brush-strokes of lightning. His moustache quivered in the wind. The Prince thought it looked like it might fall off, which was enough to make him chuckle and lifted his spirits for a moment.

'It is difficult to tell whether anything is natural in this place. But I would say not.'

'Will it end?'

The Magician shrugged.

'Perhaps I can nullify it – *perhaps* – don't get your hopes up.'

He waddled off towards the masthead. He placed a single, stubby hand on its polished wood and began muttering. Was he using the master as some kind of great conductor? Or was this just a steadying point? The Prince considered himself a creature of magic, but everything was instinctive with him – it manifested like dreams – this wilful magic was something else he did not entirely understand.

He left the Magician to it and went below decks. The water was ankle deep and rising with alarming rapidity. The Prince navigated through the twisted netting which held barrels of drinkable water in place. The netting had been made from vines growing on the trunks of the Silvenom and looked like so many xenoform eggs about to hatch ugly larvae into the bowels of the ship; he found Pike boarding up one of many leaks.

His face had almost returned to normal after the beating. This place had a strange way of accelerating the healing process. His nose would never be the same, however. It bent and twisted both left and right, forming a zigzag.

'How is she holding, Pike?'

'Don't know what's happening,' he growled, nailing a board in with such force it looked like he might cause another rupture in the hull. 'It's like she's giving up on us. Like whatever's holding her together doesn't matter.'

'Don't you get superstitious on me,' the Prince said, and watched with a glowing joy as Pike's face split into a grin.

'Well then, I guess she's just built like a sack of shit.'

'Noah lasted forty days and forty nights: I expect at least that much!'

'But Noah was a good man!' Pike said, still grinning. 'We're a bunch of sinners.'

'Now you're talking!' He clapped him on the back and then grabbed Pike's shoulders, feeling a surging energy inside him despite all that was going wrong. 'We're the worst fuckers of them all, and there's no way we're gunna let *Him* drown us!

'You're crazy!' Pike shouted.

'Duly noted. Now back to work!'

He clambered up the steps onto the deck, where he was near blinded by a descending lightning bolt. It shrieked out of the sky like a wrathful serpent, plummeting mere feet from the ship's side and striking the water with a noise like a titanic wasp's wing-buzz.

The imprint of the white column remained on his blinking, natural eye – it left no impression upon the other, darker orb. Briefly, the whiteness and its jagged shape reminded him of Fay. He thought of her, with a strange ache in his heart. What was it? The emotion posed some unfamothable mystery, like an age old philosophical question.

It was the not the first time he had felt this ache. Night after night leading up to the completion of his ark, he had searched himself with the eye, plummeting into his own darkness, unseaming his atomic structure, laying bare the fabric of his being and interrogating it for meaning. Where was the answer, the source, the definition of this thing he felt? Why did it come unpredictably? And why was it focused around her?

He had no answers save for the ones which came to him, half dreaming. Answers cloaked in heat and sleepless ecstasy and nightmares and memory. He could not understand these answers, because they seemed to him more alien than the city and its pyramid, than all the mysteries of deep creation.

After all, if his eye could not fathom them, what was there to be fathomed?

———

'I PRESENT TO YOU: *amberfire*, my lady.'

She watched the doctor bow, awkwardly low, as though semi-parodying. Behind him, slaves unloaded barrel after barrel from the elevator and set them down in the throne room.

'And what is amberfire?'

'Observe.'

Dr Monaghan took out a vial which contained a sliver of the liquid. It looked barely enough to leave a taste if consumed. The doctor also drew out a match. He opened the vial, poured a few spattered droplets on the ground and then lit the match and dropped it.

There was an eruption of flame in a small, two-foot high column.

'Impressive,' she said.

'Very. This is the most volatile substance I have ever encountered. There are lakes of this stuff below ground. Canals. Channels...' The doctor seemed to lose himself in a reverie, his eyes becoming as glacial and opaque as his steel menpo. Fay had little patience for men who lose themselves in their own supposed genius.

'What is being done to secure the canals?'

The doctor frowned.

'I'm sorry?'

'If this substance is as volatile as you suggest, then surely it poses a risk to the city? Cordon off the canals. Put guards on it day and night. Leave nothing to chance.'

She closed the distance between them. The doctor shifted. His eyes, however, still retained that impassive, unreflective quality. *He's hiding something.* Fay could always tell, even without her cards. It was a knack. Perhaps the earliest beginnings of her insight which the Prince was now developing? Dr Monaghan was a deceiver. A liar. Of course, he was also a useful asset. He'd discovered the pitch, or else, facilitated its discovery. Rumours abounded that one of the workers had found the pitch and been "ascended" by Dr Monaghan. Ascended with his six-foot cleaver.

'I will do as you command,' he said, mechanically. That's when she had the second revelation: he *hated* her. The facade was crumbling. He had made the motions of a grand gesture, but deep down, he resented everything she was. She could see it. She almost imagined a dark eye was opening within her. Why then the grand gesture of loyalty? The gift of amberfire? Was it a warning, in reality? Or was it to mask something else he was doing?

The doctor turned and began to walk away.

'Wait,' Fay said, in a tone that might have arrested a rabid animal. Dr Monaghan froze, but did not turn to face her immediately. She paced towards him until she stood at his shoulder. He was a big man, she realised. Beneath the deceptive lab-coat, his frame was bulky and muscular. No wonder he could heft the colossal weapon. Size wasn't everything, of course. The Taking Man had been bigger than her, after all. 'What do you believe we will use this amberfire for? We are not at war. There is nothing to destroy. What do you think it should be put to use for?'

Dr Monaghan did not look at her. He remained rigid, staring ahead. Beneath the static mask, however, Fay sensed a swirling conundrum, a miasma full of half-remembered shadows and inchoate thoughts, the kind of thoughts sane people instantly banished but which Dr Monaghan allowed to remain, and grow, becoming stultified beings that crept from his unconscious to disturb reality every so often. The image was so clear in her mind for a moment she forgot the sandstone walls of the throne room and the flickering palefire through the enchanted viewing window. She felt instead like she walked through his mind. *Is this what it feels like to be Michael?* The sensation was frightening, like losing oneself. *Perhaps that is why he is the way he is.*

'There's always a war,' Dr Monaghan said.

He stepped onto the elevator and descended.

———

Dr Monaghan was gritting his teeth so hard he thought they might crack. Who did the stupid fucking bitch think she was, interrogating him? The gift hadn't been for her. It'd been for the Prince. For the coming game. Yes. The great game was coming and they would need explosives. He wasn't sure why. He was never sure why he did many of the things he did. He only knew he must do them – like a calling from God, he answered with absolute obeisance.

So often these callings proved prescient. Like building the cage out of the railroad tracks. He hadn't known at the time that Fred (what he had taken to calling Larri) would fall into his hands that night, but when it had happened, he'd known that was what the cage was for.

He rubbed his hands with excitement, like a fly cleaning itself. The elevator ground to a halt and he stepped off and made his way through one of the doorways. He was always intrigued to know what vision from his past the pyramid would show him.

This time, he entered an abandoned house, a *squatter's paradise* as he used to call them. It was somewhere on the outskirts of London. He didn't remember where. But he remembered what he was watching now.

He stopped his march, clasped his hands in front of him solemnly, and observed the scene play itself out. Tying little Delano to the chair. Kicking it over. Pouring paint into his eyes and mouth. Then bleach. The screams and the thrashing. The wonderful smell afterwards.

His thirteen year old self looked up and made eye-contact with the masked man. For just a second, they shared a proud father-son moment of mutual admiration. That'd been fifteen years before he joined the police force and started working in forensics. No one had ever known. It was good to be reminded of past triumphs.

He waved goodbye to his memory and stepped through the window to the outside of the pyramid.

As he did so, he had an idea. A brilliant idea.

Why not do the same to Fred?

He bounced down the slope of the pyramid, almost losing his footing in his excitement.

Yes. Yes. Brilliant! Brilliant!

Of course, he didn't have any bleach. But he *did* have amberfire. He wondered if the substance was more or less painful. Whether Fred would be tougher than eight-year-old Delano. Whether continued exposure over a long period of time would enact some kind of mutation in Fred. Wow. That would be something grand, like in a sci-fi movie.

A spring in his stride, Dr Monaghan made his way back to the subway station and his mines, entirely forgetting Fay's instructions, or even that the conversation had ever happened.

———

FAY CALLED THE ELEVATOR. She stepped onto it and instructed Manfred to halt its progress three levels down – a secret instruction only she, Pike and the Prince knew of. He responded with his usual heroine-high lurch of the head. The platform grumbled, groaned, and then detached, dropping three floors before coming to a premature stop. She stepped off onto the platform and began scanning the doors. One had been marked with an X. She stepped through.

Within, the room had permanently moulded itself to a memory of the woman sleeping within. It seemed to be some sort of cave. Tattered rags hung over its entrance (which in reality would only lead to another illusionary chamber) battered by sand and wind. There was a small stone block with an assortment of alchemical looking devices on it and a rugged mattress, on which she was lying. Fay wondered whether the sleeping woman had once lived in this cave back in the 'Circle', where she and the cripple-man had come from. Fay didn't know much about the Circle, but she'd heard the Prince questioning the Magician about it. Wherever or whatever it was, it seemed just as dire as the city.

Hagga lay on the dishevelled mattress, eyes closed, breathing as faint as a small bird's. For all the coiled power that was within her, she looked vulnerable, fragile, as though a ghostly wind might make her slip from this world into another.

'Hagga,' she called, but the sleeping woman did not answer. She never did. She had been in a coma ever since the night the Prince brought her out of the blizzard. The Magician had enacted something terrible on her. The gaping claw-wounds had healed with alarming rapidity, but something else was at work.

Fay knelt by her bedside. The Prince had tried to wake Hagga, plunging into her consciousness with his eye. He said he'd tried to converse with her, that he could always find a projection in the mind with which to communicate, but she had been black and empty. He'd now charged Fay with bringing Hagga from the darkness, but if he couldn't do it, Fay doubted she would find a way. She had never had healing hands.

She placed her palm on Hagga's brow and found it nightmarishly cold. Fay closed her eye and practiced the techniques of self hypnosis the Prince had taught her, sinking into herself, falling, like a pendulous droplet of liquid detaching itself from a suspended body of water, through the waves of her brain.

She entered the blackness.

In the blackness she was clothed and formed much as she was now. Three-dimensional infinity stretched in all directions, yet there was an invisible platform on which she could walk.

'Hagga, can you hear me?'

Nothing. Vast emptiness. How low had her mind sunk? What could wipe it? People in comas were said to dream vividly. Why was her mind empty?

She walked for what felt like hours but she knew would be moments in the world outside. Occasionally, beneath her feet and the invisible platform, she saw flickering imagery: a labyrinth, a city made of bones, sex, and a white horse with blood-flecked lips. *You have tasted horror,* Fay thought.

'Yes.'

Fay froze. Had that been a response? She waited, hoping the voice would speak again. Nothing.

'Hagga. Please. Speak to me.'

'Horror,' the voice said, mournful. 'All there is. Horror.'

And then the darkness exploded.

CHAPTER 15

It took a while, but soon he realised the abyss was not empty. There was a floor and walls. How he had survived the fall was beyond his ability to fathom. He only knew that he must go on or utterly lose his mind in these depths. The darkness was so oppressive that it pushed like a reeking hand over his eye-sockets. His legs were weak and jellied. Even his sense of up and down was distorted. He could not tell what his own head was doing; it was as though the lightlessness had stripped him of matter, rendering him a lost spirit.

A few shuddering steps were all he could manage at first. Then he would stop and put his hand on his knees and curl up, somehow breathless. The will it took to force himself from this position and go on was rending – like a hypodermic needle being pushed slowly into his heart. But he knew if he did not, he would be destroyed.

He knew this because he had a growing certainty that there were others here with him in the blackness. Coiled, like the first life discovered in imprinted fossils, barely more than bio-organic many-legged shells, they lay in this place, transfixed as though under a lead mantle. He could hear them, sometimes, though the darkness also seemed to suppress sound as well as sight. At times he felt as though his feet brushed against something – a back or a limb. Being was obliterated in this place. Meaning. Mind. Disintegrated by absence.

But the Taking Man had more than one being. Throughout his life he had used his *gift* to take souls, more than he could now remember. As the darkness stripped him, it only found more layers, spiralling downward without a core. The darkness was a fire but the Taking Man merely peeled flesh like a serpent, each new skin deeper than the last.

And so, he reached a wall. In reaching it, the space became terminated, fixed: it had an end and shape. It was not limitless. With this revelation, the ravaging oppression sank away. He traced the wall like a blind man with the fingertips of his one hand and found an opening into which he stepped.

He began to walk down a long, dark tunnel, but froze as he saw a green light begin to throb, like an awakened consciousness, or perhaps an eye, scanning and searching the deep darkness with an intensity to challenge even the Prince's.

For a moment, he was transfixed with a kind of fear he had not ever experienced before in his life. Then he broke the spell and began to walk towards it.

The light pulsed, as though in welcome.

———

THE STORM HAD CALMED, but the Prince was still afraid.

The dark waters had settled down to a kind of pawing motion, like a pet wishing to attract its owner's attention. It lapped at the hull, leaving traces like slug-trail marks across the greenish Silvenom boards. He was concerned the layer of pitch would fail, that Dr Monaghan had miscalculated its durability.

Seven of their oars had broken during the storm, which was nearly half of their rowing strength, but they had brought many spares. Pike was now bringing up these oars and distributing them amongst the galley slaves. They received them gratefully, with sharp nods of the head, as though a great honour had been bestowed on them.

The Prince smiled.

The twenty had apparently been volunteers. In reality, a careful selection process had taken place. He had used the eye to scan their thoughts, their feelings, their motivations. He only wanted crew-members who would give anything to get back to the other world – who would defend the ship's life and indeed *his* life with their own no matter the cost. Any who were infirm of purpose posed the risk of breaking and persuading others it was time to turn back. The Prince knew enough about betrayal to know it only ever took one.

He grimaced. Shadows gathered in the socket. The ship creaked.

The memory brought a pain to his chest, a different kind of ache to the one he associated with Fay. This was a poisonous burning, like Silvenom smoke, or slow-acting acid. Brian Mor. His best friend. His murderer. If Brian was still alive in the world they found on the other side of these waters, he would kill him. Not only that. He would *annihilate* him, unmake his soul and shatter it. *No eternity for you my friend. No place of suffering.*

No, if he ever found Brian Mor again, he would erase him from the universe.

'Prince!'

Pike's voice disturbed his thoughts. Like a diver returning, he surfaced to consciousness again. The gypsy was beckoning to him. The men were standing in a circle and looking at something on the deck. The Prince cursed and made his way over.

'What is it?'

Pike pointed.

A creature flopped about on the wet boards. It looked like some weird mix of jellyfish and octopus: a multitude of tendrils branched out from a gelatinous 'head' which was transparent. A brain, which resembled fungal growths, could be seen through its semi-transparent flesh.

Everything about its movement was repulsive.

'Wave hit the side of the ship and threw this thing on deck,' Pike explained, unable to take his eyes off of it. There was something pathetic about watching it scrape and scrabble with the deck. It seemed to be trying to right itself but its limbs had no bones or rigidity. It was all tendons and jelly. A kind of ooze started to leak from it.

'What does it mean?' one of the crew-members asked.

'Mean?' Pike asked.

'It's a sign, clearly.' She'd started to mumble.

'What makes you say that?' the Prince cut in.

She tried to lift her eyes to him, but couldn't. Instead, she spoke with her head half-bowed.

'Everything in this place is a sign. The weather. The shape of the city. Haven't you noticed it changes? Its geography shifts depending on its moods.'

'Moods?' The Prince was angry now. He crossed the distance to her, stepping over the jelly-thing and coming to within inches of the woman. He unleashed the eye and it shot forward like a ravenous dog spying a morsel it wishes to track and kill. He felt it blast through the barriers of her psyche, pummelling down the walls and entering the caverns of the unconscious. Normally, he tried to slip in relatively unnoticed, but his rage had made the entrance clumsy and she let out a cry of pain. Her eyes rolled back into the top of her head. The other crew members leapt back from him, muttering and making strange signals with their hand.

'Mara,' the Prince spat. Names. So many names he had raped from the mind. 'Explain to me what you mean. Now!'

'The...the...city... it's made up of people. In the stones. In the grave-yard. You can hear them. People don't die. That's why some... some eat the flesh. To stop the soul from becoming part of the city.'

'A mood is singular, Mara,' the Prince said, easing off, drawing the eye back. For some reason he was finding it more difficult to control. It had been a while since he had used the eye. There'd been little reason to on the Ark. Maybe it was restless. 'You said the city has a *singular* mood. How can that arise from all these multitudes of people?'

'I don't know. I don't know. Please.'

The Prince showed his teeth.

'We'll see.'

He drove back into her mind, shrieking down her spine like a razor blade cutting the bone. She screamed, so loud that the sound seemed to flee to the sky and touch the clouds, creating an echo of lightning. He ripped open every chest, every trunk, every locker, ransacking thought until he was sure she was telling the truth. She knew nothing more.

He withdrew and she collapsed, one of the other crew members catching her.

The Prince turned. The thing still flapped on the deck, like a bird soaked in an oil-spill. He stamped on it, and the creature exploded. Pike leapt out of the way of a segment of brain, or perhaps it was tissue, it was hard to tell.

'This place will not beat us!' he roared. 'We have come so far, but we must not lose faith now. If this place is emotional. If this universe has a personality. Then I think it has shown us one thing clearly.' He turned and took in every expression. 'IT IS AFRAID OF US!'

They surged forward, cheering and clapping him on the back. Some reached out to touch his jacket and shoes – he let them, letting his energy flow out from the eye like boiling water frothing over the rim of a cup. *Let my passion make them mad!*

'I'm afraid, I must humbly disagree.'

The Magician stood on the other side of the deck, leaning against the side of the ship. His eyes focused on the Prince. Unlike Mara, he was not afraid to meet the disfigured gaze, the socket that was not a socket.

'How so?' The Prince shook off the adoring followers and walked towards the dwarf. He was beginning to sense an inner disturbance with Yin. It was nothing that he could obviously detect – more like bubbles beneath the surface of water that indicated there was something breathing down below. Something unpleasant. He would have to be careful. He needed the Magician, but he could not stand to see him turn.

'I agree with Mara. Everything here is a sign. Whoever built this place thought rather like myself. The best prison is a prison of the mind.' He tapped his temple with a pudgy finger. 'This creature was sent as a *warning*. I would expect to see a million soon enough – a sea full of them. Or else one that is two hundred feet tall.' The dwarf grinned in a way that even the Prince found aberrant. 'This is them, *it*, whatever this world is, giving us a chance to turn back. I suggest we take it.'

The Prince stood for a moment. He appeared to be still, but inwardly, every fibre of him shook with a kind of blossoming pain that attacked his insides like a hornet swarm. He felt the eye expand, suddenly, without warning. The dwarf's mouth fell open and he staggered back – but there was nowhere to go so instead he lost footing on the lurching deck and fell down.

The Prince took two strides forward until he stood over the Magician. All the while the eye expanded, becoming a black, circular shield which seemed to swallow colour, swirling and yet utterly still as the darkest depths of space. A portal was within the bounds of darkness, but also, nothingness.

The eye grew until there was not even a ship. The blackness of the water seemed diaphanous colour next to the null of self-swallowing abyss which emanated from the Prince.

'If you speak of turning back again...'

But the threat was never completed. It seemed it did not need to be. Perhaps the sentence had been finished in Yin's mind. It did not matter, because the dwarf laid his head against the deck and began to whimper and cry like a beaten school-child.

The darkness receded, the eye withdrawing back into the burned flesh-hole. The Prince looked almost normal, mortal. He turned and walked back towards the crowd. He put a hand on Pike's shoulder.

'Prepare for the worst,' he said, and returned to his private quarters.

———

LARRI SHIVERED IN HIS CELL. He didn't shiver with the cold. He shivered with the afterglow of pain which seethed through his whole body. He didn't know how many days he had been in the cell, but he knew if he didn't find a way out soon, he would die.

Or become part of the city, whatever happens in this place.

The most worrying thing of all was that this prospect no longer terrified him. It would be a kind of release after the torment at the hands of the masked man.

Thinking of the screwball eyes, the hideous war-mask where a face should have been, the grimy coat covered in fluids, and, perhaps worst of all, the stench which flowed from him, made the pain return. Scalding wax across his nerve endings.

God, I can smell him now.

Larri did not know if this meant the lunatic had returned from whatever venture he had embarked upon or whether his mind was slowly eroding under the pressures and strains. Either way, it clogged up his nostrils and made him gag.

The masked man smelt unmistakeably of *war*. Of course, Larri only had a small window of insight. The war he knew of from the Circle had been waged with bone-swords and cudgels. So, he smelled the blood, the rage, the dirt. The other smells formed a disorientating smog he could not decipher but which made him afraid. A soldier in the trenches of a 20th century war might have known those smells more readily however, because Dr Monaghan smelled like a walking Somme: gasoline, the noxious venom of exploded warheads, the sulphuric aftermath of dissolved skin (a smell which was beginning to emanate from Larri too).

'Hello Fred.'

Larri shut his eyes so hard his eyelids began to ache, and willed this to be imagination.

No, he had returned. The game was about to start again.

'*Fred...*' A dangerous insistence made Larri open his eyes and sit upright. The motion awakened fresh waves of pain all down one side. He scrambled towards the edge of the cage and regretfully met his captor's eye.

'Yes, doctor?'

'It's time for your tests,' he said. Through the grill of the menpo, Larri saw white teeth.

'I don't need tests. I'm not sick!' He said it as though rehearsing a script. He wasn't even sure why he bothered anymore. He had about as much chance of breaking through to Dr Monaghan as restoring him to sanity.

'We're all sick,' he said, keeping to his lines. 'But it's not about being sick. It's about the *game*. Don't you see? We need to see if you're fit enough to play.'

He drew out a glistening vial. Larri put his hands on the bars, gripping them so tightly the grooves in his palms began to bleed. He grit his teeth, closed his eyes and rested his forehead against the cage.

'Not again. Please.'

'There, there, Fred,' Dr Monaghan said, patting him gently on the shoulder.

But not gently enough: he had touched a section of burnt flesh. Larri howled and withdrew, clutching his shoulder and whimpering.

Dr Monaghan tutted.

'You know what they say, Fred.' He unstopped the vial and held it up. 'What doesn't kill you, makes you stronger.' He leant forward and made as if to throw the liquid over Larri. Larri darted, surprised at his own speed, evading the throw.

But Dr Monaghan had been fainting. He'd covered the lid with a gloved thumb. Now, as Larri recovered from his violent exertion, he threw the liquid over him.

Larri clawed, trying to scrape off as much as possible.

Dr Monaghan lit a match.

'Radiance! Radiance!' he said, setting the prisoner alight.

———

A HURRICANE of thought surrounded Fay. It was like being stood at the centre of Times Square, with every screen enlarged tenfold and showing scenes of soul-rending depravity. She twisted and turned, but the imagery was all around her, springing to life like some enchanted and malignant wood. Every atom swam with an electrical sea of further visions, moving too fast to capture, but leaving a kind of imprint on her nonetheless.

'Hagga! Hear me!'

The thoughts continued to blossom, gyre and turn, closing in on her, becoming a relentlessly folding and unfolding origami, each crease revealing infinitudes of memory. If Fay had not already touched the fibres of time, not already dabbled with the forces of the universe, her mind might have instantly broken at what she saw: the impossible scale of a human being rendered absolutely and in an instant. But Fay was unlike anyone. Even the Prince.

She stood amidst the pandemonium and closed her eyes, drawing into herself despite not having a self, being a single current of probing thought amidst someone else's universe.

'*You cannot understand what I have been through. You cannot understand...*'

And then she heard a roar, a roar that might have shattered the foundations of a cathedral. Fay's eyes sprang open. She wheeled and saw the origami confusion being torn apart by something bestial and colossal, something which was inside the surrounding darkness and yet forming it, creating it.

'NEEEEEEEEEEDDDDDDDDDDDDDDDDDDDDDDDDD.'

Hagga's voice, a scream as though of mutilation. The beast ripped through the thoughts and came shambling towards Fay; whether it was a wolf, a bear, a dragon or a corpse, she couldn't tell. Its eyes changed colour a thousand times a second, hypnotically violating all possibility of understanding.

Fay took a step back.

'This is your beast?'

Hagga no longer seemed to be able to answer her. The Need opened its mouth and revealed motes of teeth.

Fay reached for her sickle and then remembered she was not in the physical world, if the city could be considered that, and she had no weapons except her mind.

'Stay back.' The words felt pathetic on her lips.

The Need grinned and lurched down, its mouth becoming an oval void. Slaver sprayed from its lips like an acidic burst.

Fay danced back, light on her feet as she might have been in a corporeal state.

The beast swung a humongous limb, expecting her to have let her guard down already, but she knew well the kind of relentless attack only beasts and ugly men were capable of. She somersaulted back, the clawed limb swiping air beneath her, and landed on one knee, palm to the invisible floor.

'Hagga, this isn't you.'

The beast pounced. Fay rolled to the side. She felt the air quiver, disturbed; a strange reality her mind had created. There was no air here.

'Hagga.'

The Need came again, slashing wildly. This time, evasion was impossible and so Fay dived between the creature's jackal hind-legs. It wheeled, nightmarishly fast, swinging again. She evaded, bending at the hip. A single claw caught her across the cheek and made a thick red line, like the beginnings of a Japanese rune.

Fay skirted back, giving distance.

So, I can bleed and die here.

This was something the Prince had not told her. Or perhaps, it was not the same for him?

She looked into the psychedelic eyes of the Need. It waited, it seemed, for her to balk and make a false move. It would leap on her and snap her neck like a fox might a rabbit. But she was well trained. She wasn't going to make the first, wrong move.

Think. You have no weapons. Eventually, it will wear you down...

She looked around. The crazy maelstrom of thoughts was still blooming in every direction, walls of memory like fifty-foot television screens threatening to topple and crush them both.

Memory.

Somewhere within here would be a memory she could use to subdue the creature, or perhaps to reach Hagga.

The Need seemed to sense her intention, because it snarled, a sound which reminded her so many animals, but no species in particular.

Fay smiled.

'Come get me, bitch.'

It roared and lunged, mouth opening impossibly wide, like the dislocated jaw of a snake. Fay, rather than moving to the side, rolled back, raising both her legs.

For a moment, she felt a buckling weight – she could not hold it!

This isn't real. There is no weight. We are in the mind.

She forced with all her will to believe it, and the weight vanished. As though the Need was nothing more than a pebble, she kicked out and sent it hurtling into a wall of memory. The wall shuddered, shimmered, and then exploded like a stained-glass window hit with a shockwave. The dark form of the Need disappeared through it as though dragged down beneath opaque waters. The pieces of memory tumbled around her, a hailstorm of broken glass, and Fay leapt forwards.

There was no floor beyond the shattered wall. She dropped into something.

An acute sensation came to her.

That of treading on a grave.

CHAPTER 16

He hid in the shadows. Whatever it was that had passed him in the corridor was not human. Not remotely. And it terrified him.

He had not seen it clearly (that was always the way with frightening things, was it not?), but what was more, he felt if he *had* looked at it, his mind might have stretched and torn with the vast pressure of what it perceived.

Shivering, he peered out from the alcove in which he'd been curled and looked down the tunnel where the creature had passed him. Phosphorous green light had shone, or rather *shed* like a cloud of emerald snowflakes, from its entire body, revealing the walls to be raised from a midnight black stone which glistened with untraceable moisture. Most disturbing was that the light seemed to remain long after it'd passed, like luminous, radioactive fragments, lighting the corridor in patches.

There had been a sound which accompanied the sight too. Static – rising and falling as though composing the syllabics of sentence and language. If it was speech, it could only have communicated suffering.

You have to leave. That thing may come back. You have to get up.

But he felt with the surety of dream-logic that as soon as he stepped out from the alcove he would see the green light blossoming once again, hear the static, this time weakening and allowing himself to stare beyond the veil which the luminosity created at the *thing itself.*

Foolishness! Weakness!

His inner voice berated like some worn military general. He placed his hand and the stump around his knees and began to sit like a schoolchild with his chin rested on his knees. It was perhaps the first time in fifteen years he had allowed himself to adopt such a submissive posture.

But he had nothing to draw on. This was not the world he knew. There were no people to capture and manipulate. He had even been cut off from his Slaves, who were poor substitutes at best for the pawns he had moved in London. What could he do? His power was the power to *take:* life, meaning, strength, secrets. He doubted very much his gifts would stand against a creature like the one he had just seen.

It was then the Taking Man realised that alone, he was powerless.

All his life, he had considered himself to be acting alone. He had devised his plans for London in the dead of night in gutters not even the criminal scum attended to. He had set out to destroy his own brother and bring him to his knees. He had lied, killed, and stolen.

But always, he had used his agents. What was he without them? What was he in this place? Beneath it all?

You will die here, then, the voice said. This time it was not the tuckered out General. It sounded almost like Albric, the man who had pretended to be his father for 15 years.

'Liar,' he whispered, unaware he was breaking the spectral silence of the tunnels.

I only tried to protect you, Albric seemed to say. His voice was coming from the walls – or was it from the inside of his own skull? *I raised you. I cared for you. I taught you everything you know. I was your true father, not the one who abandoned you.*

The Taking Man plunged his head as though into his hands, forgetting that now he only had one, and then scratched at his scalp. Flesh came away in snowfalls of dandruff. His rotten face felt weighty as a planet.

'To hell with you, old man,' he said.

The darkness swallowed him for a time. It was as though he gave up being and became assimilated like those ignorant slaves spoke of. There was no alcove, no corridor, no awful chamber in which basking sinners lay paralysed beneath the infinite weight of darkness. He became less than a thought, bodiless, meaningless, and strangely, calm.

He was brought from his reverie by the sound of static. There wouldn't be a second chance. He had to move. He had to survive. It had been repressed and beaten, but that instinct still lived in him.

He climbed out of the alcove, like a sub-human creature accustomed to the caves. He looked both ways. He thought he saw a pinprick of green that was more than an afterglow somewhere down the corridor into which the creature had moved. He turned the other way and began to move lightly. This, he was expert at as someone who had studied ninjutsu their whole life.

As he passed the discarded green 'snowflakes', a buzz of static returned. His palm was slick as though bloody. Some of that might also have been the oily surface of the walls. Was that some kind of disintegrating mortar? Moisture from some kind of imperceptible heat (it was cold in the tunnels)? Was it applied or naturally occurring?

There were too many questions clogging his mind. He knew he must remain focused now. He must remain alert and ready to act.

Then, like the shrill alarm of a military base flaring into life, an intruder detected, he heard a shriek which made his marrow feel like it would snap. He opened his own mouth in a silent scream upon hearing it and wheeled around. A second later he realised his mistake, because the sound had come from somewhere far ahead.

When he turned back around, he could see a haze intensifying to blinding levels. Through it (he was tempted to look just as he had feared) he saw two semi-circular iridescent pools as though two of the creatures approached one another.

He gritted his teeth and went down to one knee. Focusing on his breath, and ignoring the scraping dryness in his throat, he summoned the gift until his fingertips felt as though they might burst like over-ripe boils.

'Come then,' he snarled. 'And see if you can take me!'

———

THE STORM HAD RETURNED.

Pike clung to the masthead as the ship plummeted down the side of a near-vertical wave and was enveloped by water so cold it stung like a swarm of insects. The force of the jerking crash almost dislodged him and sent him hurtling overboard. The oarsmen were abandoning their posts, clinging to the side of the ship as though it was the last real thing in the world. He supposed it might be. The sea no longer looked like a sea. It looked like the edge of a wild canvas. And there was this light beneath the water – disturbing, *shaped,* as though it had many sides like a dodecahedron. Rays of the light burst up through the darkness. Pike wondered what would happen if they intersected one of those points of light. Would it cut the ship in half?

He did a head count. One of the oarsmen had already been lost, flung overboard. The Prince hurled his voice at them – matching the storm's volume – but not even he seemed to be able to control them now. The Magician was below decks somewhere, holding together the belly of the ship with his magic.

But his magic is just illusion. It can't hold anything. It's not real.

It could if this whole place is an illusion itself.

Pike pushed this disturbing thought aside. Now was not the time to question reality. Now was the time to *do something* and help these flimsy planks of wood hold together.

'I'm going up top!' he yelled to the Prince.

He didn't hear him. Pike didn't have time to cross the deck and tell him again. Besides, he'd probably be thrown headlong into the sea if he tried to move without holding onto something. Only the Prince seemed to be able to keep his balance whilst the ship was rocked. Pike wondered whether an earthquake could shake him.

He began to climb the mast. They had dug crude nails every few feet along it to make for a makeshift ladder, the kind of thing you saw on the side of a telephone pole. The mainsail was still unfurled – the oarsmen had needed a rest and the sea had looked calm. Pike was not a sailor, but he knew enough about boating to know that sail was imminently going to drag them all to an early grave.

Unless he could cut it loose.

The climb was slippery, and after only a few feet he could no longer feel his hands. The rust of the ugly metal discoloured his hands so he looked like a coal miner.

He could have climbed the distance without thinking and in seconds had the master been still, but the ship was rolling like a spinning top losing momentum. He felt at times he was crawling towards a vortex – the mast was near horizontal, and the sky, a light-show of impossible colours. At others he was most certainly climbing, heaving his weight up the uneven rungs. One broke under his grip and he had to throw himself up to the next. His hands were covered in slashes, red mixing with the orange rust-stains.

Rain beat his body until it felt amorphous.

The ship lurched violently. A spear of light shot past him, the colour of uranium. He took one hand and leg and swung around the mast to avoid its passage, still afraid it would obliterate. Like a firework, it popped upon reaching a certain height. Then a wave washed over it, slapping Pike in the face. His fingers started to feel like they had been stripped to the bone. He groaned, pulled, and brought all his extremities back to bear on the narrow rungs.

The mast creaked ominously. Another wave slapped it, this time lower down, drenching Pike's feet, making the shoes heavy. Pike cursed and then kicked them off. They would only slow him down and his toes would afford him better grip. They fell. Oddly, he did not hear them touch the deck.

The creak sounded again, only now it was a ripping noise which sounded like the cry of a living thing about to collapse under torture. He supposed it was not far from the truth: the tallest of the Silvenom's they could find had been stripped of its flesh and made to serve their industrial purposes.

He had to hurry before it gave.

The last few rungs were like a beating. Pike had experienced more than a few of those in his time. Some of them had been bloody, like the time he'd gotten into an argument with two Arabic men at a cheap chicken takeout and ended up having his nose broken twice. The worst he'd experienced in what he had started referring to as 'life before' was when he'd split up with Lizzie and walked out into the streets of Brighton in the early hours of the morning with nowhere to go and no one to call. Lizzie was about the only person he could have ever fallen in love with. She talked like a guy (which he loved), had Mediterranean skin (a plus) and a face that was eternally impish and yet capable of teasing, sultry beauty. He'd wandered around for a bit and found a bench to settle down on, sleeping rough for the night. He'd woken up with his head being kicked in by five or six guys. They'd stomped on his legs, broke his ankle, stomped on his cock and balls, made him spit out more teeth than he had ever been able to afford to replace, broke a few ribs and fractured his skull. He'd barely been able to say his own name after it. That'd been the worst beating of his life. Physically.

Of course, the beating at the hands of the Taking Man had been worse *emotionally*.

He burned with sudden humiliation, and his hands and legs faltered. He felt as though the muscles had been surgically removed; all of a sudden he had no agency or ability to move.

Come on. One more. One more push.

But he couldn't, because over and over he saw the Taking Man discarding his suit jacket, felt the bone-shattering punches, and then saw his face. *I'm going to take everything.*

He had not succeeded in killing him, but he had taken everything, hadn't he?

Pike quivered. He had an urge to let go of the mast and let himself fall back. It was the same kind of sensation of peeking over the edge of a cliff, that idea of how *easy* it would be to just say 'no' to existence.

He beat you, he heard the Prince say. *But he did not break you.* Was he remembering words the Prince had spoken to him whilst he lay recovering or was he hearing him now?

He forced himself to look down. A darkness in the shape of an eye glinted back at him. The Prince's face was solemn and granite – around it everything moved but the face seemed like it had been etched into the fabric of the universe. If all other realities failed he would not. The Prince was a constant – all else, variable.

I was beaten once. We return stronger. You are better than him. You will have your chance for revenge. I promise you.

Pike shuddered, in a way that signified life-strength returning. His limbs no longer felt dead and inchoate. He hauled himself to the mast's top and flung his leg over the horizontal beam , straddling it and using his thighs to maintain balance.

He had no blade but he drew his trusty lighter from his pocket, lay flat along the beam, and then flicked it into being. Despite the cold, the rains, and the roiling ocean, the fire lit on the first thumb-swipe. He touched it to the sail and it began to burn, smoke coiling away like an escaping spirit. He grinned and looked up at the sky. He took his hands from the mast.

'Better send us a rainbow and dove soon!'

He heard the Prince's laughter – like thunder.

The sail took quickly, the flame spreading down the white fabric and blackening it like an advancing line of crop-burning cultists. Pike hurriedly clambered down the rungs. The journey down was a lot quicker and less dizzying.

He leapt the final few feet and landed on the deck. He soon toppled as the ship jolted upwards: he hit his back on the slimy wood. When he stood up again, using the mast for support, he realised he'd lost his lighter.

'Looking for this?' the Prince said, holding it out.

Pike sighed. He'd become strangely attached to it, perhaps because it was about the only thing he'd taken from the 'life before'. He'd never been one for material possessions, he was the Tarmac King after all, who lived most his life out of a backpack, but no one was entirely immune to attachment.

'Keep it,' he found himself saying, despite how much the thought of losing it had pained him moments before. 'I couldn't have lit the sail without you.'

A wave rose up like a foamy hand and slapped the mast, expelling the fire. It was too late however: only shrivelled shreds of the sail remained. They were torn from the mast and pulled into the collective white crests of the water, as though returning to a source.

The Prince folded his cracked fingers around the lighter and withdrew his hand. He was smiling in a way Pike had never seen him smile before.

'Generosity was one of the five pillars of knighthood, Sir Malory. You continue to uphold your virtuous code.'

'It's not generosity. It's repayment.'

The Prince looked at him, and it seemed an idea formed behind his human eye, because it shone with depths Pike had previously only associated with the mysterious socket. Then, he pocketed the lighter.

'We'll see.'

———

THIS IS SICK.

Now she knew the true extent of the Prince's curse, of what it meant to see everything. There were things Fay had glimpsed in the future, in the windows of her cards, that'd made her blood feel hot and acidic, that'd kept her burning-eyed awake through the night, unable to banish the horror. Sometimes these were disjointed from anything she knew – a cataclysmic horror. Other times they were so personal they almost broke her mind. At those times she rebelled against the cards. How dare they show her her own fate unasked. How dare they show her the fate of those around her when she had not wanted to see.

But the Prince did not just see the future. He saw the present and the past and he saw *inside* people. This penetration into consciousness occurred for him at a whim. Fay had managed it on Hagga because she was comatose, had had time to prepare. But the Prince received everything and everyone at all times, like some over-trodden trade route that'd existed for a thousand years and been built by gods' knew who.

Fay was looking at Hagga and the cripple man, Larri, locked together on the mattress. Larri's back was to her, crooked, but muscular. His face was buried in Hagga's ample chest. His fingers sunk deep into her soft flesh. He kissed the areolae: they were like the dewy pollen-rich centre of a flower. Fay noticed his hands had holes through them, as though he were an incomplete puzzle. *They are both broken.* Hagga skin's was blistered down one arm and the top of her breast, but the rest of it was so sun-kissed it made Fay feel like a ghost, and oh so distant from the place she had come from, the place before the city, though it was hardly more than a fleeting dream now. There had been sun there. And monsoons. The Prince thought she came from the city, and she allowed him to believe it. She feared the day he would reach in and discover the truth: her last and only secret from him.

She tried to pull her eyes away, but was transfixed. *There is danger.* The Need had fallen into this memory too. It was here somewhere. She had to find it. Not be distracted.

Fay had prepared herself for horror, for degradation, abuse, some kind of monstrous violence, the whims and hungers of the Need manifested, but the eroticism of this took her back, made *her* feel like the violator.

Hagga cried out in pleasure and Fay flinched, retreating to the wall, looking for a way out of this place. There was only one door and a window. Fay briefly wondered that if she jumped and fell in this memory she would die, her body in the pyramid crumpling like a toy cast aside by an inattentive child.

Hagga rode her man harder, telling Larri she was going to cum. He groaned, unable to keep down the pressure. Fay clamped her teeth together.

'Where are you?' she spat, half expecting the furious lovers might hear her and stop but they did nothing.

'YES!' Hagga cried. 'YES! YES!'

She leaned back, placing her hands behind her buttocks, showing the musculature of her torso, perfectly underpinning the spreading, round breasts. Her head was thrown back, the neck taut with protruding tendons like cables, making Fay want to bite into it and suck forever. Her hair fell back like a tangle of hanging vines in some midnight, secret garden where only black flowers grew.

'*Now!*' she whispered, so soft, so suddenly tender, Fay felt her breath leave her lungs without returning. Hagga's whole body shook. Her eyes screwed up until her face was a mask as visceral as Dr Monaghan's crazed menpo. The quivering tremor looked like it might last forever, a stasis of ecstasy. But then it shuddered into a stop. Larri panted and sat back on his hands, his arms straight. He looked into her eyes; Hagga looked back. Fay could see there was love there, not just lust. Perhaps they were not aware of this yet, but Fay could *see*. She had seen many acts in the life before this one, and she knew the difference between one performed at the behest of the flesh and one performed at the behest of the spirit.

Hagga smiled, but the smile did not sit right on her face, as though it had been painted over.

She looked directly at Fay, grabbed Larri's head between her palms and twisted it fully around. There was a noise like glass being ground by metal gears and Larri fell limply to the bed. Hagga rose off of him, her sex still dripping wet. Her grin was over-wide now, pulling the cheeks of her face apart.

Fay felt the snarl rupture from her throat, like a howl of pain that couldn't be kept in. She had been deceived. But it didn't matter.

'Trying to scare me?' Fay said. 'It won't work.'

Hagga only continued to offer her demented grin, the kind of smile worn by a lobotomised patient, only, this patient was being guided by another will.

'Kill me and you kill her,' she, or rather *it*, mouthed. The Hagga who'd stood before the Prince and faced him down had been straight-backed, almost regal, but this shambling doppelgänger was hunched over, a primate unused to standing on two legs. Her fingers were spread like claws.

'I very much doubt that,' Fay said, once more feeling the absence of her sickle-blade. 'I think she'll live, better than she ever has.'

'Simon could not destroy me and neither can you,' it spat, drool dangling from its lips.

It, the Need wearing Hagga like ill-fitting clothes, was worryingly close to her now, and Fay felt naked without her weapon. *You are priestess. You are guardian. You will not fall to this.* But she had never been in this danger before, trapped in another's memory and at the mercy of a living, breathing id.

But she did have one weapon.

Knowledge.

She reached into her dress and drew out her cards. She was not surprised to find them there, just as she had not been surprised to find them the day she emerged from the dark waters, the day she received new purpose. The cards were part of her. Yes, the deck could be wiped, damaged or altered, but so long as she kept remaking them, they would be as eternal she was. She threw the cards into the face of the Need which recoiled as though she had thrown amberfire at it.

Fay snatched a card from the air and held it in front of her like a talisman.

It was The Star. Upon its face, hand-painted with the grease and oil of the dying city, was an image of a female Aquarius pouring water into an endless river, and above her, a star which eclipsed all others. Drawn in the dark colours, it resembled, eerily, the eye of the Prince. And though she did not know this at that moment, he was thinking of her, reaching out to her, the aching in his heart compelling him to seek her image.

'The Star means hope,' Fay snarled. 'Larri is alive. Can you hear me Hagga? Larri is alive. You have to come back.'

The Need in Hagga's shape launched itself at Fay, who leapt to the side, avoiding the claw-like hands which she knew could kill her just as easily as the monstrous paws of the beast. Hagga swung round, but sluggishly, a zombie obeying a voodoo sorcerer's will, but at the very limits of the spell. *She is resisting,* Fay thought, fire igniting her body, making the pale skin glow like the surface of a perfect moon. *Hagga is fighting it.*

It attacked again, swiping furiously like a sabre cat. Fay leapt back, placing one foot on the wall. She pushed and somersaulted over Hagga, an acrobat, landing behind her. Hagga screamed in frustration as she tore a gash in the wall that began to bleed, like damaged membrane. Fay shuddered.

It turned.

'You can run and hide, but sooner or later, witch, I'll tear you apart. You're just another cunt to be fucked, just another meal to be had.'

It drove a fist at Fay, with a force like a pneumatic drill.

But Fay, a cobra seeing weakness, flashed to meet her. She gripped Hagga's wrist, so deceptively slender and beautiful, and stopped the blow mid-flight. With a howl the Need tried to pull free of her, but Fay did not let go, instead she struck Hagga around the mouth. Even now, she felt a twinge of guilt. But she overcame it and struck again. Teeth went flying. Not human teeth. Needles thick with venom.

She leaned in close, putting her lips to Hagga's ears.

'I am not a witch,' she whispered. 'I am the guardian of Nekyia; you are my sacrifice.'

It shrieked, writhing to be free, blood dripping from its mouth which was no more than a ragged, lipless slit. Hagga's face was all but gone. Monstrosity warped from her eyes like caterpillar seedlings chewing their way to the light.

'Hunger! The hunger,' it said. 'I will always exist.' But its desperation made the words mewling.

Fay grinned now. She tightened her grip, crushing the arm so that the bones in the forearm snapped. She struck the solar-plexus, the centre of the false-Hagga's being, and black cracks appeared as though the body was made of feeble glass. Fay struck again and fragments dislocated from the whole, revealing writhing masses of oil-dark worms beneath.

'Yes,' she cried. 'But I am the slacker of thirsts.'

For a moment, she was no longer in the dirty room in the shadow city. She was once more at the grand altar, hundreds of feet beneath the earth. She did not wear the modern white dress, she wore two ceremonial strips of cloth which came down from her shoulder, covering each breast, and looping at the waist to form a long white tabard covering her loins. In one hand, the sickle, in the other, a bowl ornately engraved with the head of Anubis.

The offering stood beneath her, and beyond, a crowd of darkened faces, eyes lit by fire and belief. Her skin was coloured deepest gold by the endless sun so she seemed an indestructible statue, immortal on earth, a female Orion cast entirely from the substances of gods. Then, she had been a beauty that cut off the tongues of men, that gelded them, and that made women boil over like heated blood from a wound.

She felt that glory breathe again now – the vision of her old life clearer to her than the meaning which lay in the painted images on her cards.

In her mind, it was a bull who's throat she slit with the nail of her finger, but in Hagga's mind, it was the twisted doppelgänger. And as it fell, mouth open like a beached shark's, body crumpling as though it'd been propped up by invisible hands, she thought she saw something surge from the darkness of its maw.

The world was obliterated. She soared upwards, entwined with whatever spirit had been birthed from the corpse of the Need. *Hagga?* The two of them were interlocked, like twin sisters in the womb.

Thank you. Thank you. For showing me.

They had become one, a spearhead. A cocoon of burning atmosphere enveloped them as they drove into an impossible, uncreated sky. A crack, another shattering. There were images and stories in the multi-coloured flames. A sound like sound bursting, a drum exploded, everything decompressing.

Weightlessness.

Then Fay opened her eyes.

CHAPTER 17

ekyia.

He heard it whispered as though by someone at his side; he knew it came from Fay, but what it meant eluded him. A name? A secret word?

His heart became tight, as though it'd shrunk. What if she was in danger? What if the beast inside the sleeping girl had gotten the upper hand?

And what were these concerns? His missions had always led him and those who followed head to head with danger. It was the way of things. Perhaps it was because he always wished to do the undoable. Perhaps it was simply a kind of karma, a ka. Whatever the case, he had lost many servants for the sake of the mission, but so long as the mission succeeded, it was irrelevant. Except Fay was not a servant, was she? An advisor, then.

The pressure building up in his mind from the frustrated line of thought caused his mouth to crack, like a shell splitting, revealing a grimace of perfect teeth. He clenched his fist as he leant out over the edge of the ship and stared down into the water – an answering blackness to that of his eye. *These waters remade me.* But he was starting to think they had changed a few things as well. His interactions with Fay, their connection over even this vast distance, none of it made any sense to him. He had believed wholeheartedly he was one of a kind, but here he found pieces of himself inside another. *And yet she is so different as well.* It was the difference that frightened him, more terrifying than any of the blood-hot sweat-rank dreams which had terrorised his sleep for most of his lifetime. He could not define it. He could not isolate it. The eye failed him. Her memories and thoughts were shadowy and barely decipherable. She was from an ancient time, he knew that much. And she had been worshipped; perhaps not as a goddess, but approaching it.

He shivered. She was an enigma he so desired to solve, and yet, a part of him never wanted to find the bottom of it, wanted to hound the truth in an endless ecstatic pursuit.

'You seem troubled.'

The Prince was startled. He had not sensed the approach. His eye and preternatural awareness had been closed and turned inward. *Dangerous.*

Pike stood beside him, his face half in shadow and half lit like the Phantom of the Opera's ghostly mask. Palefire shone above them; the Prince could not decide whether it was one large, snake-like shape contorting, or a myriad of smaller serpents pursuing their own unintelligible paths. There was a strange, awe-full spirituality about the aurora, like the sacred smoke of Japanese incense.

'Apparently, I'm not the only one,' the Prince said, forcing the levity of charm into his voice. He straightened and pointed at the palefire. 'I've been thinking about that. I've realised what it's made of.' He looked at Pike, watching his face. The resemblance to a mask was so close it seemed it would never move.

'What?'

'Ghosts,' the Prince said, grinning. 'It explains why they come out at night, at least.'

'The ghosts I know don't give a fuck whether it's night or day.'

'Them and monsters.' There was a satanic glint in the Prince's eye. There was a time when that would have cut into Pike like a cold blade, but now he found it strangely electrifying.

'I don't know,' Pike said, following his gaze and peering at the nebulous, undulating display. 'Are monsters and ghosts the same?' He was thinking of the Taking Man, of the look on Cris's face when he realised the truth. That day seemed impossibly long ago, but it was only months by the cycles of this place. 'Memories, though, they come at night.' Pike rested his elbows on the side of the ship and looked up, his eyes catching the light like ignited chips of magnesium. 'It looks more like memory to me.'

'Ghosts, memories, aren't *they* the same?' It was the first time Pike had heard the Prince ask a question with any uncertainty: usually he already knew the answer or he wished to rip it from whoever kept the secret. Pike hadn't forgotten the way he treated the oarswoman. Still, there was something which made him add:

'Perhaps. I suppose it depends whether you think the old masters were being literal when they spoke about ghosts, or just spinning metaphors.'

They heard cumbersome footsteps on the deck and turned. The Magician stood on the deck. The palefire somehow made his features uglier: emphasising the shadows and pits in his face whilst also drawing attention to the pock-marked flesh on his forehead and cheeks.

'Haven't you seen it?' he hissed.

'Seen what?' the Prince did not withhold the growl in this throat. The Magician seemed unperturbed by it.

'The water! Look at the water!'

They peered overboard and didn't have to look long to see what he meant. Thousands upon thousands of glinting shapes bobbed just beneath the surface, like a fragments of a colossal gemstone shattered by a lightning bolt. It was the jellied bodies of the same octopean creature which had been washed on board the Ark, catching the palefire and sheathed in foam. Pike saw a sea of cocaine, granules glistening like perfectly cut diamonds. He remembered his weakness and turned away.

All of a sudden, they all heard, as though someone had just turned on a sound system, a noise like water being drained down a sink, only magnified to earth-quake volume.

'What's going on?' the Prince bellowed, the near-serenity he had experienced moments before dissipated in an instant.

'You were *warned!*' The Magician yelled, and he turned and fled across the deck.

The Prince cursed and turned to Pike.

'Come on.'

They went to the prow of the ship. Most of the oarsmen had abandoned their rowing. One was even trying to throw himself overboard, two of his friends holding him back.

Mad! They've all gone mad! The Prince thought, and for once, he wasn't sure he could control the situation.

He stood at the prow. Ahead of them, somehow dark despite the palefire, lay a circular disc in the water. The Prince cursed the deception of his natural eye as the black orb in his socket expanded, opening. Not a disc, a funnel into which the streams of creatures were being sucked and then regurgitated.

'Whirlpool!' one of the oarsmen cried.

It was miles upon miles in diameter. There was no hope of them ever steering around it.

'Turn this ship!' the Prince roared, but none of the oarsmen leapt to obey him. He grabbed one at random, who was chattering hysterically. The Prince hurled him over the side with a single, almost careless jerk of his hand. There was a splash, and the hysterics abruptly ceased. The sucking noise grew ever louder and the black disc grew as though swelled by the gallons it consumed. 'Turn this ship around!' he roared. None of the oarsmen cared. The one who had been struggling for release finally broke free and cast himself into the waters freely. The Prince's face showed a network of veins, like a bloody cobweb.

'Yin!' He turned to the Magician, who watched the whirlpool with fatalistic eyes. 'Yin! You can turn the ship.'

'If I could do that, you wouldn't have needed the slaves.'

The Prince screamed. He climbed up onto the prow. Pike was suddenly afraid; the dark eye was giving off waves of energy like a powering up generator. What was he about to do? Surely he could not unmake a whirlpool?

'You can try to keep us here all you want!' the Prince roared. The ship heaved as the surging pull of the whirlpool became more powerful. The Prince maintained balance effortlessly as a panther upon a swaying bough. 'But you will fail! Do you hear me? You will *fail!*'

The Prince threw back his head and the eye birthed tendrils of darkness which spread out, at first like tentacles, but then, like jointed limbs. Membrane sprouted between them. The darkness crept down the Prince's body like vine, rooted itself in the deck, began to solidify itself with the ship. One of the oarsmen began to laugh as though he had been saving all the humour in his lifetime for this moment. The bat-like, symbiotic mass began to flap unreal wings, lifting the ship from the water.

The Magician recoiled in horror. It was clear this kind of magic was unknown even to him. His eyes were like a pig's in the grip of a butcher. Water sloughed from the ship, as though unwilling to relinquish its hold.

Something emerged from the whirlpool.

It took Pike a moment to contemplate what he was seeing. The Prince's feat had rattled him. But what now came from within the funnelling chaos of water was another story.

It was an orb. Perfectly spherical. From it, a myriad of tendrils hung, each large enough to cleave through a skyscraper. Its limbs hung vertically, limp, straight into the pit of the whirlpool, a small moon moored to the abyssal depths below. There was no eye or any other distinguishable features but Pike sensed it could see, just as the Prince's socket saw. What it was, what it meant, and why it took such an ugly and incomprehensible form were all questions which flashed through Pike's mind like dogs gone wild with heat. He could not catch the thoughts. All he knew was that the whirlpool-thing impressed upon him a feeling of utter, chilling dread.

He looked at the Prince, who was almost levitating. The prophet trembled, his natural eye fixed on the creature, the unnatural one continuing to spew the eerie symbiote.

'I don't fear you!' he cried, but his tone betrayed him.

The orb began to move towards the floating Ark, its tentacles creating furrows in the water like those made by a crashed plane. It dwarfed them. It dwarfed everything.

The Prince curled inwards, as though with a stab wound and the symbiotic creature was sucked back into his dark eye. The Ark tumbled from its flight, momentarily weightless, then hit the water hard enough to throw Pike to the floor. He scrambled up, the ship less stable and grounded than the water.

The oarsmen abandoned all remnant of sanity. The Magician was huddled by the rail of the ship, muttering what might have been spells or prayers.

The Prince rose from his hunched position. The eye seemed to be gathering shadows, swelling like a cancerous tumour. Then, a beam shot from it, red, violent, a scar across the retina and the air. It scored the surface of the humongous creature from the whirlpool.

And did nothing.

The Prince growled and gathered himself again, unleashing a barrage of flaming beams like the shellfire of a tank. Still, it remained unscathed.

That was when Pike saw the Prince's hands were trembling, his throat constricted. *Impotency. That is what he most fears.*

Pike threw caution to the wind.

'Michael!' He had heard Fay call him that once. Now, he thought it was the only thing which might reach him. The Prince turned, looking like a lost boy hearing the call of his mother but still not able to see her.

'Pike...'

'It's no use. Abandon ship.'

'But the mission...'

'It's over.'

Pike ran over and grabbed him by the shoulders.

'We can't kill it! Don't you see? If you can't: no-one can!'

The Prince seemed distant, as though he had just been dosed with heroine.

'I... but to turn back...to fail again...'

The sucking sound of the whirlpool, the noise of demolished hopes, of garbage heaps, was so loud Pike could not hear his own voice. He couldn't think clearly either, his thoughts were drowned.

'We have no choice. If we turn back now, we can still - '

He didn't know what they could do. He shook the Prince, who was vacantly staring into an oblivion quite separate from the one which lay in the water.

'Pike...'

But that was when the orb lashed out with one of its gigantic limbs, cutting the ship in half with the ease of a grown man snapping a twig.

AS THE SHIP SPLINTERED, ruptured, twisted and then broke in half, Larri's flesh pulled, blistered and tore beneath the violent acidic touch of amberfire. He screamed: a sound shockingly like the squeal of the deck's boards springing apart as the deep rushed up to covet them.

THE ARK FOLDED LIKE A V, drawn down by its centre; just as it did so, miles and miles away within a room in the pyramid, Hagga's legs jerked inward, bringing her knees up. Her stomach muscles contracted, and she sat bolt upright. She sucked in a long, rattling breath, as though filling herself with air to the very bottom of her being. Then she burst into tears.

'It's ok,' a soothing voice said. Soft arms embraced her. Once, before Hagga had become the cursed thing she was, her mother had held her like this. 'You've been asleep a while.'

'Like Larri,' Hagga said. She laughed bitterly. 'Asleep like Larri.'

———

PIKE FLEW THROUGH THE AIR. He had the sensation of being plucked from the ruptured deck, as though by the scruff of his neck, dangled for a moment, then tossed like a spinning knife. Palefire and black sea flashed alternatingly and then he was plunged into water so dismally cold it paralysed him. He sank beneath its surface. Not even the highland lochs of Scotland had chilled him this deeply. There was no cold to compare. He wondered that his heart had not been instantly stopped, but then he remembered, that death didn't work the same way in this world.

Move, a voice within him said. *Move or you're dead.*

He forced his arms into motion, pulling at the water uselessly, clawing as though up a cliff-face. He kicked out, his legs feeling as though the bones within had solidified into one un-bendable bar.

Breaking the surface in a cloud of foam, almost swallowing the limb of one of the diminutive creatures. This close, as it drifted helplessly by him, he thought they might be the acorn-origins of the colossal sphere-creature.

He glanced around him. The palefire swathed the scene in fragmented light, like sunlight through the bars of a cell. The ship was being dragged under, folding like a closed book. Where was the Prince? Pike started to beat at the waters, heading for the wreckage. He had always been a strong swimmer and it'd saved him more than once in his lifetime. The water was thick with the jellyfish creatures, making his strokes sloppy, but they did not seem poisonous which was a boon.

He found a rent plank and attached himself to it, panting heavily. The cold was draining his energy faster than the act of swimming ever could. He looked around him. Many of the oarsmen had already gone under. *Once you allow the cold to take you, it's over.* He wondered whether they would be assimilated to the bottom of the ocean (if it even had a bottom), or, as the Prince had said, become part of the hideous skyscape: to be forever a tormented and forlorn display of human suffering. That thought was worse than anything. Pike had come to accept there was a second life after death, but deep down, he still craved the silence he had thought the Taking Man had sent him too.

He glimpsed the Prince amidst the collapsing wreckage. The prophet was unconscious in the water; face down. Behind him, something cut through the ocean, just below the surface of the waves. Like an oilspill, it spread its darkness around him, or a shadow created by an impossibly huge carrion bird. A snaking tendril glided out of the water and wrapped itself around the Prince. At first it merely seemed to cradle him. Then, with an effortless twist, it dragging him under.

Pike did not know what emotion seized him, but he felt a tearing cry come to his throat.

Tears burned at the back of his eyes. They would not fall but they stung as though needles pressed at the back of the corneas from inside his skull.

'He is lost,' a voice said.

Pike kicked and turned the driftwood. The Magician was beside him, standing with perfect balance on a segment of the deck. His arms were folded, head bowed. For all the sobriety on his face, he seemed pleased.

'He can survive. If anyone can.'

'Perhaps,' the Magician said.

Pike glanced back at where the Prince had gone under. The monster glided away from the shipwreck, its mission achieved. It sank slowly down into the whirlpool, which continued to hiss and churn for a few moments before spraying up a column of water. The column hovered for a few seconds, a translucent pillar, as though made of tinted glass, and then descended, wiping away all trace of there ever having been a whirlpool.

'What was that thing?'

The Magician paused a moment and then looked at him. Pike saw, not for the first time, that there was a chaos behind the frosted surface of his eyes, a kind of emotional maelstrom, tethered, like a rabid dog in chains. Pike realised then that the Magician perhaps could have saved the Prince. But he had *chosen* to do nothing.

'Tekeli-li,' the dwarf said.

For all its strangeness, the phrase felt familiar to Pike, as though, like a Japanese character, it contained its meaning within the sound and image of the word itself.

The Magician unfolded his arms, took two stunted strides and leapt from his makeshift raft. Mid-air, he transmogrified, becoming a black, sleek shark. He plummeted into the waters, diving out of sight.

Pike spat and swore.

This place gets weirder and weirder.

He shivered as though something diseased had touched him, and knew it was the cold pushing beneath his skin. He began to kick, limbs numb and oddly weighted, like tools he was unused to using.

Before long, he could not feel anything.

Not even the sting of tears.

———

LIGHT EXPLODED, flushing down the corridor like floodwater. He sensed parts of his eye being touched by spectrums of colour he could not decipher. Then a noise, exactly like the sound the Border Collie he'd owned in his childhood had made as he slit its throat: mewling, guttural, fading.

A death-scream.

Only one of the points of light remained. The other had vanished as though it'd never been. The remaining light was fading too – whatever birthed it receding down another passageway. The Taking Man breathed. He allowed the gift, still weighing down his palms and finger-tips, to dissipate and clear. He took another breath and let it out as though reeling silk.

Like the most cautious thief, he crept down the corridor. His breathing had become indiscernible. His footsteps were silent as a ninja's. He reached a crossroads where the two lights had faced one another. His eyes were still startled from the dazzling colour. They tingled, like the aftermath taste of something exotically spiced. They struggled with the darkness even though the Taking Man had lived in darkness most of his life.

He began to search the crossroads, keeping his ears and eyes alert at all times to the reappearance of one of those fatal green lights. The walls felt like the scales of a serpent. He wondered whether this underground place had been built into the earth or whether it had been built above ground and sunk with time.

Stumbling over the thing he was looking for, he caught his breath. It lay at his feet. It could have easily been mistaken for a pile of rags. He knelt and began to search it with his remaining hand. Robes. Robes made from some kind of web-like silk. These things were not animals, then. They had civilisation. His hands roved upwards. Arms. A chest. It had a human body.

He touched something which gave beneath his probing fingers like a sponge. He hesitated a moment. Its surface had been slick. He could not stop himself thinking of an octopus's tentacle. He forced himself to return to his investigations. Two. Three. Four. Five tentacles. He lifted them and found an orifice: its mouth, the instrument which emitted such sickening music. He let the tentacles flop down. He explored higher, finding a squid-like face. Two eyes. Were these what gave off the ghostly aura or was it the flesh of the thing itself? His hands went to the back of the head: a hairless dome. At the place where the skull (if it even had a skull) and the neck intersected there were more tentacles, but these ones were long and thin, unlike the ones which covered its mouth. They also ended in bulbs, like plant-heads not yet blossomed. *These must be the source of the light.*

He took his hand away. It itched, as though sprayed with a chemical irritant. He had no way to scratch it and so he wiped it on his thigh.

Something's not right.

The surface of its flesh had been oily like the walls, and so he dismissed it. Now he saw that was a terrible mistake. Phlegm rushed into his mouth, a white flood. His groin tightened. He choked, staggered to his feet. *No!* The darkness started to fill with – colour? He could not tell whether it was the approach of one of these beings or whether it was the substance working on him already. He took three steps, unsure which corridor he had chosen. His footing uneven, as though walking through a bog.

He gasped. All the effort by which he had controlled his breathing was made redundant as he struggled for air. Visions started to swarm from the darkness. The walls were lined with faces: the faces of everyone he had ever taken. *We are inside you,* they mouthed as one. The young, the old, men, women and children. He lashed out at one, hoping it would shatter like the fragile, illusionary mask it was, but his hand passed right through the face.

This is not real!

He had once before tasted the effects of a hallucinatory psychedelic. Nothing could have prepared him, however, for the speed with which this one took hold.

He tripped and fell. He looked up dazedly. The body of the creature. He'd been walking in circles.

'Please...!'

What did he mean? Did he think some great saviour would come for him? He did not believe in god. He did not believe in anything except that only by becoming nothing, accepting that nothing, could the realities of existence be faced. This nihilism had always empowered him; his enemies could not take from him because he had nothing *to* take.

But now, the nothing dragged him into a mire of tar.

He was kicking, screaming, frothing at the mouth. The stones glowed violent red like coals heated over a fire. His cock unslung in his pants and he came down the side of his leg. That sensation was dull compared to the firework display within his mouth. He spat, trying to cool down the sensation, but it only renewed itself, like a tide coming back in.

He rolled onto his side, staring at the creature which had poisoned him, even in death.

It seemed to be looking back.

Hello, Jack.

'You can't know my name,' he growled. 'No one knows my name.'

We know everything, Jack.

He rolled onto his back, but he felt the creature was now standing over him: he could see its fish-eyes glinting in the dark.

Green light erupted, forming a mane around the alien and unknowable face. Like gunshots the light struck him and he howled. The drug made the light physical.

'What are you?'

The shining and flowered bulbs descended, eerily like the implements of a surgeon, and attached themselves like electrodes to his skull. Static erupted, for a moment so loud he thought he would lose his mind. It cut out, as though a channel had been changed.

He stood in a dark space, teleported from the present agony. He wore his suit jacket again. He had both hands. The thing stood before him: unlit, plainer, somehow, virtually human.

'What are you?' he repeated.

We built this place, it said, gesturing with one hand, as though showing him a prospective home. *The pyramid. The twelve. The entire citadel, the shore. Everything.* He could not see its mouth but he sensed a smile.

'Why?'

Human minds are – how should I say it – sustaining.

The Taking Man swallowed.

'Is that what you're doing now? Eating my mind?'

It shook its head, the tentacles swaying like pendulums. He

wondered how much time was passing as he lay convulsing beneath its touch and the hallucinogen.

One of our number wished to, but I had to destroy him. You see, no one has ever crawled from the pit before. You are the first, and this intrigues us.

It took a step closer. What was the purpose of this vision? To make him feel more at home as it probed his thoughts? To give him the illusion of safety?

'You think I might be useful to you?' he sneered.

A noise like chimes. Was this its laughter?

Less foolish than your counterparts. But our goals are the same, Jack Orton. The Prince. The one called Michael Banner. He stands in our way.

A multitude of shadows seemed to breed in its face. Its flesh, which had been tinted faintly green like a toad, now turned to onyx. The eyes resembled a pair of angler fish's lures.

Rage filled up the Taking Man and made him tremble. He felt his hands clench, both of them.

'I will destroy him.'

The sound of chimes again. Was he being mocked?

He strode forward and swiped at the vision. Predictably it had no effect.

Then he was pierced by a thousand needles. It was his turn to emit the squeal like a dog; the pain was like no pain he had ever known. Nails in every joint, nerve and tendon and cancer in his heart. He collapsed to one knee. The pain vanished. He whimpered. For a moment, he struggled to even move, frightened that in doing so he would reawaken the pain.

He expected the creature to chide him, to deride, but it did nothing, merely continued to stare. That was when he realised that his perception of nothingness had been incorrect. Now, next to the vast power of this being, he was truly void. As an ant was to a human so he was to it.

'If you are so powerful then why can't you destroy him yourself?' he breathed.

A wise question. Its tone suggested that nothing had happened, but he knew it was the originator of that mind-bowing pain. *It is partly because we do not yet fully know the limits of his power. We have not come this far through taking inane risks.* A sensation of deep humour now.

The Taking Man realised that just as it was scanning his thoughts and memories, so too he was experiencing minute flashes of its emotion. What he could see was no doubt nothing to what it perceived, but still, it was something he could use. *We are cautious, by nature. To come to the surface and face him might risk the destruction of all we have worked so hard to build. Imagine if all your plans for London had been thrown away overnight, that you carelessly got into a fight an opponent whose full strength you had not calculated? That would be the end of a mere ten years planning. Imagine a thousand years. To throw it away...*

'You will use me?' he said.

Consider it a karma. He felt the lash of this sentence and almost fell from his kneeling position. Instead, with a grimace, he forced himself to stand.

It regarded him, gaze colder than a planet without atmosphere.

Resilient. Good.

'What now?'

A parting gift.

It raised its hand. The pain returned, duller than before, but with the added sensation of a kind of soldering, as though runic emblems were being burned into the marrow of his bones. He screamed, fell backwards but did not hit a floor, instead he toppled through whirlpools of green light.

You will know what we are, its voice still sounded, from everywhere and nowhere at once. *Your legends have spoken of us. Your myths have drawn our silhouette; the sketches of ignorant children making sense of what is and always will be beyond them.*

We are the Mind-flayers.

Seething heat. Colours. A receding aftermath of light, like the shedding spores of a fungal disease.

He woke from the trip in darkness, beside the body of the slain mind-flayer. His hand went to the stump and he cursed. For a moment, the vision had tricked him.

Clambering up with difficulty, using the elbow of his stunted arm for support, he gained his footing. He felt no different. No more powerful. There was a light ahead, but this was yellow and grey. Could it be a way up? He began to walk towards it, barely able to think. His feet found steps and he climbed up them. It was a life age of ascent, dizzying and difficult. His feet bled, leaving prints behind him which the darkness washed away.

He emerged from a tomb's mouth; it sealed itself behind him. He was standing in a graveyard. The palefire dissipated in the sky like milk steadily diluted with water.

The city seemed a three-dimensional jigsaw, cracked and unreal.

Somewhere, the sounds of suffering and rage. He thought of London and ached to hear sirens again.

CHAPTER 18

'We have to save him.'

Hagga was on her feet even though her legs felt like they were missing a few key muscles. She almost fell over as she staggered through the door, out of the chamber of the past, and into the cylindrical interior of the pyramid. Fay made no move to stop her, but followed through the door, her face conveying a kind of proud sadness which made Hagga think of her mother again. It had been a long time since she thought of her.

The elevator was waiting for them. Fay shouted to Manfred. After a few moments, the platform began to descend. Doorways upon doorways streamed past, a humanised honeycomb.

'You're not strong enough to face Monaghan,' Fay said, casually. 'I don't know what's happened to your Need either. It might be I've exorcised it forever, or just put it into remission. Either way, you may find it's not there when you call.'

'I'm not going to face him,' Hagga said, thinking as she talked. 'That place is full of tunnels. I can sneak past him.'

'If he finds you he'll kill you,' Fay said. 'Or do what he's doing to Larri. Worse, perhaps. He's afraid of women.'

Hagga laughed.

'Aren't most men?'

Fay offered a smile which Hagga sensed did not mean she necessarily agreed with her.

'In my experience, men and women are afraid of each other, but for different reasons. W-'

Fay let out a whimper and doubled over. Hagga lurched and caught her, barely keeping her own footing. Fay groaned and shuddered, her skin crawling and hot beneath Hagga's grip. When she straightened, her nose was bleeding.

'What's wrong?'

'Something...' She swallowed. 'Something...'

She reached into a slim pocket in her dress and pulled out her tarot cards. Moments previous, she had used them to find Larri. Now she began shuffling them with eye-dazzling complexity, folding them over like the metal of a katana, or the passages of a labyrinth. Finally she drew a card. It was a Tower.

Her lips peeled back to reveal a skeleton's grimace and for the first time Hagga saw a look of hopelessness cross the fortune-teller's face.

The elevator ground to a halt.

'What do you think's happened?'

'The Ark,' Fay whispered, slowly. 'It must be. He's failed.'

Hagga wanted to comfort Fay, but right now there was only one person on her mind. The Prince's mission, the mysteries of this place, all of that could wait. She cared about the man who'd carried her out of the City of Illusion on broken legs. The man she'd taken to her bed after so many men and finally found solace in. The man she'd only just gained and then lost.

Hagga staggered onto the platform, having to hold onto the railings. *This is crazy,* she thought. *You can barely stand. You should rest. Recover.* But something was gnawing at her. Not the hunger of the Need. Something different. A kind of prickling sixth sense that insisted Larri needed her *right now*, and that to wait a few days to recover would make her too late to save him.

Fay went no further, but as Hagga went through the door which led to the pyramid's windowed exit, she called after her.

Hagga stopped and turned.

'Just remember not all madmen are stupid.' She swallowed. 'I'd come with you, but I have to see. I have to know if he's alive.'

Hagga nodded.

'So do I.'

––––––

DEELA PACED BACKWARDS AND FORWARD. In one hand she held a metal pipe, jagged at one end like a crude spear. Its tip had been brought to an orange glare in the coals of the brazier. It was her summoning staff, her ritual totem, and the congregation followed its glowing tip like cats would follow a dangling charm. The chapel was full: fuller, she noted, than it had ever been with the psychopathic man in white at its head. She smiled. Patience like the Nile crocodile brings its reward.

'The Prince is gone. Lost on his fool's quest. The child-killer is dead, thrown into the pit by the witch. We have a chance now to act. To bring this city into a place of light and stop the assimilation of souls.'

The ghostly god-beams which fell through the shattered ceiling of the chapel flickered, as though the souls of the city heard her and grew concerned. Murmurs ran through the throng at this, as though they had witnessed a spectacular miracle. *Minds are too easily bent,* she thought, with sadness. It had been so in her life. Why did thousands obey the will of the one even when the one was mad? It never made sense to her.

'This time of grace will not be open for long. A new dictator will take the place of the old one. A new monster will rise. The pyramid still stands: all it represents, all the evil, still unchallenged. I ask you -'

The doors to the chapel burst open. A man entered. His appearance was like the arrival of a wolf in the midst of a crowd of sheep. Bleats and squeals rose up. People scrambled to selfishly put distance between themselves and the arrival, only to find themselves confined by the crumbling chapel walls. Not a single one had the courage to raise a hand. This was no surprise. Half his face looked like it was falling off, or degenerating into slag, yet his eyes still pierced with the intensity of a nail-gun to the forehead. He had only one hand, but that hand was blackened like the enchanted gauntlet of an ancient pagan warrior. To even think of being touched by that hand induced convulsions in the stomach, a taste in the mouth that meant leprosy.

Worst was the light which his flesh gave off: a shine the colour of sickness that caused everything within its radius to appear dead. There was a noise that accompanied his footsteps, like an out-of-time backing vocalist; continually rising static.

He began to walk the aisle between the pews, towards Deela, who remained frozen and clutching her spear.

'I'm back,' he said. 'Did you miss me?'

Deela gritted her teeth. She had seen such horrors before, seen the embalmed walk, dis-organed corpses rise and cry for their mothers, seen oblivion in the teardrops of Anubis.

'You smell of the pit,' she spat.

She raised the red-tipped spear above her head, javelin-like. The arrival paused, as if contemplating the danger that spear posed. Then, as though he had decided it was of little consequence, continued walking.

Deela screamed and hurled the spear.

Moving with an abomination's speed, the arrival snatched the spear out of the air with his one hand. He flipped it around, so the burning end faced Deela. He advanced. She did not retreat or back down, but stood firmly, lips curling back to reveal the teeth of an angered simian.

'I'm not sure I like what you've done with the place,' he said, almost at the altar.

'You'll never rule the city,' she said, and the anger vanished to be replaced by the amusement of a vulture. 'You'll never be able to beat him. He has *courage*. You just have your hate.'

The arrival rammed the spear through Deela's belly. She gave the smallest grunt, froze, as though every muscle had suddenly turned to stone. She collapsed to her knees, still locking eyes with her killer.

He stared at her.

'This was your first death.'

From the back of his head, she thought she could see serpents unfolding, serpents made from the green smog of the city's poison wood.

'What are you -'

'Now, for your second.'

Torn from her body and into the arms of jackal-headed agony. She had never known such agony, never known it was possible for a mind to break so swiftly. But that was what was happening, in barely a second, her mind cracked like a canopic jar; all the dust of her being spilled out.

Lost forever.

———

HE SLITHERED from out the water onto the shore, a legless slug, but one slowly gaining mammalian shape, a parody of evolution. A bloated mass, pushing upright, waddling on stunted legs (whose feet still ended in flippers), looking like a crooked frog. Then two upper limbs dropped forward. A dog. A jackal. A cat. The spine grown longer. Two legs.

A dwarfish man emerged, the last vestiges of a tail fading into the ragged end of his cloak. He was exhausted beyond measure. The transformation had been one effort. The swim another. And the whole venture his powers had been slowly drained in holding back the storm, keeping the ship together.

But no more efforts for the Prince.

A savage grin split his features. The shadowed eyes lit like a night sky penetrated with the sudden manifestation of stars.

Free!

How long he had waited for this moment. It had taken all his patience, all his deceptive cunning. The Prince had almost come close to discovering him many times; he had felt the eye drawing near to the secret, seen the glimmer of something on the Prince's face: a half-understood revelation. But Yin had always just managed to turn it away at the last moment, to escape it.

The Prince was not dead. Of that, he was sure. Partly because he understood that nothing could truly die here. Partly because even now he feared his power. What had happened when the Guardian emerged had shaken Yin to the core. For a moment he'd thought all his plans might be in vain: the Prince could still triumph even against such impossible odds. What was that magic, the thing which had emerged from the eye? It was an illusion, but more than that. It had life and being. Yin had tasted its energy - pulsing, orgasmic spasms, a star dying and recreating itself over and over. Dazzlingly complex, irradiating, pneumatic. Like being inside a bomb at the instant of detonation, before the epilogue of fire and heat and shockwaves.

He tasted vomit in his mouth. After all he'd done, the Prince's magic was deeper than his ever could be. He wretched. Nothing came up. Nothing ever did.

Focus now.

The job was not done. He had to disappear. The Prince would be back from the deep before long. Enraged. Yin had to meld with the city, to use his knowledge to gain further control. There was a mystery at the bottom of the pyramid, perhaps if he sought there.

His flesh tingled. He knew the thought had brought about some primal connection with the world around him. The black sand tinkled as the thin, surface layer shifted over the more settled sand beneath.

He saw him, shimmering in a heat-wave that could not have been created by heat because there was none. The Taking Man. The enemy of the Prince. He carried a spear and wore a look on is face as though he meant to unmake the world. A pallid glow shone from him, turning the sand beneath his feet white, as though he was Time itself bringing the pale horse of age with him.

Words came into the Magician's mouth.

'The Pit Arisen.'

The Taking Man nodded.

'You went into the abyss?' Yin said, but he did not need an answer. He knew. He could smell it, far more powerfully than Deela, who had known the pit well. As though he had seen the illuminating answer to a puzzle, images and fragments seemed to be rushing together inside his head. The city's secret was about to be laid bare. He was at that tipping point where he both understood everything and nothing; the truth was inchoate. He needed to articulate it, but the words now were faltering. Instead, he listened as the Taking Man spoke.

'It's time for his reign to come to an end.'

'What do you mean?' He knew very well.

'We have to destroy him. You can lie to yourself that you could escape, you might even succeed for a short while, but you're forgetting he has the eye. He would find you and kill you, or make you a slave again.' The Taking Man smiled. Despite how grotesque his features were, it still managed to convey a sense of wryness. 'Either way, he wins. You lose.' He locked eyes with the Magician. 'But if you want to win, then we have to kill him once and for all.'

'Is that what *they* want?'

He could not bring himself to use the name. The Taking Man nodded.

'How can we do it?' Yin bit his lip and began pacing, head bowed. He was glad not to be looking at the Taking Man directly. Every time he did, an ache started in his brain, as though a blood vessel had burst. 'He's too strong.'

'It will take three of us.'

Now Yin turned sharply.

'Dr Monaghan as well?'

The Taking Man offered a very different smile, one like a hyena guzzling on the intestines of a slain behemoth.

'Yes. We'll need to talk him around. It shouldn't be too hard. He craves anything that will give him sport. And what better sport than killing the biggest monster of them all?'

Yin did not think the Prince was the biggest monster anymore, not as his nostrils filled with the repulsive odour of something not only dead but unholy, of something *not supposed to exist*. It was the only way he could define it.

Still, he needed to be free of the Prince. And after the deed was done he'd find a way to extricate himself from the Taking Man too. He would certainly be easier to deceive. He did not have the eye.

He extended a hand. The Taking Man bowed and took it in his; it looked like it'd been thrust into a black hole and retained some of the void as it was drawn out. Yin finally thought he understood what it was like to make a deal with the devil.

And wondered whether once that was how the inhabitants of the Circle had thought about him.

Chapter 19

C ocooned in ink. A landscape as indecipherable as pre-human hieroglyphs. Crushed beneath the weight. What created it? How had he gotten here? He did not know. He only knew that Atlas could not have borne this burden. The titan's bones would have splintered and then caved like ancient beams.

He struggled to uncoil. Did he have a body? It seemed at once he did not and he did. He felt, he had feeling, but he could not see himself or understand himself within the emptiness. Emptiness like the pupil of a whirlpool.

And then he remembered.

Was he in the bowels of that Thing? Or had it dragged him to a subterranean prison?

He breathed, expecting a flood of water. There was none. He tried to feel his face for a bandage or covering that was blocking his sight (both natural and unnatural). He could not feel a face. He understood then, that if he was in a cell, it was not physical. Somehow it had put him to sleep and entered his dreamspace.

They never learn, he thought, with a smile that split the pelagic darkness like the rays of a diseased crescent moon. *This is my place. Here, I am strongest.*

In answer to his light, there was an orb which shone green. It stretched, becoming an oval, and then, a slit, with three-dimensional space dropping away behind it like an endless series of archways.

Someone emerged from the doorway. Someone he knew.

A hiss escaped his teeth and he clenched fists which did not exist.

'Hello, son,' the man said, with a smile to rival the Prince's.

'Dad.' The Prince gave a curt nod. *Honour thy father and mother.* How he wished that rule was possible to break. It wasn't. He'd tried so hard. 'I seem to remember throwing you into an abyss.'

His father laughed.

'You did. But I'd have thought someone like you would know sometimes the abyss throws something back.'

'So, what did you find down there? Beneath the pyramid.'

He took a few steps towards the visitation, but never, for a moment, let down his guard. Every atom of his being quivered like an animal on the edge of striking its prey. He had confronted his father at the pyramid's head, overcome him, and thrown him down into the blackness, a blackness which, as Yin and the twelve shadows had led him to believe, utterly broke the mind of any who entered it.

Well, it wouldn't be the first time father surprised you. Besides, he was a little broken to begin with.

His father put his grubby hands into the workman's pants. His vest was patchy with stains from half a dozen different meals, sweat and what might have been faecal matter. His face was hungry and alive, as though he rode a drug high. The green light gave every edge of him a disturbing glow; he seemed a picture drawn by an artist possessed.

'I found creation,' he said. 'I found the roots of it all.'

As he spoke, tendrils appeared from the slit behind him, wriggling their way out like maggots from the slaglike guts of a rotten body.

'What roots?' He had one eye on the tentacles. One on the wraith.

'Things older than you can imagine, son.' His father's smile kept widening. It didn't fit his face. None of this fit anything. The Prince tried to feel the power which breathed in the empty socket, the *real* eye which stared always into the truth. He couldn't. It was as though it'd withdrawn or been closed. That, more than anything else, made a current run through him, like feeling the tip of a blade at the throat without seeing to whom it belonged.

'I'm older than you can imagine, father. This, you never understood.'

'Oh but I did.' Pacing forward, breaking the invisible ring they had been circling. 'I understood it all too well. It's why I obsessed over you. Tested you. It drove me mad.' He laughed. The Prince knew he should divert, alter the distance, but he was paralysed to the spot, as if the creeping tentacles had grabbed his ankles. 'You. The son. You drove me *insane.*'

And then the Prince felt it, what he hadn't felt since the age of twelve, the hammerblow of his father's anger searing across his consciousness. It made him reel, but also, threw off the paralysis.

He raised his fist, ran forward and lashed out. The blow could have killed anything, could have shattered concrete (at the cost of the Prince's hand), but his father was no longer where he had been. He was *behind* the Prince. And he glowed.

Slowly, the Prince turned. His father's face flickered, like an old VHS tape. Beneath it a squidlike monstrosity.

'I see you,' the Prince said. And he finally understood. *Nekyia.*

'No,' the mind-flayer said. 'You see nothing.'

The vision closed, crumpling like a discarded sketch. The Prince found himself cocooned again, buoyed up by an unseen anti-gravity. He was gaining form, acquiring bones and flesh and finally even clothes with the rapidity of rising bread mixture.

A gasp. The eye exploded.

He was born for the third time.

———

FRED WASN'T LOOKING TOO good. It was a shame really. He'd proved quite the remarkable test subject, but everything ran its course. There was more to find out, of course, but he was fairly sure Fred might die the next time he was exposed to amberfire. His skin had almost entirely dropped off or shrivelled to a blackened husk. He urinated himself more often than made it to the bucket in the corner of his cell

(Dr Monaghan had cited animal-protection clauses as he placed it next to Fred, who'd groaned like an ape). A stink came off him that Dr Monaghan knew was necrotic, of something turning bad.

He had to be grateful for this place, this magical city. If he'd been conducting these experiments in the before-world, Fred would have died a long time ago. As it happened, this place made everyone a good deal more durable. And then when they did die...

Well, that was the secret Dr Monaghan hoped to unravel. There came a moment of transition, it seemed, when the body became one with the city. He'd seen it countless times as he cleaved the heads from disappointing miners. Their bodies collapsed, jittering (as he expected) and then, after a few moments, they transformed, melding with whatever surface they fell on. He'd seen rent chests explode into fungal gardens, severed arms raise themselves into miniature trees, heads turn into dusty, insect hives. Remarkable. Bizarre. But at the bottom of everything there was a dirty answer. Science destroyed all myth. That was its colossal power. Cultures and religions could be ended by its mighty arm as though they had never been. Hiroshima. Chernobyl.

If you thought sex was a thing of beauty, you could guess again at the bare reality of men's disappointing concupiscence. If you wanted to believe in a soul mate, science could show you women were biologically made to be with as many men as possible.

Science was the magic-killer.

And at some point, Dr Monaghan would figure out how to kill the magic of this 'assimilation', as he'd heard one miner call it.

Fred screamed. He often did that out of the blue. It was possibly because his skin was re-knitting. *I should put him out of his misery.* Now there was a strange thought Dr Monaghan found most troubling.

'I'm coming dear,' he called.

'Don't keep me waiting.'

Dr Monaghan turned. He had not heard the new arrivals enter. The Magician and a one-handed man. Well, now he knew why he hadn't heard them. The Magician had suppressed the sound.

'Can I help you two gentlemen? Perhaps a tea is in order?'

The one-handed man laughed. The Magician shifted nervously

from one stunted foot to another. It had never occurred to Dr Monaghan before, but the Magician and Fred were really quite alike.

'We've come to make you a proposition,' the one-handed man said.

Dr Monaghan's eyes narrowed beneath the steel mask. He didn't like business talk, and he mistrusted all who used it. The one-handed man seemed to sense this. He glided into his next sentence like a bird changing direction mid-flight.

'We have a game you might like to play.'

'A game...?'

You should not trust them. But his curiosity was piqued. Besides, he had a six foot cleaver strapped to his back made of a near indestructible metal; he could make them into spare parts for Fred without really having to think about it.

'The *Ultimate* Game.'

The one-handed man had stepped forward, into the sphere of Dr Monaghan's reach. The doctor didn't retreat or lash out, but let him remain there. He was shaking all over. Had the one-handed man read his mind? He'd thought only the Prince was capable of that.

Or was he too, a zealot, a believer?

Because there was one magic science could never destroy.

'The game is unplayable. It cannot be begun. The pieces are too many.'

'The pieces have already fallen into place.'

Another revelation, one which set his spine alight.

'How so?'

'The Prince, the great beast, is ready to be hunted.'

Briefly, a vision of him standing beneath the sloped pyramid's flank, hearing the words roared from the pulpit-like balcony, feeling the energy of all living matter ejaculate into his bloodstream, a high unlike any drug.

But then the vision was gone. The Prince had left him. It'd been so long since he'd heard his voice in his head. The Ark, what had been the point of it? It accomplished nothing.

But the stocks of amberfire in the pyramid's peak. The one's he'd been forced to give to the witch. Yes. Those could be taken back. And the silvenom poison; he was so close of finding a way to harness it as a liquid as opposed to a gas, to imbue his weapon with its deadly touch. Yes.

'He is weak?'

The one-handed man nodded.

'He is alone?'

The one-handed man nodded again.

Dr Monaghan began to laugh, the sound turned into the churning of a machine by the metallic grill of the mask.

'Then he is *ours.*'

———

THE STRANGE CONVERSATION didn't flow right, like a melody played at the wrong tempo. There were two voices, but she was sure there was a third man.

She crouched in the bend of a mining shaft, hugging the wall and glad, for once, of the dreadful and long shadows created by the eerie candlelight.

She was in more danger than she had ever been. Fay's warning rang in her head; it was the most powerful of ironies. Just when she needed the Need, it would not come. Still, she was glad it had been banished, removed, she wasn't sure what yet. She could not feel the painful stabs, like she'd swallowed a spiked shell, poison tipped, in her belly anymore. But when you grew so used to something it's absence became discomforting.

The voices stopped. She waited for them to resume but they didn't. Footsteps sounded on the stone. She unconsciously squashed herself closer to the wall. The shaft in which she hid led down, deeper into the mines, and the footsteps seemed to be going the other direction.

She put her ear to the rock and closed her eyes. The sounds were indistinct, as though further away for a moment, and then the footsteps rang clear as though someone was approaching her from behind. The closeness startled her and she took her ear away. Quiet again and growing faint. She replaced her ear and listened, counted. Definitely three. And the third, softer than the rest, as though with less weight.

Yin.

Both fear and anger surfaced, like two serpents rearing to bite at each other. She swallowed something which tasted vomit-like even though she hadn't eaten in days (and hadn't needed to). Thirst suddenly fell on her, like the oppressive weight of a thundercloud.

She forced herself to concentrate. The footsteps were barely audible, even with her ear to the wall. *Time to move.* She stood. Dizziness robbed her muscles of stability and she had to place a hand on the wall to steady herself, head feeling like it'd been dunked in formaldehyde. She took a couple of steps, like a blindwoman, hand propping her up. What was that old riddle: *what walks on four legs in the morning, two legs in the middle, and three legs in the evening?* It was as though she'd skipped straight to evening in a few moments.

Warmth between her legs. The dizziness had taken her away from it, but now she realised it. She looked down, expecting yellowing urine stains between her legs (although clueless as to what would have caused her to suddenly lose control). Instead, there was a red patch like a bullet wound.

She gasped. Pawed at the denim and looked at the blue-dark blood. Rubbed it between her finger tips. Smelt it like a wolf.

She swallowed.

Ever since the Need had first taken her over as a girl, she'd stopped bleeding. *No more periods for you Hagga* – what she imagined it whispered to her with a voice like an undead jackal. *No more eggs.* It'd meant she could fuck like a donkey all year round. No risk of children. Made the guys she was with even hornier. There'd been a desperate moment in her life when she'd thought that maybe if enough of them came into her she'd *start* bleeding again. But no. So long as the Need was inside, she remained barren and eternally 'on'.

Until now.

Summoning herself, with a back straighter and prouder than any soldier's, she began to walk down the shaft. The haze was slipping away, as was the pain. Bloody jeans were the least of anyone's worries now.

She got to the door from which she'd heard the voices and peered in. A singular beam of light, like a violent brush-stroke designed to wreck an otherwise perfect canvas painting. It illuminated the glittering edges of a cage – it looked holographic and unreal, immersed in so much darkness.

The Need could see in the dark; rather, it saw only in black, white and red, and therefore, the dark no longer held any obscurity to it. Hagga was less fortunate. She had heard them leave, but a warning remained in her consciousness, like the glimmer of a lighthouse, telling her that something waited in this dark and would seize upon her if she rashly stepped in.

But there was no other choice. That cage was where Larri must be being held. She could not see him, but she suspected that was because he was lying down, right where the darkness pooled thickest and deepest.

She crept within. Her foot brushed something warm and liquid. She withdrew it hastily, catlike, but realised it was only the heated wax of a recently extinguished candle: nothing untoward...

The cage seemed to gather the shadows to it. The beam of light coming from the exploded opening in the 'ceiling' did not touch it directly. She was right up within touching distance of the bars before she saw anything at all.

A foot.

There was no skin.

'Larri?'

Hagga had never watched a horror movie. She came from a world without electricity and in which there was enough of real horror to render the concept of watching it for pleasure masochistic. She had lived her own horror movie, of a sort. Of all the things she had experienced, one thing stood out in her mind, transcendent of the rest. The sound which had come from the lips of the one they called Blood Mare.

The sound of his skull cracking, like brittle plastic. The sound of his brain pulping beneath the impact, spilling hungrily to the desert floor. Neither were anything next to the whistling groan which came from his lips *after* she had struck the killing blow. A sound of a body without mind or soul struggling to retain life. The sound, though she did not have this word in her vocabulary, of a zombie.

That was what she heard now, and she recoiled from it.

Biting her lips, she forced herself to return to the bar.

The foot moved: the heel slid back, the toes pointed down.

Someone (or *something*, her brain could not help but add) was getting up.

The darkness swelled, created an impression, and then withdrew.

'Oh god,' she said. 'Oh god, Larri.'

They called Larri the cripple. But now he might also be called deformed. There was nothing left of his face save the eyes and the bony protrusion of a nose, no hair, lips barely more than cracked flesh framing bleach-white teeth. Veins pulsed beneath a grimy, semi-liquid fascia. He had no eyelids.

'Hagga?'

The hope in his voice made looking at him even worse.

'Yes,' she said. 'Yes. I'm here.'

'You're bleeding...' he said.

And then, for the first time in twenty or more years, Hagga felt scalding heat at her eyes, liquid on her cheeks.

'I'm fine.'

She reached through the bars, stretching her fingers. For a moment, he remained hesitant, then, with excruciating slowness, he clasped her hands. To her surprise, the feeling beneath her palm was one of dryness, like coal-ash. He winced, the muscles unnaturally-visible on his face.

'Does that hurt?'

'Not enough to make me want to stop,' he said.

For a few seconds, seconds which felt like years, they held one another like this.

'I need to get you out of here,' she said.

'The fire. Amberfire, I think he called it. It'll melt right through these bars. He never let it touch them, never let me get anywhere near it.'

Hagga searched around the room, eventually she came back with a vial of orange liquid.

'That's the one,' Larri said, and he almost sounded like his old self. His visage made it impossible to think of him that way. Hagga choked. He was a ruin of a man. He'd been a cripple before and now he was beneath even that. *A wretch.*

And it was because of her. Recklessness. Pride. The Need had driven her to take on Yin without thinking about anyone else.

Hagga knelt.

'Larri, I...I would have come sooner...' What was she saying? Couldn't she own up to it? Say what she really meant?

'Don't you dare apologise.' He took a pause to breathe. 'You tried to save me, fighting Yin. When he... I thought you were gone. I thought you were dead. *I'm* the one who should be sorry.' She saw the heaving movements of his chest, the way his head was jerking forward as though in the throes of a minor seizure, and realised he was trying, but had no capacity with which to emit tears. 'I ran. I left you behind. I ran. But you...'

She reached through the bars and put a finger on his lips. He fell quiet at once, though the silent, tearless crying continued.

'We both blame ourselves. And when you're out of here, we'll talk more.'

She unstopped the vial and poured it along the cage. It began to hiss, twist, warp and melt; with a shudder she realised the extent to which Larri had been damaged if amberfire could do this to metal.

Larri rocked forward, onto all fours, then stood. Though he seemed unsteady, he did not need assistance to stand. *In the morning of its life... In the middle... In the evening...*

'I know it looks bad,' he said, thickly. 'But, I'm not sure it is. After a while, the amberfire didn't seem to be hurting me as much anymore. Of course, I kept up the act. Screamed.' He straightened, almost as tall as Hagga. She realised his legs looked more muscular and shaped than they had ever done. 'But it was almost like once I passed through the baptism, the rest was *building* me somehow.'

He swiped and the slagging framework of the cage collapsed. He stepped out, red-garbed, looking, for an eerie moment, like the Prince had when they'd first seen him emerge from the throng, proclaiming that they must make a journey back to the world of the living.

Hagga forced herself not to take a step back from him.

Tenderly, he reached out, as though not to startle her. He put his hands on her arms.

'Can you love me like this?'

Hagga grinned.

'If you can love a fucked-up wolf.' She kissed his lips; they tasted of meat, which she liked. 'Then I can love a fucked-up man.'

———

A SHAWL of seaweed around his shoulders, he looked like the Ancient Mariner, trawled up from some unplumbable depths. He sat with his legs against his chest, looking out over the black ocean, fearing and disdaining it. Driftwood was continually washing up on the shore, the bones of a once proud creature discarded by a monstrous predator.

'The tower,' he said, through chattering teeth. 'The tower.'

Two of three cards had come true. The third and final was the Devil Reversed.

'It means breaking free,' Fay had said, as she pushed the card towards him. 'The Devil is control, bondage, slavery. Upside down, each card means its opposite. Many people would desire this card in their reading.'

And once upon a time, when he had lived in a coastal town in England and drunk Carling and smoked cigarettes and lived as travellers had lived for millennia, he would have desired nothing more. Freedom seemed to be his meaning in life; his definition.

Now, he wasn't so sure he wanted to be free.

Maybe, he just wanted to be happy.

'Cris,' he said. He thought of his friend, the eyes which never ceased to burn with warm hearth-fire, the kind of fire which invited you to stay after walking on a long winter's night. His energy, belying the gut which hung over his belt. The laugh which came so suddenly, like a violent wind, and caught everyone around him up in it. He'd give anything to see him, to sit with him, to share one more story, even if it was one he'd told him a thousand times.

He wept on the black sand, as the tide shushed him, like a mother might shush a child. Only, Pike's mother had never shushed him when he cried as a boy, kind though she was. A matter of fact lady who did not understand the depths of people.

'Where are you Cris?' He looked to the sky, which offered only a growl of thunder (that reminded him more of his father). Fay had told him this place was not hell. Yet she'd drawn a card with a devil on its out of her pack, and the Prince, the one person she felt might understand him, had been claimed by some kind of leviathanic thing formed from nightmares. He still wasn't sure what he saw.

Something was bobbing in the driftwood. It looked like it might be a cluster of planks roped together with seaweed. He peered closer. No, it was a person. Someone was being brought in by the tide.

His eyes widened.

It couldn't be.

———

MICHAEL BANNER PULLED himself from the black slush of the wet sand; a kind of primordial emulsion, he thought, and stood. He felt none of the surging energies the last time he had emerged from the dark waters. In fact, he felt … *old.* Not in the way he felt like the knowledge of the universe, of all time, had been inseminated into his consciousness. Not in the way he sometimes felt when he unleashed the eye – like he had been made before even the world was made. No. He felt mortally old. And frail. It was disturbing.

He staggered up the shingle-less sandbank and met with concrete.

'The Prince! The Prince has returned!'

He watched the herald run off into the city, shouting over and over again. People appeared at the windows, their yellow eyes like corroded gemstones. For the first time he sensed that there was little fear behind those eyes. Again, disturbing.

There was a tramp wrapped in seaweed on the beach. He looked like he had been made by the old Greek sea god Poseidon. There were two other city-dwellers on the street. They watched the Prince with the idle curiosity of children. One, a woman with proud arms folded (her fore-arms were massive with muscle) pursued her lips and said:

'Where's your Ark?'

He snarled at her.

'At the bottom of the ocean,' he spat.

She snorted and turned her back on him; went into the building behind. The other, a man, continued to watch him.

What is happening?

He felt as though some fulcrum had turned, the stars suddenly against him, or rather, the city itself malignantly opposed to him. Distantly, out of the past, words came to him. They were the words Yin had spoken to him when he first slunk out of the dark waters to claim the city.

I will give you the choice to go back into the darkness, if you so wish. That might be better for you.

He'd laughed at the dwarf then. Now, the words rang true.

'Send word to the pyramid I have returned,' the Prince barked at the bystanding city dweller. He didn't move.

Another shout. A different herald.

'The Three are coming!'

The eyes at the windows grew more numerous, as though colonies of nightcrawling creatures bred like insects within the ancient skyscrapers. People were filling up the avenues, their dark bodies looking no more substantial than shadows.

The Prince growled.

'What the fuck are you all looking at?'

Ahead, emerging from the distance like a desert mirage, were three shapes. One, he knew instantly. The dwarfish silhouette could only be Yin. Light refracted off another's face – the metal mask which belonged to Dr Monaghan.

But who was the third?

Closing his natural eye, and unshackling his other, the Prince sent his gaze forward. Like a miniature cyclone is swept through the grey-monochrome until it hovered face to face with his adversary. A name surfaced, like a submerged chest bobbing up to the top of the water.

Jack Orton. The Taking Man.

A vision of green fire curling; the Ark disintegrating. Pike lying at his feet, beaten half to death. A flash of silver and his hand spinning off into the darkness. And then, most vividly of all, a little boy in the woods slitting the throat of his beloved dog.

Both natural and unnatural eye widened.

This is my enemy. The strength of the thought made the Prince stop walking, his bones began to vibrate with carnal energy, as though, like an earth-titan, he drew strength from the ground beneath him. *And I made him.*

The deformed flesh seemed a mockery of all human beauty, and the Prince hated it, hated it more strongly even than he had hated the girl Lucy, back in the winters of dead New York. She had defied him, mocked him, made a shambles of centuries of work. A girl, a waif. He had seen her in the dreams and the dreams always told him who to kill. But Brian Mor had failed. His once-friend had let her live, to the ruin of all.

Thinking of her brought a scream to his throat, like a blood-hungry were-creature. But then, something happened which paralysed him.

The Taking Man looked *at* the hovering eye, reached out with a hand made out of the substance of wormholes, and grasped it.

'Peekaboo,' he said, and hurled the eye to the ground where it shattered like a glass phylactery. The Prince reeled as though struck. *Impossible! How? How?*

The eye was invisible and saw into the invisible. How could he see it in return?

He blinked, breathed. The eye was still there in his socket, a suspended darkness. Though, he sensed, with the intuitive part of himself that always made decisions, it was shaken.

He had never backed down from any fight (he knew one was coming), not as long as he'd lived, but now, for the briefest flicker, he considered it.

'No.' He turned and regarded the onlookers. 'I will not be cowed. *I AM THE PRINCE.*' But for the first time those words didn't sit right in his mouth, they slapped hollowly against the walls. Meaning nothing.

He shivered.

At last Yin, Dr Monaghan and Jack Orton stood before him.

'I hope, for your sake,' the Prince said, looking at Dr Monaghan and Yin, 'that you are bringing me this wretch as a prisoner.'

They said nothing.

'It's over,' the Taking Man said. 'The pyramid and this city are ours now. You have failed to succeed in your mission, reneged on your promise to the *people.*' His grin was revolting, like watching a wound being slowly pulled wider. 'Bow to us, and we might just spare you.'

The Prince laughed; a cutting sound.

'You think I can't see through that lie? I can see your soul, *Jack,* and I'll be damned if it isn't blacker than mine!'

Jack Orton grinned.

'If it is, you made it so. You think you see everything. But you're blind. Don't you get it? You're not going to win this fight. The city is against you.'

Those words caused a ripple of nausea to creep up into the Prince's throat. He thought, distantly, he could hear the sound of hornets. Or was it static? The crowds were gathering, like wasps to the body of their fallen kin.

For the second time, the Prince considered running. As the thought manifested itself, he thought he heard Fay too. Urging him. *Go. My love. Go.*

Love?

He gritted his teeth, drew his fists into shaking hammers of gathered power. Began to stride towards them. Traitors. Traitors all. First Brian Mor. Now Yin and the doctor. No one was loyal to him. Dogs.

'Dogs!' he screamed.

With a flash Dr Monaghan had drawn his immense cleaver and swung, his strength superhuman. The green and black blade swept through the air like an incision in the universe, momentarily glimpsed. The Prince barely ducked it, came in smashing his fist into the Japanese war-mask with all his might. It crumpled, dented. He felt bones in his hand shatter. Dr Monaghan screamed and toppled, his blade flying.

The Prince reeled, Yin was writhing, twisting, becoming a shape like an upright wolf.

A hand grabbed him from behind. He turned and lashed out with a back-fist, sending the Taking Man crashing to the ground in an explosion of blood: one of the tumour sacks had split and spilled clear liquid.

Then teeth; agony.

The Prince screamed as the nine-inch nail fangs burst through the flesh and muscle of his shoulder. At least one of the teeth had transfixed a bone. He writhed, the eyes of the wolf so close to his he felt he might momentarily cross into them.

He grappled with its bear-thick neck, its fur sharp as procupine needles, cutting his hands. A massive paw struck him in the kidney and he crumpled to one knee.

He grabbed the wolf's snout and began to squeeze. It yelped, squealed.

'Down you fucking dog!'

He readjusted his grip and smashed the wolf's snout down onto his knee; tearing a chunk from his own shoulder as he did so. Blood spurted onto the pavement. It was nothing the Prince had not seen before. The wolf, Yin, squealed and leapt back.

A singing noise. He threw himself down, the blade scraping along his leather jacket. Dr Monaghan stood over him, his coat covered in bloodstains that looked like pagan runes. His mask was semi-concave, and the eyes behind it were so white they looked like granules of cocaine.

'It ends!' he screamed, bringing the blade down like an executioner's axe.

The Prince rolled. The blade crashed through concrete, embedding itself in the earth like Arthur's sword in the stone.

He scrambled to his feet.

The Taking Man had acquired a six feet metal pole. Its end glowed, like the tip of a volcano.

'Still a fucking coward,' the Prince said, grinning. 'Still a boy in the woods.'

The Taking Man jabbed. Once. Twice. Each time the Prince edged just the right distance back. The third lunge the Prince sidestepped and grabbed the pole. To his surprise, the Taking Man let it go, leapt forward and placed his blackened hand on the Prince's forehead.

The eye immediately exploded from its socket, blackness rushing out like a dire crow, and as it did so, an answering green light erupted from the Taking Man, serpentine. The two met. There was a cataclysmic hush – the ground became translucent and gridded, like a blueprint.

Each was drawn into the other. The Prince found himself lost in seas of disturbing green rays and white noise. The Taking Man found himself in a darkness filled with the voices of his past, hounding him, like bloody mouthed dogs. Understanding flowered between them, but never empathy. And this understanding only meant that each became more set on destroying the other.

Like a sculpture, they had become frozen, a battle taking place on a plane none of the others could ever reach. They began to quiver together, almost like lovers, the light between them melding and separating, melding and separating, and with it the dichromatic sky changing: alternating between aurora and thunder.

'Nekyia!' The Taking Man screamed.

The Prince flinched, the eye wavered. He tumbled back, smoke billowing from the empty socket.

Behind him, Yin changed into a many limbed octopus. He enveloped the Prince, wrapping his tendrils around arms, legs, neck and torso. The Prince struggled, but something had been drained out of him, and the shape still held terror for him because of the guardian which had destroyed the Ark. His fingers lost their grip. He was a climber who had scaled half a cliff-face only to discover they no longer had the strength to go on.

He choked, spluttered. Blood dribbled from his mouth.

Yin held him.

Dr Monaghan stood, drawing his blade from the concrete. The Taking Man grabbed his magma-tipped spear.

'So,' he said, 'Here we are...'

'Show me what you've got,' the Prince said.

———

AND THEY DID.

Dr Monaghan began the proceedings. Smashing his fist again and again into the Prince's chest until he felt his ribs crack and bend inwards. A lung was punctured, he coughed a nugget of gore and spat it out into Dr Monaghan's face.

The doctor forced it through the grill of his mask, chewed it, made an *hmmmm* noise, and continued his work. He began using a ridge hand technique, hitting the sternum again and again until the Prince thought the bones of it would unlink themselves and fall apart.

The blows then varied. A strike into the side of his neck snapped the other collar bone. A blow to his stomach made him vomit, though all that came out was blood and water. A blow to his natural eye's socket made the skull fracture and blood wept from his tearducts.

At some point he realised: this was only the beginning.

———

PIKE WATCHED with horror as the Prince was beaten.

First, Dr Monaghan lay into him with his fists, punching with such ferocity it seemed he intended to pulp the Prince's insides into sludge. He heard ribs crack audibly. Blood poured from the Prince's shoulder and mouth. Teeth littered the ground around them like discarded dice.

With each blow, Pike flinched. He knew what it was like to take such a beating at the hands of a monster.

Slowly, he crept around the back of the spectacle. If he took them by surprise, he had a chance of rescuing the Prince.

As he did so, he sensed something, a tickling at the back of his neck. He touched it but there was nothing there. Then he heard him.

Leave me.

Pike swallowed and look at the Prince's face. He was looking directly at him, half slumped in Yin's chain-like tentacles, the face broken and distorted, eye weeping blood.

Leave me. They'll kill you.

No, he thought, hoping the Prince could hear him.

He didn't respond. Dr Monaghan stepped back. The Taking Man came forward.

'Strip him,' he said.

Pike tried to watch. His lips curled back to reveal his semi-rotten teeth. He clenched his fists. It did not good. He had to turn away.

Because when they removed his clothes, there was just a hollow ruin of a body. All the magic and enigma was gone. The Prince was just a mortal man with bones protruding through his flesh, unwashed skin, and ugly scrotal sack. His penis was shrivelled and unremarkable.

'Doctor, if you would commence the operation,' the Taking Man said.

'Gladly,' Dr Monaghan said, pulling a knife from the folds of his labcoat.

Go, he heard the voice again. *I am lost. I am lost. Go.*

Pike fled.

———

DR MONAGHAN WAS breathless as he approached the shamed Prince. His face stung, or rather, it ached as though it'd been smashed in with a baseball bat. *Such strength,* and yet it still had not been enough to save the prophet.

'Pity,' he tutted, bending so that his head was level with the Prince's cock. He considered the veiny, wrinkled worm of a thing for a moment. He imagined whether he could get it hard if he sucked it or stroked it. He shrugged. Pussy was far more intriguing. Mysterious. What happened when you cut off the little bump just above the slit?

Far more interesting than what was about to happen. Everyone knew what happened when you cut off a cock.

With one swift slice he took it off, balls and staff.

The Prince let out a scream that would have stopped the heart of a sane man. He screamed so loud Dr Monaghan wondered if the dark ones who had given the one-handed man his gift could hear him, below, in their kingdom.

He caught the dropping sack in his hands, turned and raised it up above his head for the crowd to see.

Then he turned and threw it into the Prince's face.

'I expected more,' he said.

Blood dripped from between the Prince's legs, like a fruit being squeezed of liquid.

The Taking Man stepped forward.

'Now time for the main event.'

He raised the hot-iron spear. Yin forced the Prince to his knees.

'Anything to say?'

The Prince opened his mouth, choked, spat blood, swallowed, opened his mouth again.

'Go fuck yourself.'

'Apt,' the Taking Man said.

He drove the spear into the Prince's natural eye.

And this time he screamed even louder.

———

PAIN LIKE NO OTHER. The pain of a universe collapsing. There was flame and then darkness. The world closed, winking out in an instant. The dark eye unfurled vistas to him but without the corresponding reality, it made everything no more sensical than a dream sequence.

Not even death had hurt this much.

He heard them, through the convulsions of pain like seismic quakes in his body.

'Now for the other.'

Fear flooded him, filled him up to the mouth. A taste like ash, snow.

'No!'

It wasn't possible. They couldn't destroy that eye. Surely? It was the one thing which set him above, the source of all his strength.

And it was not enough to save you from him.

'No!' he screamed again.

But then the red-hot blade pierced the darkness. For a moment he had a dream of foam blossoming into sculptures of serene decay, like ice-statues; mould creeping along a loaf of bread, disintegrating it, then the foam being set alight, shrivelled into blackness and ash. He felt a sensation like something sucked at the back of his head, a vacuum. He did not scream, but felt his skeleton being pulled from his body and sputtered jabbering, incoherent sentences.

'Lucy... in the blizzard... Lucy... in the sky...'

A wrench. An anchor heaved up from unknowable depths, dragging with it a tangle of messy life, the roots of something. Darkness became absolute and no longer filled with anything: no voices, no dreams, no memories. Even thoughts seemed remote, like petals falling on the abyssal waters of a well.

'...with diamonds.'

The dark eye shut forever.

ACT IV: THE FIFTH HORSEMAN

Chapter 20

The Taking stood back, smiling the smile of a necromantic creature. He turned to the crowd.

'Your Prince is no more!'

Yin released the Prince. He toppled to the ground, a broken doll. Blood spread from him like a two-dimensional flower. Dr Monaghan bowed his head in mock reverence.

'Slaves! His flesh is yours!'

But the Slaves did not answer the Taking Man. He pulled back his thick, black lips to reveal horse-teeth.

'Consume him. Not a trace must be left to assimilate. You know the city.'

'There's bad meat,' one of the crowd called – was it from a window or the shadows of an alley? 'Ain't none of us gunna touch it.'

The Taking Man's fist became so tight around the spear that it seemed like it might shatter it. Then he relaxed. He turned back and looked at the decimated body of his enemy. Dr Monaghan was pissing on it.

He laughed.

It's over. He's dead. The city will claim him but who cares? What can he do as an aimless spirit? Nothing.

'You now have three Kings!' Yin declared, feeling himself grow, expand. *The old power is returning. It was the Prince who kept it down all along.*

'And our first command is...' Dr Monaghan raised a hand. 'RUN!'

They set on the city-dwellers like bloodhounds on a fox.

Yin birthed his virus.

And then the people set on each other.

———

A PROSTITUTE FUCKING a woman doggy-style bent down and grabbed her throat: he slit it with his fingernail in one swift motion, then continued to fuck the corpse.

Another prostitute brained him with a lump of rubble.

Two lovers began to argue and one went for a knife.

Someone cast themselves from the peak of a skyscraper, making a red ghost on the street below.

Within minutes the quiet of the city crumbled into the sounds of a trench war turned massacre. Yin's tendrils spread, like unearthly music, haunting the streets, possessing people with visions of malignant faces and steely teeth; whatever frightened them most.

'A god again!'

Yin laughed and laughed, as, like Turner's ghost, he swept through the mortar of the city, spreading and spreading and spreading.

A group of women stormed the prostitute's camp (with their ORGASM GUARANTEED banners), stoning the sex-workers to twitching heaps. They stripped the bodies and ran wild with the tears of cloth through the street, shrieking like banshees. They ran too far and met a man in a labcoat and a Japanese war-menpo; he blocked their passage.

Cut them into body parts with his blade, scooped the remnants into a bag of viscera, and dragged them along with him like a demented Santa Claus dragging his present-sack, leaving a bloody rivulet behind.

———

HAGGA AND LARRI clambered up the last few steps of the subway and emerged into the half-light of the city. Chaos had taken hold. Green silvenom flame sprouted from windows. People were running senseless, sometimes seizing on the companions with which they ran and beating them to bloody messes. *For what reason?*

The air was smog-thick and Hagga mistrusted it. She tore off a strip of her shirt and wrapped it around her mouth like a bandit's snood. She repeated the process for Larri.

'It's him,' he said, as she wrapped it around his broken mouth. 'Yin.'

'But the Prince? Wouldn't he stop him?'

'Maybe Yin got tired of following orders?'

Or maybe something happened to the Prince, Hagga thought. She wasn't sure why that thought filled her with dread, but it did. However evil the Prince may or may not have been (even now she wasn't certain), the death of something great makes the heart ache.

And as the madness of the city unfolded around them like a twisted child's cootie catcher, she grew to believe that he must be dead. It was the only thing that could fully explain *this*.

'Come on,' Larri said, 'We can't stay.'

He began to limp towards an alleyway, dragging her with him. He was worse than his speech had made out. She would have to protect him.

How?

———

PIKE RAN AS THOUGH from his worst fear incarnate; his eyes white like slaver.

Go, he'd said, he'd commanded. But Pike was not the kind of person to go. He was the Last Knight; wasn't that what the Prince called him? With his grand eloquence he'd make Pike feel like the last honourable human being alive. Why was he running now?

Because trying to save him was pointless. They'd have killed you and him.

Coward.

Was it the word he ran from or did the word allow him *to* run? He didn't know. In all his life he'd never backed down from a fight, no matter the odds.

You're not afraid. You're doing the right thing.

Perhaps they wouldn't be able to finish the job and Pike could come back later? Perhaps he could avenge the Prince? Picking off the Three Kings one by one like some hero in a corny action flick.

Coward.

He'd never backed down from a fight. Not in his entire life. He wasn't afraid. Only. Only... He remembered a rain of grubby, dirt-black knuckles, a sloughing face, laughter. He'd never been beat like that before. And deep down beneath all the rational reasons he threw up, Pike knew *that* was the reason he was running. He'd lost his nerve.

A scream, so loud, so chilling, it could only mean one thing.

He stopped in an alley, doubled over, and vomited what looked like tadpoles.

The Devil Reversed.

Perhaps Fay had gotten it wrong. It wasn't anything as abstract as breaking out of bondage. It was that the Devil, the Prince, with his Machiavellian charm and crazed dreams (the word 'Miltonic' sprung into his head like a newly formed god) would be overturned. With all his reading, Pike could not articulate why he felt this was profoundly wrong; as though something good had been undone.

'It's over,' he said, and wasn't sure what he meant by it.

Distantly, he could hear the sound of the city tearing itself apart.

He breathed, hands on knees. He knew he had to get moving. Things were about to turn ugly. The impulse to flee had left him, however, replaced by listlessness.

He straightened and began to jog down an alleyway. Sounds of conflict came from its end, so he turned and doubled back, broke out onto a main road and began to run towards the pyramid. Across the highway two women were clubbing a man wearing nothing but an overcoat to death.

Smashed glass – a shriek equally as bone-jarring – and something splattered on the pavement feet in front of him. Pike looked up, someone was leaning out of the window six or seven floors up, staring down at what they'd done.

The city has lost its mind.

Crimson grass stems sprouted from the mulched corpse. *Assimilation,* he thought. The sensation he'd forgotten something, something dreadfully important, came over him like a dizzy spell. Something was trying to connect at the back of his mind. It couldn't. Not yet, anyway. He let it be.

He leapt over the grass and ran on.

Three men appeared from a sidestreet, carrying bloodstained crowbars. They had moonsick eyes. They made for Pike. He sprinted across the highway and leapt a trashcan. In the alleyway beyond a couple were tearing at each other like worst enemies.

He had expected collapse, but not this quickly and not on this scale. Something was happening.

The Magician.

It had to be. He was the only one of the three who could influence so many people. But how? He barged past the couple, who spat after him and then continued to assault each other.

He glanced over his shoulder. The three men still followed, moving like orcas on a chase. They stopped when they reached the couple. As Pike turned to look ahead again, he heard the sound of metal on skin, a splash of liquid, and then the patter of footsteps.

He rounded a corner. A man stood, holding a flaming brand of silvenom wood. His belly hung three feet below the line of his belt; pale like fish-meat, covered with pubic-looking hair. His face was lost in beard.

'It's all going to burn!'

He held the fire so close to his eyes Pike wondered whether he'd blinded himself.

The torchbearer looked straight at him, lifted the brand of green fire.

Pike threw all his weight into a bull-tackle. The torchbearer went catherine-wheeling backward and finally toppled, brought down by his own immense bulk.

Pike stood, hazily, aware with the heightened consciousness of a drug-user of the footsteps in the alley.

He sprinted, ducked right into another alley and crouched behind some detritus: old pipes, girders, slagged rubble.

He breathed once heavy, then again, smooth as silk.

Waiting, his knees began to give way. He was good at stealthy. More than once he'd resorted to stealing to keep living, not that he ever mentioned that to Cris much. Cris had been very straightforward in his moral views: black and white, right and wrong. Pike had always thought he was naive. Now, he wasn't so sure. He felt like he was in the midst of something that might well be as clearly defined. Determining which side was the right one; that was the difficult bit.

The footsteps approached. Half-solid shadows cast into the alley in which he crouched.

He moved back, farther into the darkness of the alley.

Coldness in his heart, like a window had been opened on his soul, and outside, winter marched dauntless and eternal. His foot touched a wall. A dead end.

The three men entered the alley. Perhaps they'd heard him scurry back? Perhaps they'd acted on a hunch, the kind of preternatural instinct predators always seemed to possess.

Pike scrambled in the dark for a weapon and found one against all expectation. A thick wooden pole rested against the wall of the alley. His fingers brushed it. The first thing he realised was that this wasn't made of silvenom. It was red oak. He'd know the feel anywhere. He stood, still concealed, though not for much longer. He grabbed the staff.

Like driftwood brought in from a tide: memories. The smell of chrysanthemums, unwavering sunlight, mountain air, siang pure, sweat. He remembered the temple more vividly than he remembered his own mother. The monks out on the hillocks day after day, earlier than the first rays, training to fight *tang shou tao*. The favoured weapon of the shifu had been a staff, which he pretended was a walking-aid; in reality he could stand on one bent leg from dawn till dusk.

That temple in China had been the one place the Tarmac King had ever considered staying.

He couldn't. Pride, wanderlust and too many other things got in the way. 'A restless soul', the shifu had said, quaffing wine in a way that was irreconcilable with all the movie kung fu masters Pike had seen. 'I see you will not be schooled by *anyone*. But...' He leant forward, face a musk of training oil, biting tea, and the wine. 'I'll share one thing with you. A traveller's gift, if you can accept it.' He smiled, the smallest of gestures. '*There is no room for death in the heart of the shaolin master.* What do you think it means?'

Had Pike ever answered him? Had he even spoken? He couldn't remember. All he remembered was that he'd never understood it.

But now he thought he did.

He grabbed the staff, surer and surer it was a totem to the world he'd given up in the name of a friend. He leapt from the shade and in front of the three crowbar-wielding lunatics.

No words exchanged. They looked beyond speech and far beyond thought.

They set on him like automatons.

He swept the staff in an arch, catching the leftmost assailant on the temple and knocking him down. The other two were staggered by the swing but not harmed. They growled and lunged again. Pike dodged, struck out, using the staff more like a two-handed greatsword. The monks, no doubt, would have called it barbaric.

The wood connected with his aggressor's face and split it. He half-completed a somersault, landed crumpled and upside down against the wall. The third got a punch through, a graze, on Pike's chin. As he went back he threw out his leg so he formed a fencer's lunging stance.

'*Blood for...*'

Pike jabbed the tip of the staff with his left hand, aiming it with his right which he'd formed like a tube, the motion of a snooker-player potting the black. His aim was perfect, breaking in the thug's teeth with a semi-musical tinkle and driving into the back of his mouth, making him choke.

The thug swung, blindly and stupidly, hitting air, fell to his knees, grabbed his throat.

He looked into Pike's eyes.

'Wrong turn, 'fella,' Pike said, and left him choking.

As he emerged from the alley he was bowled over and slammed against the wall. The shape had moved so fast he hadn't seen any details of his attacker. His head smacked back against the concrete of a building and he almost let go of his staff.

Dazed, he slid down the wall, despite his best efforts to prop himself up with his weapon.

'Hagga, wait!'

Pike blinked. Given the injury in his head and his perspective, the woman, Hagga, seemed gigantic. *Not a giant, but she's almost taller than you.*

Next to her, a man appeared. He had no skin.

'Jesus,' Pike said.

Both were wearing rags of cloth around their mouths. A gang identification, perhaps?

'What do you want?' he asked, still fuzzy, though things were starting to sharpen again. He tried to tighten his grip on the staff without them noticing.

'How come he's not like the others?' the woman, Hagga, said.

'Not sure. Let's ask him.'

'We don't have time.'

The skinless man, Larri, knelt.

'Why haven't you lost your mind?'

'I see a therapist.'

With his recent triumph, some of his old stubbornness was coming back to. He fully closed his grip on the staff. *Come a little closer you fucker.*

'The air you're breathing is poisoned. You've got no cover.'

'Beats me.'

'I -'

Larri's eyes glanced at the staff. He threw himself back just as Pike swung it.

In a second, Pike was on his feet and throwing forward his staff horizontally to butt away the woman.

But she didn't charge as expected, she dodged to the left, swept out her legs and brought him toppling on his back. She jumped and planted her knees in his chest, driving the air out. The staff went flying.

The woman had bared her teeth, and for a brief moment, he

thought he saw a wolf's fangs inside her mouth; a wolf's eyes behind the hazel orbs.

'See, you never needed the Need,' Larri said to the woman, rising. Closer, Pike saw he *did* have skin, but it'd been burned and disintegrated. *Amberfire?*

And then it clicked.

'You were tortured. By Dr Monaghan.'

Larri nodded.

Pike stopped struggling. He held out his hands in a gesture of surrender.

'We're on the same side.'

Hagga looked less than convinced.

'Let him go,' Larri said, the way an understanding sober-companion might. Her eyes were cauldrons, but she acquiesced, rising. Pike got up slowly and made no moves towards his weapon.

'I used to follow the Prince, but now he's dead, and the Three, they've taken over.'

'The Three?'

'Dr Monaghan, The Taking Man, The Magician: they've all come together to destroy the city.'

'That's who I must have heard,' she said, looking at Larri. 'In the mines.'

'They killed the Prince,' Pike said, and a part of him within trembled, as though somewhere someone had trodden on his grave. Of course, that was a very real possibility. 'Broke his eye. I don't know how...'

'Where do we go?' Hagga said. 'Nowhere's safe.'

Then something rushed into Pike's mind.

'Fay!'

They looked at him as though he had started speaking tongues.

'The woman in white,' he said. 'The fortune teller. We have to get to her. She was the Prince's lieutenant; she'll know what to do.'

Larri nodded.

'But first I think we have to pay a visit to *him*.'

Hagga raised an eyebrow.

'You think he'll know?'

'I'm sorry, who the fuck's him?' Pike said.

Hagga ignored him. Her attention was uniquely on Larri in a way that made Pike suspect they were intimate. If not physically (how could she be with someone as broken has him?): emotionally.

'It's worth a shot. We've nothing to lose.'

Hagga looked at Pike.

'I'll explain on the way.' She turned to go, then looked back at him. 'And you might want to take your staff.'

CHAPTER 21

Now he knew the meaning of the word magic.

Like guttural poetry, it animated his being. Faultless, his faulted body moved like a perfect killing machine. His spear was a dancer, and he, its partner. Droves fell. A green haze enveloped him, a nebula of warping agonies; in the cloud those he struck down saw reflections of their past, mirages, and always, felt stabs of pain like neurological syringes through the skull.

A man fled from him; he seemed slow as a beetle.

The Taking Man launched his spear and it impaled him right through. A forty-yard throw. The strangest thing was the Taking Man knew he *couldn't* have missed it.

He clicked his fingers and the burning-tipped weapon withdrew itself, cauterising the wound (reminding him, bitterly, of the moment he had lost his hand). It hovered back to him, gently lowering itself into his coal-black fingers.

The darkness was spreading across his whole body. He had shed his shirt, baring his deformities to all. It looked as though he'd dipped his arm into tar up to the bicep. Those who looked at the blackness long enough saw that no light lingered on it.

The Pit Arisen.

That's who he was now. Not the Taking Man. Not Jack Orton. The Pit given form.

A god.

In the distance he saw the pyramid lying like the discarded piece of some colossal puzzle. He knew what he wanted. The throne room.

As he looked at the pyramid, it seemed to change, warping like a mirage in heat. It rippled, as though only a reflection in a pool of water. And then he was flying towards it, drawn by an invisible and irresistible force. He reached it, hovering suspended. He saw now, emerging onto the balcony from which the Prince had once delivered his great sermon on the return to the world above, a figure.

The mind-flayer.

A gasp which became a choke.

Its flesh looked impossible under the skylight. Its robes were the stuff of tattered nightmares; a priest of some monstrous brotherhood assembled at the end of time against the end of all. Its eyes burned him.

Your part is done, Orton. You have delivered us the Prince. Now for our end of the bargain.

'I never made a bargain with you,' he growled. 'It was of my own volition.'

The flayer ignored him.

You have taken the life of one we desired dead. Now, we will take the life of one you desire dead. The eyes, drawing and repelling simultaneously. *You.*

'No!' But it rang with demonic truth. Even now, even with all this power, didn't he want the suffering to stop? 'I climbed from the Pit. I wanted to *survive.*'

The instinct for self preservation changes nothing. It is present in the suicidal, the depressed, the mad. It must be relinquished, of course, for them to achieve the end they desire. And so we give you a chance to relinquish it willingly. Come to us. Come to us and do not draw out the suffering.

And then he was standing in the street, drooling. Chaos around like the aftermath of a hurricane or an earthquake. People moved past him as though he was invisible, savaging one another.

The Taking Man shook himself.

Reality returned like sound crashing through an open door.

If they thought he would lie down now, after all the power he had attained, they were wrong. A grin split his face.

Time to find Dr Monaghan.

———

He whistled as he leapt up the last few steps of the pyramid, wiping his blade clean as though polishing a favourite household decoration. It'd been a wonderful day, with so much good work done. And the game was in full flow. It was about to get even better.

He stepped into the window and crossed the room. Watched his younger self pouring paint into a child's eyes idly for a few seconds (still whistling) and stepped through the door, entering the cylindrical spine of the pyramid.

He clambered onto the elevator and called to be let up.

Manfred, who had been half asleep and forgotten whose side anyone was on, obliged, pulling the lever and mumbling. He tucked himself back into his makeshift bed.

Dr Monaghan ascended, examining his sword.

'I ought to give you a name,' he thought, out loud. 'Every great blade needs a name.'

He thought for a few seconds as the platform clanked and groaned upwards.

'Bloodthirster? Bloodletter? Blooddrinker? Bonecleaver?' He sighed. 'All the good ones are gone.'

The elevator came chuntering to a halt.

He entered the throne room, considered killing Manfred (curled like a babe swaddled in blankets), decided it was beneath the mighty Foes-licer to take such a meagre life. Foeslicer. He liked that.

He looked around. One glance told him they were gone.

He swallowed.

Blinked, looked again.

Gone.

He tried to rub his eyes but the mask got in the way and he shrieked with rage.

Gone.

'FUCKING WITCH!'

Manfred started awake, panicked, stood. Saw Dr Monaghan drawing his blade and begin swinging it pointlessly round his head in a blind, berserk rage.

'FUCKING WITCH. YOU FUCKING TOOK IT. YOU FUCKING BITCH.'

The doctor wheeled, saw Manfred.

'She took it,' he demanded. 'She took it, didn't she?'

When all that left Manfred's lips was a mumble, Dr Monaghan leapt forward and cut him in half with a single blow.

He shrieked at the still-standing legs, shedding blood like a cherry blossom sheds petals in winter. He kicked them over where they did a kind of drunken dance and then went still. Manfred's mouth, on the other half of him, was wide open as though about to bite into an apple.

The witch. The witch had taken the amberfire.

How then, could the game be played and finished?

And the one-handed man. He would be disappointed. Dr Monaghan sensed his threat, his strength. He grit his teeth.

'I'm coming for you you fucking cunt. I'm coming.'

Before now he had not truly plumbed the depths of his imagination. But for her, oh yes, for her he would.

Leaving bloody footprints, he left the room, like a storm seeking new territory to rage over.

———

THE MADNESS of the city was muted here.

The gravestone-sculptures each seemed to emit whispers which hushed all other sound, a lullaby eternally sung just below the register of real understanding.

Pike glanced around nervously; he half expected something to jump out, like in some tacky horror movie. He followed Hagga and Larri, who seemed to know the way through the maze of statues and thorns. His staff tapped a metre which he found comforting.

'What's that?'

Hagga stopped. Larri, ahead a few paces, paused and turned. Pike slowed.

She was staring at one of the tombstones. There was a square of darkness in its centre. Pike blinked. It was a door. He hadn't noticed; the shadow was so impenetrable it looked solid, like a slab of black onyx.

'That wasn't here last time, was it?' she said. She took a step closer and Pike's heart squeezed. *Don't go near it. Don't trust anything in this place.* These thoughts were eclipsed by the light of a suddenly kindled desire to go through the door himself.

'No.' Larri stood by her side and also stared into its depths.

Pike followed their gaze and thought he could make out a sliver of silver light running horizontally, near the lip of the entrance. A stair?

That kindled desire grew brighter, became a beacon and floated before him, guiding him towards the opening like Macbeth's dagger towards the bed of the sleeping Duncan. Where did it lead? To somewhere far deeper and darker than Dr Monaghan's mines, that was sure. His heartbeat was loud in his ears, like a summoning drum. His foot edged forward without him willing it.

Mixed in with the desire, the pull, was an alchemy of fears, sprouting like erupted fungus, like the crimson stems from the body of the fallen man. He wanted to go down there; didn't want to go down there for anything. A reek wafted up, like breath from a long, dark throat. The same awful smell which clung to the Taking Man.

A smell of something so dreadful, it could never be confessed; a stumbled upon secret that ravages the mind. Pike saw, as though projected from the doorway, a montage of images from his life, all things he'd tried with all his might to forget. Bodies in Hyde Park torn by explosions; like so many gutted fish. Corpses in Shang Hai, lying half dissolved in the waters. Ugliness. A flaying whip on his brain forever.

A hand pulled him back and he allowed it to. He would not, could not, go down there. 'Come on,' Hagga said, shivering. Had she seen similar things?

Pike nodded and they went on.

Eventually they came to a ringed area in which a colossal statue sat, looming over them like a Pharaohic visage.

'We need your help,' Hagga said, to the statue.

Pike noted how he did not even question these things anymore. Maybe he'd lost it. Maybe all this was inside his head. Maybe after he'd collapsed in the prison cell from the tumour-pain he'd actually been taken to an asylum, and here he was, living out his miraculous delusions, wrapped in a straight jacket. Maybe Cris visited him sometimes, peering through the bars of his door. Did Pike recognise him? He liked to hope he did.

Only, this world felt realer than the old one.

The statue's face fractionally shifted, so small and subtle it could barely be detected, but enough to suggest it's attention was focused on them. A half-smile curled one side of the face into a chubby-cheeked grin, the other, into despair. The eyes were unevenly crafted, as though the sculptor had been working on two different people and then spliced them into one.

You brought a friend!

Whatever Pike had expected, it had not been the high, half delirious voice. He noticed some kind of black sludge was beginning to seep from the statue's base.

How kind of you. The more the merrier.

'The city's in chaos. The Prince is dead.'

No one dies in this place, sharp, harder, *haven't you listened?*

'Gone, then,' she continued. 'What do we do? We can't stop the Three Kings.'

Can't you?

The question threw Hagga; she stuttered and looked at Larri.

'What do you mean?'

Have you ever tried?

'Yes,' Pike growled, stepping forward, his feet inches from the black liquid. 'I fought the Taking Man, and that was before he... changed. I barely survived. Wouldn't have, if it weren't for Fay. Can you tell us where she is?'

The statue's eyes were closed. Pike knew they hadn't been before.

He blinked and they'd opened again,

I cannot find her. Tricky lady, that one. Very powerful, very proud. But even the proud know when to hide when the odds aren't good.

Pike felt his insides burn. Was that for him?

You'll have to find a way without her.

'Can't you do anything?' Hagga said, accusation barely veiled. 'You said you willingly gave yourself to assimilation. You're part of the city. Can't you help?'

Silence for a long time. The liquid spread and Pike and Hagga had to draw back from it. Larri watched the statue with unwavering eyes, as though he was studying it for weakness.

There is little I can do now. A note of terrible sadness, of regret, like a mournful minor chord. *But I can tell you this: the Three are at the pyramid now, in the throne room. You may never have another chance to fight them on their own.*

The liquid receded.

It's a shame about the Prince. I was almost beginning to like him. He's changed. Changed so much. Yet still the same.

The statue returning to placidity, stillness.

'Who are you?' Larri said.

Just a fool... Teehee.

And then the graveyard fell silent.

CHAPTER 22

What was his name?

The one thing perforating the nothing. Sound interrupting silence. Light dark. Epiphany stillness. It kept coming back, caught in a circular flow.

He couldn't remember his name. He couldn't remember a lot of things. Pain had a habit of erasing the past. Cancer survivors struggled to remember aspects of their life before the operations, the suffering, and so with him, everything before the blinding spear seemed irrelevant and unformed. The past had become a future not yet born.

He felt like he had become one with the concrete. Something warm and sticky was glued to his face, chest, arms. Was it blood? Was it a kind of emulsion that would draw him into the city? That's what happened in this place.

No!

He would not accept it. He would not accept assimilation, to become part of some hive-mind, unimportant, diminished, buglike. He was...

Who was he?

Prideful, clearly. Unable to accept defeat. Here he lay in his own blood, torn apart, blind, and still imagined he would rise. No. It was over. The mission. The dreams...

He stirred, nothing more than a spasm virtually invisible from the outside.

The dreams. How horrible they had been. Torture and death. And how he had misused them. Yes. He was starting to remember now. The days in New York, hunting down children and babes. Slitting their throats. Sometimes even drinking the blood. That, he'd never told his apostles about. Never anyone.

Memories...

M...

Yes, his name began with M. But he couldn't think of any other word except Monster.

I am a monster.

Burning holes in his face; empty sockets, smouldering like the craters of some atomic blast.

I deserve to die.

A sound breaking through. A real sound. What was it – hoof beats?

Footsteps.

'Michael?'

He screamed. He screamed like a child waking from a coma to discover thirty years have passed. Screamed and screamed: the blunt instrument of reality was too much. All at once his memory returned and unlimited horror filled his soul; where it overflowed it spilled out in his screams.

'Michael, please.'

Soothing like balm. Like sunlight melting snow. He knew that voice and he knew who it belonged too. He would have recognised it even if he had remembered nothing else.

'Fay,' he choked.

'Yes. I'm here.'

He reached out with a failing hand. Hers found his, then she lifted him out of the muck, easily as a child. Her grip was alarmingly strong, and comforting at the same time. She cradled him. A soft hand touched is face.

The gentleness of that hand made him expect the darkness to melt away.

'I'm here,' she repeated, again.

'Why? Why did you come for me? There's no reason... No reason...'

'Isn't there?'

And then he started to shake. It sounded like a cough emerging, as though a venomous tooth was trapped in his lung. Heaving, body-trembling coughs.

Not coughs. Sobs. He had no tearducts, yet he wept. The pain he had so often felt thinking of Fay exploded in his heart as though every vessel of blood had burst and he gasped for air. Struggling, like a child that couldn't swim. He tried to free himself from her hold, her warm arms. But she held onto him. He was too weak.

He began to quake and the weeping redoubled, coupled with a terrible frustration that he could not free the tears.

There was not a trace of self pity. He did not weep for himself.

He wept because even now, he still did not understand why she had come back for him.

———

LIFTED INTO THE AIR. He was being draped over the flank of something. He felt its strong muscles against his thighs and its hair beneath his fingertips, bristly.

A horse.

Then.

The white horse!

It could only be. He heard Fay mount, kick; it leapt into a gallop.

She took him through the city, weaving through conflicts and flames. Her face flickered with the doubt and turmoil she felt. She knew she had to save him, but how much was there left to save?

Eventually they reached the city's edged shrouded in the shadow of the pyramid. She rode deep into the silvenom wood, through the tangles of bent trees, until they reached her hidden place.

It looked like the kind of place a 'witch' might live in, which made her smile to herself. She called it the Last Hope.

She dismounted. A tree wide as a small house loomed over their heads, two humungous roots bifurcating six feet from the ground, creating a kind of doorway. Beneath the tree, the rest of the roots formed a teepee shelter. A small, half-dead fire burned in the dwelling place, emitting trails of greenish smoke which escaped through small gaps between the roots. Across from the cave she had erected a tent out of worm-silk weave. Underneath it she kept the accumulated tools of centuries: parchment riddled with hieroglyphics, jars of ancient mixtures (their lids shaped like animal-heads), Roman pauldrons, an ash longbow and arrows, a gas-lamp and musket. It was always funny what people brought with them and what left behind.

Surrounding the equipment were piles of tarot cards. Each set was drawn differently, as though it held its own unique secret. Some were dark, the imagery reminiscent of old idols. Others promised light.

She helped the Prince down. No sooner had his feet touched the leaf-strewn ground than his legs buckled and he fell. She carried him, his arm over her shoulder, through the root doorway and laid him down next to the embers beneath the tree.

She kissed his forehead. It tasted of urine and she felt rage surge inside her.

Animals.

'Give me a moment.'

She went and gathered a stack of branches and returned. She drew out the lighter which she'd taken from the Prince's discarded jacket and lit the fire. The Prince shuddered, as though the warmth were discomforting to him. With the greenish light on his body, the damage was made plain. His flesh looked like bark which had been hacked at for days. His face was broken apart by two drill-holes.

The wound between his legs gaped like a toothless mouth. She shivered.

'Fay?'

She went to him, laying his head on her lap.

'Fay...' he swallowed. 'I think I understand... why you came back... why...'

A guttering noise of pain that made her feel cold.

'Lie still.' But part of her didn't want him too. Part of her wanted to hear. *Needed* to hear.

'I always... always tried... to reach the next world. Even before Nekyia I was never content with the one I was in.' He gritted his teeth and blood wept from between them, trickling over his lip and chin. 'Never content. Never seeing. Imagination became... a god. Always looking; never seeing. The eye... lies... lied to me.'

'Enough.'

She stroked his brow, tried to push him down. He attempted to shrug her off. She allowed it even though she could have overpowered him.

'I have to finish...' His eyes widened, as though staring over the edge of a well down into limitless horror. His mouth hung open. For a few moments he held this posture then shivered and went on as though nothing had happened. '...I was wrong my whole life. About everything. Everything was wrong.' A sucking breath that seemed to catch several times as it was drawn. 'I thought if I controlled...the dreams... if I mastered... I could...' A growl like a harpooned beast. 'I couldn't! I couldn't! I failed...'

He reached out, gripped her neck with slackening fingers. Stared at her without eyes.

She held him in return.

'But you... you changed me...' A red grin. 'When I no longer believed it was possible.'

She placed a hand against his cheek. Cold, like the dismal wind of space. The firelight couldn't seem to touch him anymore. He was grey as stone.

'It's not over,' she said, knowing it was, knowing it surer than if the hateful card had been turned over. She held him too tightly now, the last tether to anything. Her face burned; her eyes were globes of fire. She was shaking.

'No...' So quiet. Barely a whisper. 'You have to save Pike. Save...' A moment of stillness that made her heart stop with it. 'Fay...?'

As the word broke, so too, two silver streaks. She was rocking him, like a babe.

'Yes?'

'Ki- ki-'

She bent, seeming to move towards him for an age. Her lips parted: his were already open, slack, the lips of a man dying of thirst, awaiting a droplet of water. There was hair-raising second of contact in which she felt he might surge with life, return the kiss, feel her tongue with his.

Instead, he exploded into a cloud of wings.

Her heart tore as she shrieked. His body disseminated, parts breaking off like dried leaves, morphing into butterflies which soared into a hurricane of fluttering beauty. She clutched at them, as though trying to piece him back together. One alighted momentarily on her arm and she saw that stamped on its white, curvaceous wings were eyes that shone like midnight stars. A thousand eyes. Ten thousand. Shimmering and staring down at her as the cyclone of butterflies ascended and began to spread through the forest.

She stood; they circled, momentarily a halo. She wept aloud, stretched out a hand. The butterflies descended and converged, moving in an oval that created the impression of a deep portal. The portal warped, shifted, became the silhouette of a man, his entire body shining with eerie and impossible eyes, an elder god.

Did he stretch out her hand to her? She thought he did: a final farewell.

The shape disintegrated and the butterflies swept away, like sea foam, a galaxy ceasing to swirl as the stars disassembled; currents floated through the forest, an eddy of the milk of paradise.

Whispering with it: a dream.

CHAPTER 23

'This way,' and she darted through the ruins of a building, ducking cables like transmogrified vines in a far-away jungle. Larri followed her, stumbling slightly. Pike caught his arm.

'Steady,' he said. Larri nodded.

'Whatever it was, that surge of strength, it seems to be fading.'

He sounded like he was talking in his sleep.

'Just keeping going,' Pike said, patting him on the shoulder. Larri nodded again, slower than at first and bent at the hip. He staggered through the ruins. Pike checked the area and went after him. The staff was slick with blood. Strange, he thought, how the blood still hadn't changed into anything, but the body had become a tussock of weeds.

Pike had never been in a war, but now he thought he understood all those war poems. Wilfred Owen. Sassoon. He thought he knew what they meant. The waiting. Crouched in some ditch. Hearing the sounds of destruction. Always round the corner, 'just over the hill'. And the sights: like poetry itself, imprinted, eternal, soul-changing. At times he questioned whether there really was an assimilation happening, and wondered whether it might be his struggling brain overlaying the horror with strange natural beauty.

The asylum was never far from his mind.

He caught up with Hagga and Larri both squatted like hermits in the grey dust of collapse. There was an open stretch, and at its end, the pyramid. Between them and it were hundreds of city-dwellers, all savagely locked in conflict.

'Nothing for it, but to run.' Hagga said. Her eyes had a kind of desperate determination in them. *She must sense Larri is weak, that time is running out.*

He grabbed her arm as she began to rise.

'Are you sure this is the best way?'

There were a lot of them.

Hagga shook him off.

'You know the pyramid. If there's another way in, just say.'

Pike bit his lip.

'Okay, but let's be careful.'

'Most of them are wrapped up in their own fights,' she said. 'Let's leave them to it.'

She started and Pike had no choice but to follow. Larri struggled to stand, so Pike grabbed his arm (again that strange dry texture) and helped him up. He nodded in thanks, clearly too exhausted for speech.

They hobbled towards the fray, Pike holding his staff horizontal so as not to make too much noise. Hagga went in front, crouched like a hunter.

Two women fell beside her, one on top, digging into the other's eye socket with index and middle finger, black pouring from the wound like ants from a disturbed nest. Hagga, unperturbed, side-stepped and went on.

Pike forced himself not to look and skirted them. Larri's breathing was heavy.

Then suddenly, all the fighting stopped.

The city-dwellers, even those with awful wounds, picked themselves from the concrete and stood to attention like regimented soldiers. All the eyes looking around were unfocused, the eyes of somnambulists.

'What...?'

But Hagga seemed to know what was happening. She turned and looked at them.

'Pike! Staff!'

He let Larri go and raised it.

'Yin,' Larri cried. He sounded hysterical.

The Magician heard Larri, from his vantage point at the peak of the pyramid, looking through his mystical window, and remembered the blade. He remembered Larri ending his power with the brutal stab; remembered the immortal form he had created for himself shattering as though made of nothing more than glass. His attention had been diverted. He'd been concerned with the woman, the hidden wolf. He wouldn't make the mistake again. He'd get them both.

Behind him, Dr Monaghan paced.

'You're going to miss the show,' Yin said, raising his hands like a conductor. He felt as though power-cables had been attached to his fingertips.

From the throne, the Taking Man watched him. Though he could not see it, the Magician was eternally aware of the awfulness of the face.

'The show!' Dr Monaghan ran forward, gleeful as a child. He peered through the window at the still city-dwellers. He frowned.

'Why can't you take the Knight too?'

Yin grimaced. He was working a miracle here, one which not even the Prince could have achieved in his wildest dreams. Did this stupid doctor know what it took to possess the minds of hundreds? The energy? The knowledge? He was drawing from the pyramid itself, using the power of the mind-flayers against them (this had been particularly pleasing to the Taking Man). If this was nuclear fusion, he was the conduit through which all the kinetic explosivity flowed.

'I don't know,' Yin said. He had tried. Fed his mind with delusions and weaknesses, but the Knight either didn't seem to feel them or else shrugged them off. 'It doesn't matter.'

He flicked fingers. The city-dwellers turned as one to look at the three intruders in their midst.

'Those who are about to die, we salute you,' he threw his voice through the screen, down so that it could be heard at the concrete below.

Dr Monaghan grinned behind the metal grill.

'Time to place your bets!'

———

PIKE MOVED WITH INSTINCT; in one blissful second all doubts were gone. Muscles awoke. Kinaesthetic eruptions snared along his nerves. He sidestepped, twisting with the staff as his centre, avoiding the lunging automaton. He brought the staff round and down with a speed that made the air *chug*. It cracked over the back of his assailant's head and felled them in one.

And then he was boxing.

Ducking, lashing out with one end of the staff, then the other. Tripping, batting aside crude attacks that were like assaults from drunks. One went at him with a bar of metal, a piece of girding which'd been sharpened into a blade. Pike only just craned his back far enough to avoid the slash, pivoted and sent the bottom end of the staff out in a piston-thrust. Broke in the face of his attacker. They staggered but did not drop the weapon. Pike swept the legs, caught the blade-wielder at the knees and broke one. He screamed and fell. Pike finished the fight with a double handed blow that produced a sound like striking a sack of grains, only wetter. The brains became an eggless bird's nest.

'Hagga!' He fought. 'Larri!' He'd lost them in the malaise.

Hands seized his throat. At once they were frightfully strong, but also clumsy. He elbowed back, snapped the rear of his head into a nose and sent them reeling. He turned and lashed out. Other hands grabbed at him. He shook them off, like a wild bear stabbed by the blunted spears of inadequate hunters.

But even the worst hunters could win in numbers.

He swung his staff in an arc, clearing an area of six feet and sending two of the slaves falling. He used the time to charge off through the host. Not all of them were quick to attack. Many twitched, their eyelids flickering as though still dreaming some unnameable dream. Spasms riddled them, like the onset of a fit.

They resist.

And apparently, so did he, but he didn't know how.

He glimpsed Hagga, fighting bare handed. He'd never known anyone as ferocious as her (he thought she might be a match even for him) and that thought brought a weather-beaten smile to his face. He bashed aside two more slaves and began to make towards her, feeling like he was swimming in some bizarre contest.

A ring had formed around her. At its heart was Larri, prone. He looked like he was bleeding but it was hard to tell from his burnt up flesh. Hagga clawed and swiped at them, a lioness fending off jackals from her wounded cub. One stepped too close and she tore off their ear. Another found her heel in their groin.

Larri was saying something, incoherent words.

'The word... compels you... the word... of... Simon... Simon...'

Hagga took a blow to the face, a blow that would have knocked a boxer down, but Hagga rolled with it and returned a hook that made her assailants jaw audibly crack. It dislocated, hanging off like a serpent's about to swallow a live animal. Drool and blood flecked the corners, foamed, became a gruel which dripped. Like an animate dead thing, the slave ignored its wound and grabbed. Hagga was not prepared. One hand found her throat and the other grabbed between her legs and lifted. The thing, it couldn't be called human anymore after The Magician's powers had raped its mind, held her up, like a babe at baptism. Larri began to shriek but seemed unable to move.

'THE WORD. THE WORD. CAN'T YOU HEAR THE WORD! THE WORD!'

Pike growled and ran forward. Slaves intercepted him, acting like part of an ant-like hive mind.

He lunged but they danced nimbly, no trace of the jerkiness that'd previously made them slow opponents. They began to circle, probe with slashing swipes, like knife-fighters. *The Magician. The Magician is doing this.* He was fighting one man with a hundred bodies.

More closed in his periphery.

Over the shoulders of his latest foes he could see Hagga, scrapping, scratching, but unable to break the hold. The slaves were gathering around her, like worshippers drawn in a demonic ceremony, anticipating the sacrifice like a hungry orgasm.

A blade glinted. They were going to slit Hagga open and watch her bleed.

Pike smashed out his staff in a butting move and tried to break past them.

No Pike!

It was Cris's voice he heard. Cris's voice which had always been the only voice which could ever call him back. But it was too late.

An unseen limb smacked the back of his head and he went toppling face-first to the ground, though he felt like he'd spun three revolutions before hitting it. His staff broke under his body; iron rushed into his mouth. He spluttered with burst lips.

They began stamping. Crushing weights on his back.

Dimly, he saw Hagga. From this angle it looked like she was floating, suspended, above everything. Slowly, as though time had become addled in a mire of its own making, the knifeblade ascended with her, and rested, with sadistic delicacy, on her scarred and beautiful neck.

A thrum which ran through the ground. A rhythm. Not the boots and heels raining on his spine. Another rhythm. Deeper and yet lighter.

A whistle.

Hagga screamed and Pike felt his heart tear.

And the tearing set free the rage.

Like a mountain rearing, he stood, feeling like he had those days of snorting up white lines and beating whoever stood in his way. He knocked down a slave nearest him with a single backfist strike which caved half of their face. He picked up the jagged end of the staff and rammed it fully through the throat of another. Blood spattered his face and he screamed into it, opening his mouth to receive the spray, revelling in the taste of another's vital fluid.

'Have it you FUCKS!'

More whistling. Thuds of impact.

He wheeled and saw Hagga, unharmed. At her feet lay three slaves with arrows in their heads and throats.

The rhythm was getting louder.

And the slaves were breaking.

Slowly, Larri stood. His face was overly expressive without the mask of skin, the wiring of his muscles moving as though self-animated. His eyes were fearful and awe-filled both at once. He was staring into the distance.

'A horseman. He has sent a horseman.'

'What?' Pike turned, following his gaze. Something was emerging from the distance, and from it, the slaves were turning and fleeing, the control which had so enveloped them shattered in an instance, with the ease of light interrupting darkness. The rhythm was now a drum beat, the beating of their blood through their veins, a kind of pulse to which time itself was now tethered, because everything had slowed to move with it.

'A horse*woman*,' Hagga whispered.

'God,' Larri said, though Pike could not discern whether it was a statement of wonder or an attempt to name the thing he was looking at.

A horsewoman, yes, in white, riding a white horse, white glittering pauldrons adorning her shoulders, a bow in one hand and a quiver at her belt. On her back a sickle glowed like a shard of the moon seized by a Promethean hand. From her burned an energy that tasted of radiation sickness, of suns dimming, the collapse of worlds. It reminded him, faintly, of the Prince, but it was greater. Her face was terrifying, the visage of ancient Akhenaten, strange, unknowable, cursed, and as Larri's exclamation intimated, divine.

'Fay,' Pike said, not in recognition, but because the name was torn from his lips like the urge to raise a banner high upon the return of the one true king.

Like water parting, the slaves fell back at her approach. Some knelt. Some were foolish enough to try and strike at her; they were ended with an arrow faster than a thunderbolt. The rest ran, crumbling like an edifice beneath the grip of the sea.

IN THE THRONE room of the pyramid, Yin fell to his knees, blood dripping from his nose. He remained there, in the posture of defeat, aching spasms riddling his head and body. *How was it possible?* The witch had broken his hold. He'd tried to retain it, but like an implacable gladiator she had peeled away his grip until resistance was more agonising than letting go.

The shadowy figure on the throne rose.

'I see you've failed,' he said.

The Magician began to weep.

'With me,' the one-handed man said.

Dr Monaghan unslung his sword.

Yin stood on shaking legs.

'Yes, master.'

FAY FLOWED between the stragglers and finally reached Pike; she dismounted.

The battlefield had been cleared in moments. Hagga and Larri were embracing, a cyclone of dust about them. Larri sobbed – for his weakness, or was it out of gladness? Some Slaves still dragged the corpses of their beloved elsewhere to grieve, come to their senses and aware now of the horror of what had been done.

'You don't have much time,' she said.

'What do you mean?'

'I've set the amberfire at the base of the pyramid. I plan to set it alight. It's the only way. The Devil Reversed, remember?'

'We need you with us,' he said.

'Three of you and three of them. Sounds like a fair fight to me.'

He looked into her eyes. They pierced him, reached his soul. Revealed beneath the exteriors of logic, the internal labyrinth, and more than that, the way through he could not see himself.

'I have to do this, don't I?'

She nodded.

He grinned.

'You fortune tellers must get a real kick out of being right all the time.'

Fay smiled, but sadly.

'I wish that was so.'

He extended a hand.

'Not sure I ever gave you a proper handshake. This is how we Brits do it.'

Fay laughed.

She took his hand; the moment of contact was brief but electric.

'You're like him,' she said. 'Just don't make the same mistakes.'

Pike thought he knew exactly who she meant.

He turned and began to walk to the pyramid. Hagga and Larri fell in behind him.

LOOKING DOWN ON THEM, from the slopes, the Three Kings. At their centre, the Taking Man, known now as the Pit Arisen, smiled.

'A fair fight,' he whispered, watching the woman in white mount her horse and begin to gallop away from the trio. The petty, small part of him that was still human called for revenge. *Cut off both her hands, her feet, her breasts, the bump in her cunt...* But if she hadn't thrown him into the darkness, he would never have acquired the power he had now, so he supposed he should be grateful. *The witch can wait.* The horse disappeared in a plume of dust. She was surely planning something. Dr Monaghan had told him about the stolen amberfire, grovelling like a pup. *First things first.*

Pike Malory was in his grasp. And the Taking Man was going to finish what he'd started.

They descended.

'I FEEL like I'm in The Good, The Bad and the Ugly,' Pike said, 'Only there are six of us.'

'What's that?' Hagga asked.

Pike looked at her and Larri: both were confused.

'You know. The Western movie.'

'What's a Western movie?'

'Jesus Christ. Deserts. Shanty towns. Cowboys.'

'Sounds like the Circle,' Larri said.

'I'll tell you later.' Pike waved a dismissive hand. He looked up. Thirty steps above them the three shadows waited, somehow blacker than the onyx of the stone. 'If we survive,' he added.

CHAPTER 24

The Taking Man stood, spear in the midnight claw. He looked like the fisherman of souls, snaring them from the Stygian lake with his harpoon and laying them out to be devoured by some everlasting mouth. Yin huddled at his leg, like a lost child, but his eyes, rimmed red, showed emotions so corrosive they hurt to look into too long. Dr Monaghan stood with arms folded, ragged labcoat billowing like torn imperial robes of office. His mask seemed to warp and change with the light, as though it'd now become such a part of him it was no longer an emotionless slab of metal, but a second skin.

'You seem to be blessed with an uncanny amount of luck,' the Taking Man sneered. 'Twice on the brink of death. Twice you escaped. Fay seems *very* fond of you.'

'Fay's sitting this one out,' Pike spat on the ground, the hard slap of the liquid seemingly audible for miles. 'Just you and me, fuckhead.'

The Taking Man laughed.

'And doesn't that make you just a tad nervous?'

Pike clenched his fists.

'You're all the same,' Hagga said. 'Illusions and tricks. But there's nothing in you. Maybe that's why you don't die? You're like cockroaches: all shell and no substance.'

Yin's eyes narrowed into slits. The Taking Man appeared to be grinning, though it was difficult to tell beneath the engorged flesh of his tumours.

'You're impressive, Hagga. I see now why the Prince wanted you. You're so much more than these...' He waved a hand, in a way Pike was aware eerily resembled his own movements. 'Why don't you come where you truly belong? Kill them and join us.'

Hagga burst out laughing.

'You're nothing on the Prince,' she said. 'You might think you're him but you're nothing. I might have taken the Prince's offer. He called to me, a part of me I wasn't even sure existed. You're just a madman with a fucked up face.' She gave him the finger.

The Taking Man started to tremble.

Well, he's pissed now, Pike thought, grinning.

Larri limped to stand on Pike's right, aligned with Dr Monaghan. He was unsteady on his feet, hunched over slightly as though cradling a stomach pain.

'Are you ok?' Pike muttered.

Larri gritted his teeth and nodded.

'I am now I've seen *him*.' He was looking at the doctor. 'Time to pay him back.'

'You should be thankful for what I did, Fred,' Dr Monaghan said, with a high twinge of humour. 'I made you much better looking.'

Larri screamed and hurled himself up the steps.

'Larri!'

Dr Monaghan was freakishly fast. Despite the size of his blade and the fact he'd been holding it point down, he managed to bring it up, over his shoulder and down within the seconds it took Larri to mount the steps.

It bit into the shoulder with a sound like a tree-trunk tearing and something squidgy being pulped. He gasped, coughed a projectile clot of blood. Sank to his knees with the blade still embedded in his shoulder. It was a foot deep at least, reaching to where his heart must surely lie.

Hagga let out an animal's throat-burning scream but before she could go anywhere Yin leapt, twisted in the air and became a batlike monstrosity. He glided down and knocked her to the ground with a noise like air-cracking and enclosed her in membrane. Pike could not see her, but heard a *chomp,* teeth in a throat; the second scream that came from her was no longer an animal's but desperately human.

I'm going to suck you dry you fucking WHORE!

Pike experienced a moment of paralysis, familiar to him from days of waking drunk and high. Torn between rushing to help Hagga and the Taking Man, who was bounding down the steps towards him. A split second later he threw himself into a roll and heard the whoosh of the still-burning spear tip over his head. He came up in a boxer's stance, began to weave as the spear jabbed for his chest. The Taking Man held the spear like a rapier, maintaining a fencer's stance to compensate for the weight. He thrust like an angered wasp, not letting up, each jab closer to home.

Behind the Taking Man, the batlike thing was thrown back, squealing. Hagga scrambled up, shoulder a smear of blood and mangled flesh. He couldn't see Larri, he was out of his field of vision and he daren't take his eyes from the glowing spear and his adversary.

'You're ordinary, Pike,' the Taking Man was growling. 'An ordinary fucking gypsy.'

A spearthrust that went too far – Pike grabbed the haft and pulled the Taking Man towards him, smashing the hard crown of his forehead into his face. Pain blossomed and he fell back. The Taking Man also stumbled away, clutching his face and roaring.

One of the tumours popped, dripping clear liquid.

'POOR, POOR, FRED,' Dr Monaghan said, tightening his grip on the claymore. 'He played to win, but sadly, lost.' A smile lit the inside of the mask like demonic light. 'Game over man.'

He wrenched the blade from Larri's shoulder; crimson ribbons burst from the wound. Larri was lifted to his feet by the pull of the blade. Dr Monaghan stood before him, sword raised like an executioner's axe.

'GAME OVER!'

Consciousness was a thin line which Larri could barely keep in focus. But he would not die like this, executed.

He spat into Dr Monaghan's face.

The doctor smirked.

Froze.

He remained with the blade poised, like a statue.

'Ah,' a whimper escaped his lips. He whistled, breathed, as though blowing on a flame. A hissing sound had begun.

Dr Monaghan dropped the blade and clutched his face. Smoke billowed from the mask, and the metal turned white. The features of the menpo, so garishly huge, receded, mollified, then began to distort and twist as though shape-shifting into a new nightmarish creature. Dr Monaghan let out a howl, tore at the mask with his bare fingers which came away blistered and bleeding.

'WHAT HAVE YOU DONE TO ME?'

He clawed at his face and a segment of the mask came away; along with a glued slab of flesh.

Dr Monaghan looked up and screamed again, a gurgling sound. The inside of his face seemed to be being sucked into itself, like a quicksand pool.

'The Amberfire,' Larri said, grinning. 'My blood. Is acid.'

He collapsed on the slopes, still smiling.

Dr Monaghan shrieked. From the hole in the centre of his melting face erupted a tangled net of thorny vines. They uncoiled like snakes, reaching out, forming a wrangling network.

His body was slowly lost amidst the coiling tendrils of the thorns, enclosed, disintegrated.

A single red flower blossomed.

A rose.

HAGGA SEIZED the upper joint of the wing, pulled, and stepped in, hitting with the bottom of her fist, wielding her limb like a hammer. Again and again she smashed it into the leathery creature's face, feeling fangs crack beneath the weight of her strikes.

This is not a creature. Despite the transformation, the black eyes which shone in the bat's head were the same beady eyes she had come to loathe so well.

It squealed and turned beneath her blows, cowardly in pain.

It let out one virulent howl and spat something from its lips. It might have been blood or it might have been venom. Hagga turned her face away, avoiding it. When she turned back, she was no longer holding onto a wing. She was holding a small, delicate arm.

'Gwen?'

The little girl was wraith-thin and white. She wore a nightie, bare feet smudged with dust. Her eyes were black and pendulous. Hagga let go. Choked on words she had never thought she would be able to utter.

'Gwen...' The repetition stupid but impossible to repress.

Memories rose like tidal waves, breaking over her with shocking force. She flinched. She remembered the Need taking over, the ravaging hunger. Her memories in the Need were fragmented, like dreamy jigsaw pieces scattered across a blackness of infinite depth. She remembered the chicken pen in Law Town being empty (where she had directed the Need in her first days); that was a strong memory. Perhaps because she felt it, in part, absolved her.

Nothing will absolve you, a voice said, a mean voice, that sounded like her own but poisoned with the gall of all empty emotions. *Nothing will ever redeem you for this.*

'I'm so sorry, Gwen, I... I...' Meaningless platitudes. Hatred turned in on herself as though it were a beam of light that'd struck a mirror and been reflected back. 'I didn't mean... I couldn't control...'

The girl raised a sorrowful hand and pointed a finger in accusation.

'... please...' Hagga was on her knees and begging. 'I need...' She mealy mouthed the word.

Exile. Punishment. Torture. You deserve all these things.

'Yes...'

She had been cast out of Law Town, sent into the Bone Lands, an animal set loose into the wilds. So much had happened, meeting Simon and Larri, their seeming triumph over Yin, the collapse of the City of Illusion, she had begun to forget this origin, forget the terrible thing she had done.

Gwen's nightie turned red. Her tears became crimson. A gash appeared in her belly.

'No...'

Hagga sobbed.

She hated this city, this living prism of memory and pain. She hated Yin, because deep down she blamed him for the Need, for making her the way she was.

But most of all the hate burned for her own soul. If she could have clutched it and asphyxiated it, she would have.

The girl began to laugh. She burst apart and from her emerged a terrible, lizard-like shape. Hagga screamed and was swept up in its grasp, too late realising, too late seeing.

THE TAKING MAN was distracted by Dr Monaghan's fall just enough for Pike to move in. He grabbed the spear and twisted it from his grip. He kicked and the Taking Man toppled, like a ruinous tower. For a second, Pike held the spear and stood over his enemy. The Taking Man stared up at him, looking like a half-rabid dog cornered by its hunter. *He won't give up. I'll have to fight him to the very last second he clings to life.*

'Pike!'

He looked up, knowing he shouldn't, knowing the foolishness of it. The call was so stringent and baleful it pulled his eyes from his quarry.

Hagga was being carried into the air; the bat had become draconic. Pike determined its intention in a heartbeat. He levelled the spear and hurled it like a javelin. It arced, landed squarely through the wing of the beast and drew a screech from its throat that bounced from the wall of skyscrapers and echoed back at them. It tumbled from the sky, flapping, the skewer awkwardly lodged in the translucent skin of its wing.

The Taking Man scrambled to his feet. Pike ran, towards the falling Yin and Hagga. He heard his pursuers footfalls, louder than the pulse of his blood. Everything seemed quiet outside of their conflict. The city made no noise. The city-dwellers had fallen silent, perhaps still dreamily shaking off the spell the Magician had wrought.

Nothing existed outside of this moment, because Pike knew that if he failed, he failed forever. He couldn't measure life by the existential methods he once had. In an instance, a flash of understanding not unlike Fay's miraculous appearance, he realised why he'd so desired for their to be no afterlife, no continuation. It was because he was afraid to fail, had been all his life. He'd chosen the traveller's life, chosen not to believe in God or purpose, chosen to deny all that he was.

But he was the Last Knight, just as the Prince had said.

And he would avenge him.

He charged, headlong, into the creature that was Yin, knocking it from Hagga. He tumbled with it, a messy tangle of hooked limbs and fur and reeking breath and fangs. It seemed to be changing under his grip. He beat it with his fists, roaring like a lion released into the pit, tormented and oppressed for weeks prior. The bat shrank, shrivelled, like a vegetable under heat, all terror vanishing.

Suddenly there was nothing but a broken dwarf under him. Cold. Dead.

Pity welled up in him, clutched at his throat. What had he done? Beat a cripple to death with his bare hands.

He reached out to put his fingers to his neck, saw an eyelid flicker.

Illusion... he heard Hagga say.

The dwarf leapt up at him, like a reanimating corpse.

With a single, swift motion Pike grabbed his head and snapped his neck. Yin fell limp like a doll. Half a second passed which felt like an age.

A choking noise made Pike wheel around. For a brief moment he feared the worse.

'Hagga!'

But she was the one holding the spear. She had impaled the Taking Man, who now staggered back from her, clutching at thin air, mouth open but voiceless. Blood poured from the hole in his stomach. It looked like a gore-clotted eye.

'You...'

He turned and began to flee towards the pyramid.

When Pike turned back to look at Yin, he saw the head continuing to twist of its own accord. Repulsed, he watched the hands come up, like puppet's manipulated arms, join with the head, stick at the wrists and open, like a flower. The body reared itself up, also twisted; the legs became one.

Then there was no Yin, merely a strange fountain, its basin held up by two sculpted hands, its thin column carven with a spiral of stretched flesh. In the basin were dark waters in which Pike could not see a reflection of any kind.

Chilled, he turned away. The Taking Man climbed the pyramid.

'Time to finish it,' he said.

Hagga nodded. Then her eyes widened.

'Larri...'

CHAPTER 25

He limped, leaving splotches behind him, oval, eye-shaped. Everything seemed like a great big eye. He sensed him. Smelled him in the air. Albric had taught him the powers of psychic awareness, had taught him so much. *Why did I ever turn on him?* It all seemed so petty now. Albric had tried to be his father, had only not told him the truth because he wanted to save him pain.

He's a liar and a cunt. They're all liars and cunts.

He staggered and fell, steadied himself on his one arm, rose, marched on. The world around him was beginning to look like a faded television screen, composed of particles, unreal and untouchable. The pain was not even troublesome anymore, distant. That worried him more. Pain defined existence. To not feel it was to not exist.

He dug his nails into his leg, roared, looked over his shoulder.

Hagga and Pike walked after him, with the patience of hunters.

Were they taunting him? Mocking?

It would be their biggest mistake. The Taking Man was not done. Jack Orton was not dead. He had survived the Pit and would survive this.

He reached the pyramid slopes and began to pull himself up, one gruelling step at a time. He heard a squelching noise, realised a gout of meat had detached from the grisly wound. He fingered its charred edges and felt nothing.

Oh god.

Perhaps the first time that word had ever touched his lips.

He climbed, slipped in his own blood, collapsed.

No. No. Not like this. Not at their mercy.

But he couldn't move, couldn't even speak. Breathing was a painless struggle. Everything numb and empty, like a hole that had no bottom. He looked at his remaining hand, the blackness had spread all the way up his arm and was bleeding across his chest. He could see it through the torn fabric.

We will have our bargain, an awful voice resonated from the stones. *We will have you, Jack Orton.*

FAY STOOD at the edge of the circular platform looking down into the depths beneath the pyramid. She had lowered the amberfire barrels into the darkness via the elevator. With a strange twinge, she realised it was the last journey it would ever make. Now one thing remained.

She drew out Pike's lighter.

Flicked it on and held it up, like a jewel.

She threw it over the edge and swept out through one of the doors, descending on the reverse side of the pyramid which faced the woods. She found her steed, mounted and disappeared in tangles and shadows.

PIKE SMELT IT.

'Down!'

Like a fungal growth sprouting, the top of the pyramid exploded, a column of fire piercing the clouds like a colossal cannon blasting at the sky. Black rock shed from it, like seed.

Top down, with the same horrifying slowness as the World Trade Centre, it began to erupt and decompose, stone raining around them like a meteorite shower, fire licking from between the newly made openings like tongues of over-active volcanic magma. A groan, it swayed as though a being of stone waking groggily to strange life, then began to fold, sinking into a whirlpool.

THE TAKING MAN held up his hands and let out a cry of jubilation. He was sucked down, into the vortex of churning rock, ground, and disintegrated, becoming the nothing he always had been and now, always would be.

A NOISE LIKE A SCREAM, psychic, so high it was beyond hearing yet penetrated the brain.

A dust storm hit like a shockwave, blinding them.

Pike and Hagga held onto each other, each cloaking the other.

Finally, the seismic quakes and the rain of stone ended. The screams died.

The two of them were alone in the dust and ruin and rubble.

CHAPTER 26

'Larri?'

Again and again she called, but there was no trace of him.

Every second was a palpitation, felt through her whole body and, she thought, the city itself.

'Larri!'

In her heart she knew he must be dead. She'd seen what Dr Monaghan had done to him, cleaved like a butcher, but Larri had been through so much, surely it couldn't have ended like that?

She began digging into the rubble, pulling up slabs of stone that were still baked. Red burns spread across her fingertips, her palms bled from the jagged edges of everything. At one point, as she pushed aside a slab of disintegrating onyx (it now seemed so insubstantial) and found a curling rosebush.

Leaving it, she continued, trampling out further towards the centre of the formless pile. Pike watched her, neither judging nor condoning. He looked stunned, half drunk, even. Perhaps he couldn't believe it was really over?

'Larri...'

A plea, now. Then she began to punch the stone. It split and cracked beneath her fists. Her knuckles smashed, pulped, and disseminated fragments which jutted from the flesh of her hand. She howled from the pain.

Rocking, clutching her hand to her chest like a babe, she remained knelt amidst the obliteration; she didn't know how long. Her eyes closed as though the lids were weighed down. The only thing that reached her was the sound of her own choked sobs.

'Larri.'

Now she knew, he was never coming back.

A touch on her shoulder. Pike was standing beside her. What did he want? Couldn't he see? The only people she had ever called friends were dead: Simon and Larri. Who did she have left? The Circle and now this city had taken them. Taken everyone. Even the Prince was gone.

'Look,' Pike whispered.

In rage she opened her eyes, ready to shout at him, but something caught her attention. The smallest streak of colour, like a line of vibrant paint on the black canvas.

Three-legged, she crept forward, still clutching the broken hand to her chest.

It was a stem, emerging from the gap between two stones; it shifted colours with the oozy flicker of firelight: orange, purple, blue, yellow. From it, two small limbs budded, like outstretched hands.

Hagga balanced herself, sitting back on her haunches, then stretched out her hand and stroked the stem, softly, afraid to crush it.

It burst upwards.

A diaphanous explosion of colour, light, glimmering like a pillar of flame, bright and beautiful as the beam of a lighthouse, only solid. It rose in a relentless column of shifting colours, an iridescence somewhere at its heart like the internal chemistry of a star; with it, she heard the rustle of leaves, the shadows of humongous, emerging boughs. She staggered back, as did Pike. The stem had widened to the width of an ancient tree trunk. Its assault upwards seemed unstoppable; it was now a tower taller than the pyramid had ever been.

'It's... it's...'

The ascent ended. From the column the boughs continued to stretch and uncoil, sprouting leaves like wide wings. Then, at the very end of the boughs, globed fruit emerged, blood red and dripping with moisture.

'It's Larri!' Hagga said, the first childish note Pike had ever heard entering her voice.

'How can you know?' he said, still awed at the almighty tree. It dwarfed even the four thousand year old red oak he'd once seen, back in the world of before.

Hagga looked at him, a smile making her face shine with a glow he would not have thought possible of anyone in this place.

'He was nailed to the last tree in the Circle,' she said. 'And now he's the first tree here. The first *real* tree. No poison in him.'

She walked forward, Pike went to stop her and then decided against it.

Hagga reached out and touched the tree.

'Warm,' she said.

And new tears made her eyes silver.

ACT V: PERIPETY

CHAPTER 27

S he awoke from a haunting dream.

She sat upright. Last Hope was quiet, but that quiet felt like expectation; the trees swayed with invisible, unheard winds; the leaves dropped from their branches. The embers of her fire were surprisingly vivid. Though it was night, the palefire lit the sky so brightly she could see everything from the clear silvered highlights on the twisted bark (which formed patterns that looked half like faces) and the glimmer of her equipment.

She donned pauldrons, bow, quiver and sickle, and swept from her hollow. The white horse was waiting for her in the glade. She could never command it. It came when it wished, as it had done the night she destroyed the pyramid, and let her ride it for a time; then it departed. A gift from the forest. She suspected, had done for a long time, that the horse had once been someone. But all things in Nekyia were deeply obscured, like the faces on coins at the bottom of a well.

The steed snorted impatiently and stirred the earth.

'Okay,' she said, and leapt onto its back.

The steed set off immediately. In the palefire's pearly light, the thinness of its body seemed a beauty rather than a haunting mark. It galloped, smooth as running water, taking her from the woods out into the city's network. Occasionally a light at a window indicated someone was still awake, but mostly they were dark. *People sleep easy for once,* she thought. Though she did not know how long it would last.

She passed the great Flame Tree; the palefire robbed it of colour, but it was still beautiful, a pillar holding up the world. She couldn't help but think just how different it was to the pyramid, the squat, shadowy structure that drew everything to it, like a vortex.

The white horse did not slow until it reached the shores of Nekyia.

Fay dismounted and walked out. The sea caught the silvery light and reflected it, as though a second world lived beneath its surface.

'Why here?' she said, but the horse was silent and still, as though waiting.

She stroked its mane, thanked it, like an obeisant discipline keen to retain a god's favour.

Stepping out towards the shore, sudden blackness dropped over her, as though she had plunged headlong into the black ocean.

She looked up. The palefire was gone. The Aurora Borealis which hung over the city at night had disappeared as though it never had been.

Panic seized her for a few moments. She could not see anything.

No. No.

She thought she had saved the city; had it been for nothing?

Then a white column fell from the sky, and she realised, astonishingly, it was a new kind of light, or one that was new to Nekyia.

Moonlight.

The concealing clouds had at last parted. Beyond she could see something like a real sky, the kind of star-spread heaven graven on the inside of the ancient Pharaoh's tomb. Pinpricks winked at her like secret eyes from beyond the shadow of cloud.

The light revealed something else, too.

Butterflies. Thousands upon thousands of butterflies, an endless stream flowing, with gentle purpose, upwards into the light.

READ AN EXTRACT FROM THE
NEXT BOOK IN THE SERIES...

BEYOND THE BLACK GATE
THE FIFTH BOOK OF THRICE DEAD

CHAPTER 1: FORT WILLIAM

The Funeral Man sat in a pub somewhere in the Scottish highlands, far away from the world he once knew, wondering why nothing felt right. They'd won, hadn't they? Smiley, the killer that'd haunted Caleb Rogers' life for eight years, was dead and cremated, his body incinerated in a ceremonial act that was supposed to feel final, but somehow didn't. The walls of Caleb's life felt like a rubix, forever turning around one another seeking solution, but the faces were painted wrong, and the colours would never align.

He helped himself to another glass of whiskey. Clynelish. Beautiful stuff, aromatic and flavourful, not just a cheap burn at the back of the throat, but with each subsequent glass it somehow became ash in his mouth. The ash of a dead body.

Somehow, he couldn't shake the feeling Smiley was still with them. Whenever Caleb saw a light in the sky – and there was a lot of sky here in Scotland – that didn't look right, he got nervous, like it was a sign. Whenever he saw a spider, he thought about the one he'd found in the hospital, stowed away in his jacket, a little piece of Smiley he'd taken with him out of those caves beneath the Louisiana forest. He thought about all the things Smiley had said during those interviews. Most of all, he thought about the last thing he had ever said.

The Black Gate is open.

As the blood poured from the wound made by an antler in his chest.

As the haggard eyes glowed, something kindled behind them, something born.

Smiley had lived up to his name, grinning at his own death, accepting his place in a higher cosmos. Caleb wished he could do the same. Nothing felt right. The whiskey was shit. There was no rain and it was Scotland in the middle of November. Spiders were everywhere.

And he couldn't get the killer out of his head.

As he knocked back another, slouching on his barstool, the owner gave him a sneering glance. *Can't handle his whiskey, he's thinking.* Even blind drunk, Caleb had a knack for reading expressions.

He took a pause, felt the heaviness of his limbs, the treacly slow flow of his own blood through his veins. It seemed to gather at his temples, to throb there like a second heartbeat. His legs felt useless, dead mannequin limbs attached to his waist. What was worse was the ghosts of his missing fingers ached worse than usual. He wanted to flex them, pop the joints, but when he went to do it, there was nothing there, just an index and thumb on his left hand. Then there was his ear. He guessed he looked a little freakish, what with half his ear chewed off. Sure, he could have gotten some plastic surgery in one of Austin's many clinics, probably could have gotten it free what with him being a 'hero' and all, but it just didn't feel right. The wounds were a part of him now.

He was supposed to be free. He was supposed to have been purged of Smiley. The pain. His wife, Martha. All of it. As he'd laid in the hospital bed, he'd thought it was all slipping away, leaving him at last. He could finally be whole again. He'd thought: *Smiley was right. The universe has been healed.* But now everything felt dirty again. As he looked around the bar, at the sour patrons, the oily chairs and tables, the gaggle of hen-do women, it was like he was seeing everything through a grimy filter. Maybe it was because he was used to modern Austin, the space ports, the next-gen cargo freighters bustling through the sky, the squeaky clean Mars facilities...

Mars. Another bad memory. The red balloon in his mind like a tumour he'd tried and failed to cut out of himself. He remembered the prisons, the mines, the bustle of ant-like life. So different to here. Scotland was empty, still connected to the lochs, the trees, the natural world. It was supposed to be peaceful, a break from the mechanised world he'd come to loathe. But the trees seemed haunted, the lakes and lochs too deep, the grass to whisper.

The Black Gate is open.

'You havin' another round or what?' The barman said, abruptly.

Caleb blinked, looked at him. A bald, ugly face. Kind of reminded him of Hank Marshall, the prison warden. Maybe the whole story with Smiley was a lie he told himself and he was really a prisoner of Facility 06, a convict locked away in his own madness.

'I'm fine, thanks.'

'Then pay up.'

Caleb fished out some twenty pound notes and threw them down. He didn't bother waiting for the change. He hated the fiddly little coins anyway. He'd get some air.

He left the Grog and Gruel, took a walk through the tiny town. Night was just starting to creep on them, thicker, more frightening than he was used too without the light pollution of modern Texas. It reminded him of the night in the woods, chasing Smiley, the explosions, traps, gunfire, the final room.

He thought about getting something to eat, but he was dead on his feet. He'd started drinking early and already run his course. He'd forgo dinner for a big breakfast tomorrow.

Fort William was situated along the edge of Loch Linnhe. There was a small pier, crowned with a quaint but excellent fish restaurant. Fishing boats came and went throughout the day, depending on the tide, gliding like ossified swans in and out of the port. On the other side of the loch, there were mountainous hills, a few sheep grazing. It looked like something out of a Tolkien book. But it didn't soothe him. The hills cast shadows. The sheep bleated constantly, as though aware of some unseen threat, a wolf in the dark.

He found the road that ran parallel to the loch. His B&B sat on this road, overlooking the water. There was a small beach, really just a scrap of sand, but children played with seaweed on it while the parents took photos of the surroundings. English tourists. So strange to think of the diversity which existed in such a small place. Caleb had made the mistake, a casual slip of the tongue, of referring to the B&B owners as *English* on the first day of his visit. He might as well have called them bastards. They'd forgiven his ignorance now, it seemed, after he praised the breakfast of haggis and poached eggs. Though it was probably more to do with the fact they thought all Texans were stupid, therefore deserving pity.

And to be fair, he was in a piteous state.

As he went up the steps toward the B&B, he took one last look of the hills, hoping this time the clear air and the natural world would awaken something in him, a dormant hope perhaps. Instead, he saw a figure on the hill. A shape, at first vaguely human. On closer inspection, with the keenness only a detective's eyes have, he saw it had a bird's head.

What?

Even at this distance, some five hundred feet, he was sure. He blinked. Yes, a bird's head, like a crow, ugly yellow eyes, a beak festered with boils and puss. Its body was humanoid and female, naked, glinting. In its hand, it carried a double-bladed spear, something ancient but somehow profoundly at one with the landscape around her. The more Caleb stared, the closer he seemed to draw to the figure, as though he were floating across the loch. *It isn't a mask.* That'd been his first thought, but no: the eyes were too potent, the whole thing too real. Its eyes were more than just bird's eyes, there was a colour in them that hurt him, that made his guts squirmy and worm-like, that made him want to take a knife to the edges of his face and cut it off. Yellow eyes, cosmic eyes, with black slits in them that reminded him of a figure he'd once seen, a shadow, lingering in the gate, just after Smiley died.

He was seeing things, he must be seeing things.

He blinked.

The figure was still there, watching him.

'I see you,' he said, out-loud. Saying it made it real, and fear squeezed his heart, made his fingers tremble. He rubbed his eyes, an old tic returning. The bird-creature was still there. Its spear winked at him. The sheep bleated.

It was seconds, maybe; it felt like hours. He stared and stared at the figure, willing it to vanish, willing it to go away. He was hopeful that a guest would bumble out of the B&B and speak to him, break the spell, like someone always did in the movies, but nothing like that happened. The figure held him in its gaze, he was powerlessly held by it. The longer he looked, the deeper into its chasmal eyes he fell.

'Oh God,' he whispered. 'Oh God.'

Finally, the sun dropped a fraction lower, and the hills, along with the bird-figure, fell into absolute shadow.

[BUY NOW]

A SPECIAL THANK YOU TO MY PATRONS

A further and emphatic thank you is due to my patrons, my dear cultists and thralls of the Mind-Vault. The work I do is not possible without their tireless support and generosity. These heroic individuals are:

Ross Thornley, James Sale, Steve Talks Books, Lea Kaywinnet Frye, Jesu Estrada, Tom Harper, Michelle Sale, Christa Wojciechowski, Tia Wojciechowski, Iseult Murphy, Kelly Pearson, E. T. Kennard, & Erik Bergstrom.

Thank you from the bottom of my heart.

About the Author

Joseph Sale is an editor, novelist, and writing coach. His first novel, *The Darkest Touch*, was published by Dark Hall Press in 2014. He currently writes and is published with The Writing Collective. He has authored more than ten novels, including his fantasy epic *The Illuminad*. He grew up in the Lovecraftian seaside town of Bournemouth.

His short fiction has appeared in Tales from the Shadow Booth, edited by Dan Coxon, as well as in Idle Ink, Silver Blade, Fiction Vortex, Nonbinary Review, Edgar Allan Poet and Storgy Magazine. His stories have also appeared in anthologies such as *Lost Voices* (The Writing Collective), *Technological Horror* (Dark Hall Press), *Burnt Fur* (Blood Bound Books), *Exit Earth* (Storgy), and *You Are Not Alone* (Storgy). In 2017 he was nominated for The Guardian's 'Not The Booker' prize.

You can find out more by visiting his website: themindflayer.com

twitter.com/josephwordsmith

patreon.com/themindflayer

Printed in Great Britain
by Amazon